THE GINGERBREAD THIEF

THE GINGERBREAD LEGACY
BOOK TWO

CARRIE ANNE NOBLE

To my mother

Prologue

The invitation arrived by neither post nor pigeon. It came with a nudge and a whisper from a passing stranger or in a snatch of conversation overheard in a noisy tavern. Or delivered by the wind to one's doorstep, inscribed on a scrap of torn and yellowed paper. Sometimes, though rarely, a dream spoke the unexpected words:

What is your deepest desire? Take the pilgrimage to the Seven Ovens of Sainte Yvette and win the wish of your heart. Further instructions will find you if you are meant to receive them.

Most dismissed the message as useless blather, for few believed in wishes or magic in nineteenth century France. Sensible folk had bread to earn, children to tend, fields to reap. If a thing could not be touched or seen, they had no time for it—outside of a bedtime story.

But for a precious few, the message roused long-slumbering hopes, and beckoned them to believe that anything was possible.

One

FRANCE JULY, 1828

Josephine Monfort leaned over a market table crowded with carrots, green beans, and onions in the busy, small-town square. The last thing on her mind was mysterious messages. Recently (albeit allegedly) widowed at the age of forty-one, she found it difficult to focus on anything beyond breathing. To make matters worse, her housekeeper and cook had quit without notice last week, leaving her to fend for herself. If she'd been herself and not weighed down by grief, she could have made do—but she'd never felt less like herself. Simply brushing her hair felt like swimming across the sea. *One thing at a time*, she muttered twenty times a day. Currently, the one thing was shopping. She needed food to prepare supper for herself and the orange tabby cat that had shown up on her doorstep the day after her husband had (or had not) perished.

Clutching the handle of her wicker basket, she stared at the beans, unable to decide if she ought to buy enough to last two days. Her husband, Thierry, had hated green beans, but lately she'd come to crave them—raw, boiled, or fried in butter and sprinkled with lemon juice. Would her skin take on a green tint if she continued to eat so many?

"Madame," the stall owner said. "Is something wrong?"

"I'm fine," Josephine replied, blushing. She must have been staring at the beans longer than she'd thought. Everyone in Valerienne would soon be whispering that grief had driven her mad. Even she had begun to wonder if her sanity was slipping away. The things she believed about the cat...

Someone tugged at the black fabric of her sleeve: a crooked-backed old woman wearing a headscarf and a faded dress patterned with poppies. Josephine had never seen the woman before, although she did remind her of her dear departed *grand-mère*.

"I've had my eye on you, child," the woman said, pulling Josephine closer. She lifted a fat lemon out of Josephine's basket, set a folded rectangle of paper in its place, and then replaced the lemon. "Read that once you're home, and may it bring good fortune to you."

"Thank you," Josephine said, but the woman had already disappeared into the bustling crowd. For someone so elderly and bent, she'd been quick on her feet.

Focus, Josephine reminded herself. *Buy the vegetables and get home.* The cat would be missing her, and besides, she longed to know what kind of message the old woman had tucked underneath the lemon. Likely it was nonsense. The musings of senility.

Nevertheless, Josephine's heart pounded as if finally, something wonderful were about to happen, something that would change the very course of her life.

Ansgar Steuben strutted down Paris's Avenue Renard wearing the green velvet coat he'd just procured from the best tailor the city had to offer. If he did not feel young and bursting with magic, at least he felt fashionable.

How he'd missed wearing fine clothes when he'd been confined to the body of a duck! That long and miserable chapter of his existence was one he preferred not to dwell upon. Fortunately, amid the busy bustle and champagne haze of city life, he could almost forget the events that had ensued within enchanted German woodlands he'd fled, as well as its unworthy new witch-queen, Gretel. Although his darling and dreadful wife had chosen Gretel to assume the proverbial throne of the Igelwald Forest once she reached adulthood, he'd never warm to the new queen. Gretel had shoved his wife into an oven, after all. He'd only helped Gretel into power because the curse that trapped him in feathered form could not be otherwise broken. Paying the price for his freedom had been worthwhile, if unpleasant at the time. Sumptuous, jewel-toned fabrics suited him so much better than plain white plumage.

He tipped his hat to a pair of pretty, well-dressed, middle-aged women who approached on the sidewalk. One of them giggled; the other shushed her. He recognized the sisters from a recent ball. The giggler had spent some time snuggled on his lap in the host's library, if he recalled rightly. Eloise, was it? He'd meant to send her flowers and a dinner invitation.

Drat his murky memory.

He kept walking, past familiar cafés and shops. The blue-gray pigeons swooping from the rooftops to the street all looked the same. He knew every tree in the neighborhoods he frequented, every lamppost, and which parks to avoid because of an overabundance of carriage traffic. He could almost traverse Paris with his eyes closed. The city was wild in its way, but compared to the enchanted forest, it was as predictable as the phases of the moon.

After three years on French soil, Ansgar was growing not only old, but bored. Yet he could not imagine moving back to his German homeland. His practical kinfolk frowned on fripperies and indulgences, and these were the things he most relished. *Ah, well.* Perhaps he'd soon move on to Spain or Italy—if he could stockpile enough doses of the fortifying elixirs and age-reversing creams he regularly purchased from illicit, back-alley potion shops. These, he needed to maintain what remained of his good looks and vigor. If he lost his blond swoop of hair accented with a single streak of black, would the ladies still be drawn to him like flies to honey? If his limbs continued to weaken, would he be able to dance and flirt through all-night soirées?

Life would hardly be worth living if his ballroom and parlors were not teeming with glittering admirers.

As he passed the polished window of a patisserie, he barely glanced at the display of cakes and tarts. Instead, he assessed his reflection. The cut of his coat complimented his figure. But was that a new wrinkle in his forehead? Gods forbid! The sight of it made his stomach ache, which in turn made him notice the pain in his left knee and the throbbing in his lower back.

Ansgar had lost track of his real age long ago, but he reckoned he'd seen well over one hundred and fifty summers. The years had been dogging him ever since the spirit of his witch wife, Truda, had slipped away from the earthly realm, and he'd walked out of the Igelwald. It was hard to believe that he'd arrived in France in a body that appeared late-middle-aged yet spry. His magic then had been puny but enough to get by on. Now, he could hardly summon enough power to knock a spider off a chandelier.

The truth made him shudder: without a miracle, he was not long for this world.

According to the opinion of Madame Dalousse, the most venerated witch-apothecary in Paris's hidden *arondissement magique*, Ansgar's body had begun to deteriorate faster than that of an ordinary, non-magical mortal the moment he'd left the Igelwald. He had but a year or two left to live, if that.

Had his wife known this would happen? It seemed like something she might have thought worth mentioning before she'd vanished forever from the mirror she'd inhabited after little Gretel had incinerated her body. Then again, Truda had always taken pleasure in vexing him.

With a grunt, he left the patisserie window and continued up the avenue. He tried to look forward to the rich mid-day meal his pretty cook would serve, and the lazy afternoon of kisses she'd offer as dessert. Fortunately, his charm and wealth had a way of blinding his paramours to his physical decline.

Until now.

When a strong breeze drove a thin parchment letter smack into his chest, he grasped it with eager fingers. As a once-powerful practitioner of magic, he sensed a hint of enchantment imbedded in the ink. Tucking his ebony walking stick beneath his arm, he unfolded the note and read its contents.

What is your deepest desire? Take the pilgrimage to the Seven Ovens of Sainte Yvette and win the wish of your heart by pleasing the saint with an offering of a small, heart-shaped gingerbread cake. The cake is to be baked in her exalted presence from the recipe of your choosing. Assemble at the Church of the Three Sorrows in the Forêt Gernois on the morning of the fourteenth day of September. Seven supplicants will be chosen to complete an arduous journey of many days to the Seven Ovens to compete for a singular wish. Further instructions will find you.

The German stood on the Paris street corner aquiver with excitement as stylishly garbed pedestrians bustled past. He pressed the page to his breast as if it was a letter from a long lost lover. This invitation was nothing short of the miracle he needed.

A chance to win back his health and his magical powers.

His blood rushed through his body as if propelled by the heart of a twenty-year-old. He felt more alive than he had in ages. Desire burned in his breast anew to travel to the ends of the earth and taste the world's delicacies. To see the sun rise over the desert and to watch it sink beyond the horizon of the sea. He wanted...so much. He never stopped wanting one thing or another. The wanting was a beautiful and terrible ache, one he loved and detested in equal measure.

Ansgar folded the parchment and tucked it into his coat pocket. In exactly two months, the pilgrimage would begin. He would be ready for it. He was no baker, but he was in possession of an unbeatable gingerbread recipe—one magical enough to lure children through the dark forest to his beloved Truda's door. And to think he'd stolen the recipe on a whim!

Winning would be easy. A piece of cake, as it were.

A smile curved the corners of his mouth as he spun on his heel to return to the pastry shop. This momentous occasion deserved to be celebrated with the finest *tarte au citron* Paris had to offer. And a croissant or two. If ever there had been a time to spoil one's appetite for dinner, it was now.

Two

ONE DAY BEFORE THE
ASSEMBLY OF THE SUPPLICANTS

On the thirteenth day of September, Josephine Monfort was ready for the first real adventure of her life. At least that was what she kept whispering under her breath on the first morning of her forty-second year. She murmured it like a prayer in between sips of chamomile tea, while sitting by a third-floor window inside a shabby old inn. Could her legs and wits really carry her to the mysterious Seven Ovens? Excitement and fear wrestled in the pit of her stomach like a pair of puppies, negating whatever soothing effects the tea should have delivered.

The empty tea cup clattered on the saucer as she set both on the windowsill. Through the thick pane, she glimpsed the rocky gray shoulders of the French Alps. Only a blue swath of lake and a strip of gold-and-orange-leafed trees separated her from the austere mountains. The scene's beauty overwhelmed her. The four walls of her little parlor at home, hung with old paintings of the sea and forest, had always provided enough of a view. Homesickness pierced her heart like a cruelly wielded hat pin.

It should have been impossible that she was beginning her birthday alone and far from home. Well, she wasn't quite alone. She had the company of the fat orange cat that lazed among the bed pillows. In all honesty, the cat was a poor companion, as affectionate and warm as the snow capping the distant mountains. As cuddly as a sack of nails—and yet he was the reason she was about to risk life and limb on a journey any sane French housewife would scoff at: the mysterious pilgrimage of Sainte Yvette. Those sane housewives were not as desperate as she was.

For Josephine, the invitation had been hope made tangible. It had tamped down her grief and lured her away from home as nothing else could have. Only a smattering of hours and a few miles now separated her from the beginning of a life-changing journey.

If she won the wish, Josephine could save her husband from living the rest of his days trapped within the body of a cat, and thereby earn his love and gratitude. In addition, with Thierry back in his rightful form, she'd be spared eviction from their marital home.

She turned away from the view and shivered. The room's old fireplace produced more smoke than warmth, and there she stood, clad only in her linen chemise. She tugged on the pair of gray men's trousers she'd bought secondhand in the marketplace, praying they'd fit. Her fingers fumbled to fasten the button at her waist. She'd never before worn men's garments, but to her mind, attempting to hike up a mountain in a long skirt and numerous petticoats would be a very stupid thing to do. The trousers clung to her womanly curves, but she could endure the annoyance if it helped her achieve her goal.

A cheval mirror in the corner beckoned. She stared at her reflected image. Her husband would have turned crimson with rage at the sight of her dressed like a man. She imagined Thierry shouting, swearing, berating, his voice as clear as if he stood facing her, calling her a fool. Yes, she probably was foolish. Foolish to love him, mean as he was, no matter what she'd promised in her wedding vows.

Thank heaven Thierry couldn't shout at the moment.

Currently, his vocabulary was limited to meowing, hissing, and purring—if he was indeed the orange and white cat that slept on the bed. There was a chance the cat she'd toted halfway across France was just an ordinary cat. Nevertheless, she chose to put all her faith in the possibility that the sleek, amber-eyed feline held the spirit of her husband.

Josephine twisted the gold band on her finger and perched on the edge of the bed. She shut her eyes and pictured her husband's handsome face. She'd never quite understood why he'd married her, nor had she been brave enough to ask. One autumn day, Thierry had simply arrived at her family's farm asking to meet with her father, and the next day she'd been informed that they would wed. Knowing better than to refuse her father's commands, and desperately tired of keeping pigs, she'd packed her small trunk. She'd gone to church to become Madame Monfort at the ripe old age of twenty-eight.

Thierry was twenty years older than she—but in spite of his years, women of all ages still practically swooned when he walked into a room (or they had, before he'd turned feline). On the other hand, she possessed all the charm of a well-stuffed armchair: cozy and comfortable but nothing to write a sonnet about. She ought never to have fallen in love with her dashing, dallying husband, for her mother had warned against it, but here she was.

If she succeeded and saved Thierry, maybe he would finally see that she was more than furniture. Wasn't that what miracles were for? If nothing else, the reappearance of her husband would stop his uncouth brother, Jacques, from proposing marriage every five minutes, leering at her as if she were something he'd long waited to inherit. Was it not enough that Thierry had left Jacques the house and almost every penny? *Bonté divine!* The grass had not yet sprouted over Thierry's grave when Jacques had first come to call with wilted flowers and awkward flirtations. The man was too crude and strange for words.

Strange as Thierry's brother was, the circumstances of Thierry's death had been stranger. Thierry's lifeless body had been discovered in the attic laboratory where he'd spent his nights trying to turn anything and everything into gold. Although he'd sworn he'd been born with magic in his bones and a destiny for greatness, he had never once succeeded. The pursuit might have been what killed him. After examining Thierry's corpse, the baffled town physicians had proclaimed him perfectly healthy. No one bothered to consult an expert in magic.

The body, laid out in the parlor and surrounded by vases of roses, had looked peculiar to Josephine. The dead man's ears looked too large, his mouth too thin. He'd looked too old and shriveled to be the Thierry Montfort she'd known, as if someone had extracted his soul.

The morning after the funeral, an orange cat had sauntered into her sitting room. The animal had stared at her with her husband's familiar glare and climbed into his favorite chair. A shiver slithered through her. Surely this visitor was none other than Thierry. His meddling with magic had somehow sent his spirit into this cat. Her conviction was so strong that she vowed, then and there, to free Thierry if she could find the means.

The saint's baking contest would be the means—if she could win it. Six other pilgrims would compete for the prized wish. If they out-baked her, she supposed she'd find the courage to live alone—somewhere Jacques could not find her. She would seek out a job in a mill or as a maid, but life as a widow would be bleak. She certainly could never remarry in good conscience as long as the cat who might be Thierry lived.

Behind her on the bed, the cat growled low. Predictably, Thierry was appalled by the sight of her in trousers. She pivoted to face him. "I'm wearing these trousers for you, husband. We're heading into the mountains to find your freedom, and ankle-length skirts were not meant for hiking. I promise I'll never dress this way again once you're your former self and we're home."

The cat set his chin on his crossed paws and glowered. Outside, in the village square, a bell tolled ten times. She'd frittered away enough of the morning daydreaming. Less than twenty-four hours remained before the pilgrimage's start, and she still had supplies to acquire. She shimmied out of the trousers and stepped into a simple black skirt.

Today she'd shop and pack, clad in clothes befitting a lady. Tomorrow, she'd don the trousers again and set out on what might be an impossible quest. She'd be braver than she'd ever been in her life. Her future, and her husband's, depended on it.

There were feathers in Ansgar's bed. Two of them, pure white and perfect.

This would probably not have alarmed an ordinary man who'd spent the night slumbering upon a feather-stuffed mattress. But Ansgar Steuben was not an ordinary man. He knew all too well what it meant to be a duck, and the thought of becoming one again almost made him retch.

They are not my feathers, Ansgar told himself firmly. He'd not sprouted a single plume since he'd broken the curse his wife, Truda, had put him under to punish him for infidelity. He'd worked hard to undo that spell. He had paid his penance in full, and yet he continued to pay—in the coin of nightmares and wild imaginings. Truda had forgiven him in the end, but forgetting was another matter for them both.

With a groan, Ansgar rolled over and snatched his gold pocket watch from the nightstand. Quarter past eight. He'd overslept. He'd have to bribe the hired coachman to drive fast if they were to reach the village of Anneçon before nightfall. Excitement accelerated his heartbeat as he threw off the covers and sat up. If all went well, in fifteen short days, he'd have everything he desired: a healthy, younger body equipped with full command of all the magical power he'd once possessed.

The thing about wishes was knowing how to word them for maximum effect. No one in the world could be as ready as he was to milk every ounce of benefit out of the prize offered by the saint. In the event that Sainte Yvette insisted on limiting the scope of the wish, he would simply ask for a hundred years of physical and magical health. Within that timeframe, he could surely discover a way to add more years to his earthly sojourn.

With a jaw-stretching yawn, Ansgar jammed his feet into his soft lambskin slippers. *Coffee.* He needed a vat of the stuff or he'd never stay awake past noon, jostling carriage notwithstanding.

As if in answer to his unuttered prayer, the rattle of dishes outside his door preceded a firm knock. Breakfast had arrived. Unfortunately, he'd have to forgo the pleasures of a languid morning meal, down the coffee in a few gulps, and eat his pastry on his walk to meet his coachman. First, however, he needed to exchange his nightshirt for something more *chic*. Rain spattered the inn's windowpanes as Ansgar tied his cravat in a dignified knot. His exquisitely tailored suit (tan wool cut in the latest mode) was not proper attire for a pilgrimage, but he refused to dress like a pauper just because he was going rambling. Fine clothes commanded respect, and respect he would have.

He stuffed his leather travelling bag with the rest of his belongings, then slipped a paper-wrapped triangle of glass into his coat pocket. "Truda," he whispered, in case she was listening from within the shard of mirror. It was silly. He well knew she was altogether gone from the looking glass that had once held her captive. She'd been gone before he left the enchanted Igelwald. Gone long before he'd dropped the mirror onto the marble floor of an Alsatian guest house and decided to keep one thin sliver as a souvenir.

Gone for more than three years.

Those years, full of luxuries and carousing, had not been all he'd hoped they'd be. Vexed with aches and wrinkles and waning magic, nothing satisfied his soul. To find true happiness, he simply needed more time. And more magic.

Ansgar needed a new life. He needed to be the extraordinary, powerful man he'd been in the early years of his marriage. The wish would give him that chance.

When he opened the door and stepped over the gleaming silver of the breakfast tray, he felt as giddy as a boy bursting forth from schoolroom doors into an endless summer.

Three

THE DAY OF THE ASSEMBLY OF THE
SUPPLICANTS, 14 SEPTEMBER, 1828

Josephine flexed her toes inside her sturdy secondhand boots. Her belongings, including a wicker hamper containing a growling cat, sat near the door of her rented room. The town clock rang out the hour.

A fluttering stirred in Josephine's chest, a feeling that this pilgrimage would change everything, for better or for worse. She hardly knew herself this morning. Her life had been quiet for so long, a cocoon of drowsy comfort and meek concession. A life of surrendering to her husband's authority in all things.

She was about to scramble up mountainsides, slosh through streams, and wade through waving fronds of fern. She envisaged sleeping under star-strewn skies and foraging for forest delicacies. She might even find friends among her fellow travelers. Everything seemed possible, thrilling, and terrifying. The looming dark cloud of her grief miraculously lifted.

Thierry meowed plaintively, as if to remind her not to waste time daydreaming.

She set one hand on the doorknob. Still, she hesitated. Her fingers slid under the collar of her shirt, seeking the pendant she wore on a short chain. For luck, she rubbed the stone set in silver, as her grandmother often had when she'd worn it. Feisty *Grand-mère* would have approved of this adventure.

"Ready?" she asked the cat.

Thierry mewled pitifully as she lifted his basket and the double-strapped canvas bag a local shopkeeper had recommended as luggage.

"I'd trade you places if I could," she said, stepping into the hallway. Her left boot pinched her toes, and her right stocking had already started to slip down her leg. "To be carried about on a cushion sounds rather nice to me."

Ha. The idea of Thierry hauling her up a mountain to save her was as fanciful as imagining herself with wings.

"For better or for worse," she mumbled to her cat-husband as she hurried down the staircase that led to the inn's front door.

Soon after a mist-shrouded golden sunrise, Ansgar disembarked from a hired carriage at the far end of a rock-strewn graveyard. With the strap of his leather satchel slung over his shoulder, he started a slow, dignified walk toward the small crowd gathered in front of an arch of stone and iron, presumably the gateway to the Church of the Three Sorrows.

Unseasonably cold autumnal air nipped at his nose like an ornery bird, and he stiffened his posture to avoid shivering. It would not do to give the appearance of weakness. He would not be the youngest man seeking a place among the chosen. In case anyone was watching, he adopted the confident swagger of a young prince. A crow cawed from atop a statue of an angel, as if to scold him to tone down the brash display. This was a burial ground and not a street of taverns.

So many graves surrounded Ansgar. Every interment in this desolate place must have been a battle in itself. A war against rock and unyielding earth. Perhaps the gravediggers of this region used magic—although that seemed a ridiculous waste of resources. Every bit of magic was a precious thing. Since leaving duck form, his personal supply had been slow to recover—and remained paltry. Not for love or money would he ever consider wielding it to make holes for ungrateful corpses.

And the gray! Everything was some dour shade of it, save for the bright scarves or hats worn by some of the other potential pilgrims. Gray chipped headstones, gray-brown dirt, grayish-green slouching grass.

About a dozen waiting men and women stood apart from each other, unsmiling. Clearly, they had not gathered to make friends. They'd come anticipating a mysterious, hard journey to a life-changing contest, as he had. It was probably all they had in common.

Ansgar's gaze fell upon the form of a shapely woman with a domed wicker basket strapped to her back. She stood alone at the edge of the crowd, her posture straight yet not arrogant. He guessed her age to be between thirty-five and forty-five years. A few strands of silver threaded through dark hair she wore knotted at her nape. The cold had stained her rounded cheeks pink as carnations. He could not perceive the color of her downcast eyes. She was quietly attractive, like a nicely embroidered pillow—not his type at all. And what was this? She wore trousers! Scandalous! They accentuated the curves of her hips and plainly showed the shape of her thighs. The effect was not unpleasant. Doubtless this wasn't a daring fashion statement but a choice made for the sake of practicality. To wear a cumbersome gown while navigating steep rock faces or narrow ridges would be to risk one's life.

She caught him mid-perusal and cast a narrow-eyed scowl his way. He scowled back. She might possess an ember of audacity, but she'd never make it up the mountain—skirts or no skirts. She looked too soft around the edges. Even her derision seemed somehow cushioned.

"*Bonjour!*" a man shouted, drawing everyone's attention to his presence. He leaned against the black iron gate, tall and broad-shouldered, his pose effortlessly alluring. So very *French*. He doffed his cap to reveal a head of thick black hair. "I am your guide, Philippe Martel. Come forward now, all of you."

The candidates hastened to form a half-circle in front of the guide. The scowling woman now stood on the other side of the group—as if purposefully avoiding Ansgar. *Good*, he thought. The last thing he needed was for her to attempt to befriend him. She looked as agile as a three-legged footstool. He didn't need her stumbling in front of him, slowing his progress, or grabbing onto his pack and dragging him over a cliff to a shared death.

"Only seven of you may set out with me today," Martel said. "I will choose from among you, based upon your preparedness and your suitability to appear before blessed Sainte Yvette. Form a queue."

With much muttering and shuffling, they formed a line. Ansgar slipped into sixth place. His pack weighed heavy on his shoulders. Had he brought too much? Not enough? Would the guide judge him unfit? Unworthy? Perhaps the man would accept a bribe or be easily moved by a whispered word of magic. *Ha!* If his puny reserve of magic could move a fly, he'd be astounded.

Ansgar squared his shoulders and stood tall in an effort to counter the atypical anxiety that sent his pulse skittering. There had been a time when a man such as this simply dressed, shave-needing peasant-guide would have cowered before him. In decades past, Ansgar never would have imagined that he'd one day stand in line with these ragtag, desperate wish-seekers, hoping to be deemed acceptable. Thank the gods that the nastiness of this situation would be temporary. Judging by what the packing list required, he deduced the journey would last less than two weeks. The prize would make the suffering seem a small inconvenience.

He shifted the pack to distribute its weight more evenly on his back, and then for luck, he pressed his hand over the pocket that held the shard of Truda's mirror.

"No," the guide declared, and Ansgar leaned to the side to catch a glimpse of the proceedings. With a gesture of his hand, Martel dismissed a bushy-haired young man. The fellow trudged away muttering complaints.

With his hands cupped around his mouth to amplify the sound, the guide announced, "Anyone who did not bring every item on the packing list will be sent home. If you cannot follow simple instructions, you have no place on this pilgrimage."

A bald man with a bright green pack abandoned his spot near the front of the line, his face flushed. He rushed toward the gate as if pursued by wolves.

The remaining candidates stepped forward.

"Do you have a spare pair of socks?" a man whispered nervously over Ansgar's right shoulder. "I'll pay you well for them. My wife was knitting for me, you see, but our son is very ill and occupied her time. That's why I came. To win a cure for my little boy, Auguste Pierre."

"I have only the required number of socks," Ansgar replied coolly. For all he knew, the man was lying. A clever contestant would have realized the game had already begun the moment they'd lined up. No one could be trusted.

The queue moved forward again. Martel dismissed a woman for wearing unsuitable shoes, and then sent a teen boy away for a reason Ansgar didn't catch. It was hard to hear the guide's voice with the wind whistling through the nearly bare tree branches.

"You," Martel said to Ansgar when they came face to face. "You are a foreigner, I surmise."

"I am." Ansgar used an even tone to convey that he was neither ashamed nor excessively proud of his nationality.

"Our saint is merciful and good. It matters not to her from whence one came, if one's heart is true and faithful. Show me your provisions."

Ansgar squatted and unpacked his bag, mentally cursing Martel for making him undo a task he'd done meticulously. At least the flagstone on which he arrayed his belongings was clean and dry. He'd brought every last item on the list: heavy mittens, a blanket, ingredients for spiced cake, a wooden spoon carved from the branch of an apple tree, a gold coin, a prayer book, three pairs of woolen socks, a knit cap, spare undergarments... He'd also been careful not to bring anything expressly forbidden by the list, and therefore had brought a small knife rather than the jeweled but deadly dagger he would have preferred to carry.

Martel nodded, but then a stern look creased his brow. "Answer me this: would you give all that is within you and all that you possess to have the wish you seek? Your heart's blood, your spirit's very spark?"

"Without question," Ansgar replied. He stood to face the guide. "Every drop from my veins. Every ember of my being."

"Still, I sense that something is not quite right with your spirit. For the true pilgrim, the inner life is even more important than physical preparedness. Gather your belongings and wait there, *monsieur*." Philippe gestured toward a spindly spruce tree beyond a crumbling statue of a cherub.

Ansgar smiled with as much charm as he could muster, but internally he swore like a rum-soaked sailor. He headed for the spruce. Who did this Martel fellow think he was, lording it over him? He, Ansgar Steuben, had been not just a formidable wizard but the spouse of the greatest witch-queen to ever reign. Martel was nothing but an ill-mannered tour guide with ugly hair.

Ansgar kicked the tree and then regretted it. This was no time to let his temper off its leash. If he didn't want Death to gobble him up soon, he needed to win the wish. In order to secure a place in this group of pilgrims, he'd have to behave better. No kicking trees, no swearing at guides, no treating the other pilgrims like the dirt beneath his brand new, expensive hiking boots. Self control was essential. *Blast this miserable trip.*

Inside his pocket, he fingered the shard of mirror again. It sliced his skin and he gasped.

"Are you all right, *monsieur*?" the trouser-wearing woman asked as she approached. She must have been sent to wait, too. Not a good sign. She seemed as wholesome as a homemade loaf, pious as a nun. If she could be rejected, he didn't stand a chance of pleasing Martel.

"Perfect," Ansgar said. He withdrew his hand from his pocket to wrap the wound with his handkerchief.

She reached for his hand but he yanked it out of reach. "But you're bleeding. How did—"

"And you're observant. Could we mind our own business and wait quietly?"

She cringed ever so slightly, like a dog accustomed to being kicked. As the guide sent another applicant over to the accepted group, the woman set her bag and basket on the ground and leaned against the spruce.

Ansgar's nose started to itch as he watched yet another man move to the chosen group near the iron fence. As Martel nodded to a tall young woman, Ansgar's eyes began to burn.

"That's it, then," the trousered woman said. "Seven places filled." She sank to crouch beside her belongings. "I cannot believe it. It would have been better never to hear of the wish. Never to have been given false hope."

Was she speaking to her basket or to him? Ansgar ignored her as his anger flared toward the guide. *The fool.*

"Return next year if you are blessed enough to again receive the calling," Martel declared to the rejected in a superior tone. "And remember this: a true pilgrimage begins long before the first footstep. Learn patience, perform good deeds, and pray as you wait. What you think you need today may not be what you truly ought to wish for in the end."

"I detest amateur philosophers," Ansgar grumbled.

The woman stood. The scowl she wore now put her former scowling to shame. "That pompous swine. Assuming he knows what's best for us. He knows nothing at all."

A smile played on Ansgar's lips. The spite in her voice surprised him. Her disappointment had turned to bitterness quite quickly. Perhaps she was not as wholesome as she appeared.

The gold wedding band on her left hand caught the light as she lifted the basket and slid its straps over her shoulders. Ansgar expected her to turn back toward town and the safe, dull life she'd undoubtedly been leading. Instead, she declared firmly, "I'm going with them."

Ansgar almost laughed. "Don't be ridiculous, madame. The guide has chosen the seven pilgrims. Even if Martel allowed you to trail along at their heels, you'd have no oven to use on the day of the contest. Seven chosen, seven ovens. You'd only be wasting your time."

She crossed her arms and eyed him with a shocking amount of impudence. "Would I? That old woman he chose will never make it, not with that limp of hers. Neither will the dark-haired man with the big blue satchel. He's very unwell. His eyes are yellow as buttercups. My plan is to follow secretly and show up on baking day to take one of their places. It seems to me that the saint would commend such an act of tenacious faith." She met his gaze. Her dark brown eyes had a peculiar sparkle. He wondered if she was altogether sane. "You could go with me, *monsieur*. Two are better than one on a journey, my *grand-mère* used to say."

"If I were to accompany you, I'd be your opponent in the end. You would risk facing me in competition?"

"I would. What do you say? Will you wait another long year to win your heart's desire, or will you seize this chance, here and now?"

He was going to regret this later. He'd want to toss her off the mountainside before the day was out, sick of her naive optimism and the nauseating miasma of goodness she exuded. But as his bloodied finger throbbed, he heard himself say, "I will go with you."

The woman extended her hand. "Josephine Monfort. *Enchantée*."

"Ansgar Steuben." His fingers folded around hers lightly. He felt the moment, in its infinite strangeness, brand itself onto his memory. Here he was, at the foot of a French mountain, surrounded by graves, making a pact to take a treacherous journey with a woman who looked more apt to knit scarves and burp babies than to risk life and limb for a chance to make a wish.

Of all the ridiculous things he'd done in his life, both as a man and a duck, this surely topped the list.

Four

Josephine pulled her hand free of Monsieur Steuben's and resisted the urge to wipe it on her jacket. His palm had been unpleasantly warm, and the way his fingers folded over hers had felt almost as intimate as a kiss.

She had never been one to dislike anyone at first sight. It was in her nature to want to befriend everyone, as unwise as that sometimes turned out to be. But Monsieur Steuben had annoyed her from the moment she'd noticed him sauntering along the graveyard path. He wore arrogance like a foppish nobleman sporting a frilled cape to a funeral.

And on that subject...the man's attire was utterly unsuitable for the rough journey ahead. The coat alone must have cost a fortune. Her husband, Thierry, always insisted on the best tailors, so she knew what she was looking at. To see such lovely fabric torn and soiled would be a shame. She imagined the gentleman covered in dust and pine needles, his hair windblown—and only kept from giggling by biting her lower lip. If she wanted to be taken seriously, she'd have to keep that little nervous habit under control.

What had she been thinking, asking Monsieur Steuben to accompany her on an unsanctioned pilgrimage to the Seven Ovens of Sainte Yvette? If his snobbish bearing and ill-chosen wardrobe were indicative of his character, he'd be useless in the wild. She might very well end up nursing his sprained ankles or brewing teas to settle his delicate stomach. It would be like having two Thierrys to look after.

At the far end of the graveyard, the guide led the chosen seven through an ornate black iron gate. They proceeded in a solemn, silent line, like monks on their way to prayer.

Soon, the group disappeared from view. "Now we go," Monsieur Steuben said with authority. He spoke French almost well enough to pass for a native, but the hard edge of his German accent did not escape Josephine's notice. He added, "If we maintain this distance, they should not notice our presence."

So he was taking charge now, when the idea to follow the pilgrims had been hers? She sighed but made no complaint. This had been her lot since birth, living under the command of men. Never once had she been given the chance to prove that she could make her own decisions. When she'd decided to go on the pilgrimage, she'd felt as though she'd finally grabbed the wheel to steer her own ship of destiny. Finally, she could be more than obedient and docile. She could rescue Thierry and prove her mettle. The notion had been equal parts intoxicating and terrifying.

She swallowed her dismay like a dose of unneeded, bitter medicine and followed Monsieur Steuben through the gate and onto a gravel path flanked by fir trees and boulders. For the time being, she'd let the irksome German think he was in charge. What truly mattered was getting to the saint in time to compete, out-baking the others, and taking the prize.

To become Thierry's savior, she could put up with sharing the road with this unpleasant man for a week or two.

Monsieur Steuben glared over his shoulder and demanded, "Walk quietly, woman. You're noisier than a herd of heifers."

She clenched her jaw and prayed for a short and easy journey.

The late-September sun shone down fiercely on Ansgar's head as he stepped into the clearing. The pilgrims had come into view, and if he could see them, he could be seen by them. He halted and extended an arm to keep the woman, Josephine Monfort, from passing him.

The group of the chosen had stopped outside a small church built of dove-gray stone and decorated with a few arched, jewel-toned windows. The Church of the Three Sorrows, no doubt. Behind the church, a great mountain loomed, casting a shadow over the building and the pilgrims. Philippe Martel stood before the seven, gesturing and giving a speech Ansgar could not quite hear. Another annoyance to add to his collection.

How he hated the unknowns of this journey. Without a doubt, many surprises lay ahead. Tests. Challenges designed to force the pilgrims to prove their worthiness or moral purity. It would be a pleasure to watch the others fail, one by one. He would have wagered a pile of gold that half of the chosen would not make it to the Seven Ovens. As for him, he would not be daunted by whatever the saint set before him.

Ever since the day two months ago when the invitation had come to him on the wind, Ansgar had been preparing for the pilgrimage—as much as anyone could. He'd spent a considerable sum hiring scholars and bribing librarians to unearth details of past journeys, all to no avail. There were no maps of the route, no diaries penned by previous pilgrims to consult, no pamphlets offering advice (other than the letter containing the packing list and a few rules, slipped under his door as he'd slept). The only "new" information he'd gleaned came from his favorite back-alley apothecary, and it was nothing he could not have guessed: all contestants vowed to remain silent about their experiences under the threat of a painful death. As always, Ansgar would survive by his wits and wiles.

While Ansgar and his newly acquired companion lurked in the concealing shadow of a giant pine, the guide kept talking and gesturing as if everyone had come to spend the day listening to his speeches. Ansgar clenched his fists and tried to dredge up some patience, a virtue he had never owned in abundance.

"What is the guide saying?" Madame Monfort whispered close to his ear. Her breath tickled like the fluttering wings of a moth.

He shrugged and leaned away from her. "I cannot hear well enough to tell."

Finally, Martel turned and pushed open the chapel's tall wooden door. One by one, the pilgrims entered the building, heads bowed in reverence.

"Would you happen to have a map of the route?" Ansgar asked the woman.

"No," she replied. They'd walked less than a leisurely half-mile, yet pieces of her silver-streaked, dark hair had already escaped her bun. Long curls streamed down her neck and at her ears. One hung across her left eyebrow in a spring-like coil. She swiped it aside as if it were a bothersome bug. "I must have asked a dozen priests about Sainte Yvette, and just as many librarians, but it seems that almost everything about her and her pilgrimage is a mystery." The basket on her back tilted and creaked as if something weighty shifted inside.

Ansgar's nose itched. He sneezed into his coat sleeve, trying to muffle the noise. "What do you have in that basket? Flowers? An animal? Your soot collection?"

"A cat." Her cheeks turned pink as cherry blossoms.

"Great gods. No wonder I'm sniffling and sneezing. Set it free immediately. No need to drag the demonic creature up the mountainside."

"I absolutely will not." Madame Monfort glared as if he'd asked her to toss a child off a cliff.

"Are you stupid, madame? For I cannot fathom another reason one would bring a pet along on a pilgrimage such as this. It will only suffer, locked inside that basket. As will I, from its very presence." He moved around her, seeking a latch to undo.

She spun to face him. In her hand, she clutched a short knife. "You touch the basket and I will cut out your gizzard."

Ansgar raised his palms and stepped backward, although he found her as terrifying as a cream puff. "Calm yourself, woman. I only meant to help us all."

She jabbed the knife at the air. "Promise you will not touch the basket. Swear it before heaven."

"Fine. I promise. You do make a lot of fuss over something good for nothing but rat-catching."

"That is my business, not yours."

With a huff, Ansgar turned back toward the church. The woman was clearly insane. If she insisted on ignoring reason, he'd find a way to "accidentally" free the cat later.

He squinted at the closed doors. "The others have been gone for a long while," he said. "I don't think they're coming out the way they went in. Perhaps the path continues from a back or side door. I'll go peer into the window and find out if they're still present. You wait here with your little demon friend."

"He is no demon. He's my..." She stopped short and pressed her lips together as if to seal in the rest of the sentence. Her blush burned so bright it seemed possible her face might burst into flame.

Ansgar choked back a laugh. "Your what? Best friend? Your sole companion now that your husband's run off with some strumpet half your age?"

She shook her head. Her fingers wandered to touch her wedding band, as if they could not help themselves. "I have reason to believe this cat is not actually a cat. There were...odd circumstances, when my husband passed away."

And then he knew. "Great gods! You believe this cat is your husband," he said.

Now she blanched, but her voice held steady as she replied,

"Save your mockery for someone who values your opinion, *monsieur*. If you're not going to look in the window for the others, I'll do it myself."

"I'm going, I'm going." Grumbling curses in German, he rushed across a few yards of grass and flagstones to reach the church. Both his hands gripped the smooth stone sill as he leaned to peer through a square of yellow stained glass. Inside, he saw a granite font next to an arched door he assumed led into the sanctuary, but not a single pilgrim.

He beckoned the Frenchwoman with a wave of his hand. She hurried to join him.

Cautiously, slowly, Ansgar opened the heavy door. A gust of air fragranced with beeswax and roses rushed over him. He stuck his head inside the building. He tended to avoid churches, finding them stuffy and over-decorated, too full of judgmental-looking statues and uncomfortable benches. But there was something different about this place, something welcoming and soothing. That unnatural *something* set alarm bells jangling in his mind. They would not stay long, regardless. They weren't tourists with endless time to gawk at frescos.

"Have you ever seen such a beautiful place?" Madame Monfort said wonderingly as they walked into the sanctuary. Thank the gods she wasn't one of those women who'd pout for hours after a squabble.

Coming alongside him, she craned her neck to admire the vaulted wooden ceiling. "How is it possible that paint could convey such rich colors?" she said.

The deep blue boards above them were bedecked with golden stars. Even the arching ribs of the ceiling boasted a host of constellations. In spite of Ansgar's determination to remain unaffected by the decor, the rustic representation of the heavens captivated him for a moment. With effort, he turned his attention to the rest of the room, searching for clues about the pilgrimage or the path the pilgrims had taken. Rows of empty pews, five deep, stood coated in dust as thin as moonlight. At the front was an altar fenced in by dark, polished wooden railings. On a crimson silk-covered table rested an engraved silver chalice, pitcher, and plate, all of the usual accoutrements he remembered seeing in church as a boy.

Madame Monfort's voice broke the silence. "They must have gone out a back door, as you said."

"This way." He led her down the aisle, his stride long and confident.

A minute later, they slipped through a simple wooden door. But instead of ushering them outside, this door funneled them into a narrow corridor. Its wood paneling smelled faintly of lemons, as if recently polished. Shell-shaped wall sconces held short, fat candles to light their way.

The back of Ansgar's neck tingled. He had not felt this particular sensation in years: the presence of strong, living magic. Not the kind of feeble trick-magic any half-trained wizard could wield, but a deeper kind of enchantment. A glamour of sorts, actively working to deceive the senses. Was this part of Martel's game? Or some test devised by the saint, perhaps? That would be a strange thing indeed. Were not saints forbidden from dealing with all forms of magic?

"We must be nearing an actual exit," Madame Monfort said behind him as they continued to walk.

"Ha. You have not spent much time in enchanted places, have you, madame?"

"This is a church, not an enchanted place."

He cast a disparaging glance over his shoulder. "You are more simpleminded than I thought if you believe that."

"No need to be insulting, *monsieur*, just because I disagreed with your opinion. I think we should use our energy to find the pilgrims rather than resorting to petty name-calling."

He grunted. In his bones, he knew the exit would not be easily found. And with each passing second, the other travelers gained ground. If they got too far ahead, he and this *dummkopf* of a woman might never find their way to Sainte Yvette.

"I hear something," Josephine said. She pointed ahead, toward the place where the passageway intersected with another. "Voices."

Ansgar cocked his head and listened. He, too, heard the faint echo of speech. "Let's go. But mind your feet and walk softly."

They hurried into the adjoining corridor. The passage turned sharply, and they followed it. It turned again, and then again, like a hedge maze built of wood instead of plants.

"How could such a small building contain so many passageways?" Madame Monfort asked as they continued walking. "It should not be possible."

"As I already attempted to inform you, this is an enchanted place. Such places do not play by the rules."

The echoing voices grew louder. Ansgar stopped short at a doorway. Beyond it loomed an enormous chamber resembling the great hall of an ancient castle. The room appeared large enough to contain the entire exterior of the building. The pilgrims and Martel stood on the far side of the room, beyond an enormous dining table and a row of life-sized marble sculptures of robed men.

"What is this place, Monsieur Martel?" a male pilgrim asked. The sculptures blocked much of his line of sight, but Ansgar guessed the speaker was the plump, weepy, blond fellow who'd been the sixth chosen.

"If you needed to know, I would tell you," replied the guide. "We will rest here long enough to partake of water from the fountain, and then we will continue. Each of you must drink. The blessed saint requires all who seek her favor to taste this water of woe, which cleanses and strengthens like no other."

Ansgar leaned left to try to get a better view. He couldn't see the fountain, but he could hear trickling and splashing. If what Martel said was true about the water imparting strength, he could hardly wait to imbibe. He did hope the "cleansing" was a metaphorical one, however. He wanted neither to spend hours in intestinal distress nor to be somehow made pious. There was also the chance the water was tainted with another sort of magic, perhaps a spell to make the drinker submissive or numb-minded. He'd call upon his ability to perceive the presence of harmful magic before taking a sip.

His nose itched as a sneeze threatened to burst forth. He covered his face with his sleeve and did his best to dampen the sound. *Blast that cat.* If the woman would not get rid of it soon, he would.

The great hall rang with the sound of Martel chanting in somber Latin. Ansgar imagined the pilgrims taking turns scooping handfuls of water into their mouths. Was it cold? Bitter with strong magic? Upon swallowing, did they feel its effects spread warmly from their bellies to their extremities?

He glanced at Madame Monfort surreptitiously. She looked disheveled and weary—and they'd barely begun their journey. He almost felt sorry for her. Almost. A woman of her age should keep herself at home, by her fireplace with her cat, reading poorly written novels or knitting covers for tea pots.

"Onward," Martel commanded his group.

When the sound of the pilgrims' footsteps faded away, Ansgar nodded to his traveling companion. "Come along," he said.

Five

Weighed down by a ten-pound cat, a heavier bag of supplies, and an immeasurable amount of exhaustion, Josephine trailed behind the German. She barely had the energy to marvel at her surroundings as she entered the great hall. Perhaps Monsieur Steuben's suggestion that the building was enchanted was correct after all. This single room was far too large to fit within the confines of the modest Church of the Three Sorrows.

She wasn't about to tell the man she agreed with his opinion, though. That would only feed his arrogance. Monsieur Steuben could use a dose of humility. Not that she was perfect. Indeed, she had been quite snappish all morning—especially when challenged about the cat. But bringing Thierry along was non-negotiable. Her husband (cat-husband?) was the main reason she'd undertaken this pilgrimage, the one for whom she'd willingly die trying to obtain the wish. Her traveling companion would just have to get used to sneezing.

Josephine stopped to spin in a slow circle. High stone walls supported a vaulted ceiling of dark timber. The empty fireplace, large enough to host a party in, took up much of one wall. Under

Josephine's feet, wide oak planks formed a smooth floor. A row of saintly marble statues formed a motionless parade partway across the space. On each side of the room, a dozen iron brackets held flaming torches. They heated the air and shone brightly enough to show Josephine that she and the haughty German were alone.

Monsieur Steuben grabbed her arm and said, "We cannot waste time examining the architecture, madame."

She pulled free of his grip. "I'll thank you to keep your hands to yourself." Again, she'd responded to him petulantly—rebuking him in a manner quite foreign to her docile, compliant nature. She could not quite decide if she liked the naughty thrill she experienced every time she stood up for herself.

The German lifted his chin in his snooty way and hurried toward a blue-and-white tiled fountain in the room's far corner. With a huff, she followed.

"We should drink, as they did," Monsieur Steuben declared. He stopped beside the fountain and eyed her with obvious impatience. Which only made her walk more slowly.

Orange-tinted water flowed from a crusty pipe into the bowl of the fountain. A bitter scent wafted from the swirling liquid. Josephine wrinkled her nose. "It looks less than clean. I'd rather not risk becoming ill," she said. There. That was better. She'd spoken her opinion without being sassy.

Ansgar cleared his throat and scowled like an exasperated schoolmaster forced to repeat a rudimentary lesson. "We must follow the pilgrims' example as much as possible. There is magic at work in this place, and we cannot afford to turn it against us. Think about this logically, Madame Monfort. The guide is on a mission for the saint. If he were to kill the chosen with tainted water, who would remain to bake for her? I say we drink."

If she had disliked him before, she loathed him now. She simply could not stop herself. The sneer on his face, the way his fist rested on his slim hip as he spoke. True, he was probably correct, but he didn't have to speak to her as if she had the intelligence of a flea. "Fine," she said. "You drink first, since you believe so strongly that it will do us no harm."

Without hesitation, he cupped his hand under the spurting water and allowed the well of his palm to fill. He sniffed the water before tipping it into his mouth. After swallowing, he said, "It's good, in spite of its appearance. There is a trace of magic in it, but the enchantment is a simple one meant to strengthen those who imbibe."

"How could you know that from a single sip?"

"In my past life, I was the pupil of a great witch-queen, if you must know. She helped me become powerful and wise in the ways of magic. Ah, your face speaks volumes, madame. You do not believe me. Believe what you will. Your faith and your fate are your business." He drew a white handkerchief from inside his coat and wiped his hands dry.

Insulted again, Josephine felt herself scowling. Monsieur Steuben scowled back. Their eyes locked. Neither blinked.

Her pulse pounded. This staring contest could go on forever, and they did not have time to waste. Also, she knew he was right; she should drink as the pilgrims had. Heaven knew she'd need all the strength she could acquire to make it to the Seven Ovens. In her adult life, she'd rarely walked more than a mile or two in a day —and usually on level ground. She was forty-two years old, not a spry young girl anymore.

She plunged her hand into the water and delivered a palm full of the liquid to her mouth. She swallowed it quickly, amazed by the pleasant tingling sensation that trailed from her throat to her belly.

Monsieur Steuben's smile of victory was faint. Restrained, but visible. Exasperating.

"Come," he said as he turned away on the heel of his shiny new boot.

Under her breath, she cursed his name. And then she followed in his shadow in the direction they'd last seen the pilgrims, toward a tall linen screen embroidered with an image of some poor saint being boiled alive in a cauldron.

Behind the screen stood a door.

And beyond the door lay a garden.

The garden was clothed in autumnal shades of rust and gold. Leaves crunched beneath Ansgar's feet as he trod a brick pathway flanked by stubbly brown grass and thin birch trees. Overhead, the sky wore a layer of unbroken cloud. High brick walls bordered two sides of the garden, and behind him loomed the gray stone of the chapel. Straight ahead, he spied the gray stone of another building. Only one far-off door interrupted its surface, an arch of blue-stained wood.

They had no choice as to which way to proceed, which Ansgar found both helpful and unsettling. The pilgrims would have had to take this same route, guaranteeing that he and Madame Monfort would not lose track of them—unless the magic played some trick. Indeed, he strongly suspected the magic was choosing their route, shepherding them along like dimwitted sheep.

Moving forward, Ansgar tried to ignore the aches in his arms, legs, and back. In his pack, he carried a jar of the enchanted ointment he'd long relied on to ease age-related pain. If only it worked as it once had. These days, rubbing his limbs with lard might have been just as effective, and far less costly.

Evening had come in all its gilded glory, heralding the end of a long first day of travel.

A few late-blooming yellow roses clung to a trellis to his left. They'd been Truda's favorite blossom—which was fitting, given the fact that the color symbolized jealousy. With a shiver, he recalled his foolish infidelity and her wrath. He remembered the physical agony of changing from a man to a duck. He'd forgiven his wife for enchanting him, but he'd never forgive himself for betraying her.

Behind him, Josephine Monfort muttered. Was she aware of how much she talked to herself and that beastly cat? Perhaps it was something most middle-aged housewives did, like embroidery or flower arranging. A harmless little hobby to pass the hours. But was it really harmless if it drove him to rip moss from the walls to stuff his ears against the sound?

"Do you have something important to share, madame?" he grumbled. "If so, do speak up."

"Nothing that would concern someone like you, I'm sure."

He ignored her little jab. The Frenchwoman's taunt was no more than a tossed pebble; Truda had trained him to withstand the verbal version of trebuchet-launched boulders. He replied in a calm tone, "I suspect that every part of the pilgrimage will have a purpose. Every path, every trial. So let us consider what is to be gained or learned from this place. An herb, an offering, some knowledge, perhaps?"

They continued along the path, watching for clues amidst the foliage and statuary. Nothing struck Ansgar as extraordinary: wilting dandelions slumped here and there, a little pond slick with algae sloshed, a sculpture of a child clutching a lamb cast a long shadow, a few rotten pears rested at the roots of a row of espaliered trees.

"A poem," he heard Madame Monfort say from the other side of a rhododendron bush. "Could this be of use, do you suppose?"

He rounded the bush and found her staring at words carved atop a stone pillar.

> *To please the saint upon the hill*
> *A baker must perform with skill.*
> *Now pay heed to this poem small—*

Not just one part, but each and all.

Ingredients become the dough:
Honey wild from among the stones,
A pinch of sand from river drawn,
A whispered memory, most fond.

But first a bridge of pearl appears:
A passage bought with fervent tears.
Cross, and find the ovens seven
And pure sisters serving heaven.

Approach the saint with awe and fear,
A seeking soul, and conscience clear.
Whoever bakes the choicest cake
The saint's one precious wish will take.

Ansgar nodded and said, "Well done, madame. This appears to be vital information for those who intend to compete for the wish."

"I agree," she said. She'd set her things down already, and now she bent to withdraw a little notebook and a stub of pencil from her bag. She copied the words, checking and rechecking them before putting the notebook away.

"Well then," Ansgar said, rubbing his hands together to warm them. As the sky darkened, the temperature was dropping fast. "We've found the purpose of this particular place. We should move on."

"Will they—and we—travel through the night, do you think?" Madame Monfort asked nervously as she settled the straps of her pack and basket over her shoulders.

Ansgar led her back to the main path. "We must be prepared for the possibility. Martel does not seem the most merciful of leaders."

"I don't like him," Madame Montfort said.

Ansgar held back a laugh. Even the woman's spite came out coated with sweetness. She was an interesting creature, to be sure. He had known nixes and forest sprites, tree nymphs and river mermaids, and every imaginable type of mortal female, yet this one defied categorization. She was too kind to be called a shrew, and too fierce to be described as spineless.

When he reached the stone wall, he held open the arched blue door and waited for the woman to pass through. Good manners were a point of pride with him, and he'd display them even for his enemies—which she was, of course, no matter what other label he might assign her. In the end, or slightly before it, he would vanquish her. He would vanquish all of the pilgrims. No doubt every one of them had some touching reason for seeking the wish. It mattered not. His mission was to forestall death itself, and no one would stand in his way.

Finally, Madame Monfort passed by him with a word of thanks—and then a gasp. Slowly, neck craned, she took a few steps more into the room.

Ansgar followed her, trying not to inhale any cat particles leaking from the basket on her back. The blasted animal had sent him into at least ten sneezing fits since they'd set out. And was it staring at him through its little window? Great gods, if he'd had magic to spare, he would have conjured a ball of fire to incinerate the beast.

He stopped beside Josephine and took note of their surroundings. They were inside a church again, which wasn't altogether shocking. What stole his breath was the fact that every inch of the place mirrored the chapel they had entered that morning, down to the slant of the spider web hanging in the stained glass window to their right.

"Impossible," Josephine said.

"Yet here we are," Ansgar replied dryly.

Out of the corner of his eye, he saw her shiver. Close to the hollow of her throat, her fingers rubbed a pendant he'd not noticed before. "Are we trapped, then?" she said. "Doomed to move in an endless circle and never reach the Seven Ovens? Perhaps we are being punished for following the chosen ones after we were rejected."

"That would be most unfortunate, but I do not think so." Ansgar inclined his head and listened to what he'd thought at first was the hum of a fly. "Do you hear that? Martel is leading the pilgrims in song. They cannot be far from us."

"Oh, thank heaven," Josephine said. "That's something differ-ent. An eternity of senseless repetition does not appeal to me in the least."

"Such a fate does seem dreadful. I would prefer to cease to exist at all. To sink into the utter blackness of oblivion. To be free of…being." His unintentional frankness made him cringe. He wasn't one to share his personal thoughts with a near-stranger. Blaming tiredness, he rushed toward the voices before she could respond to his rambling with nonsense of her own.

In the future, he'd guard his mouth. This journey was a mission, not a jolly frolic through the countryside with a new friend. Sharing personal thoughts and feelings led to foolishness, he'd learned that lesson well enough when he'd fallen for the larch tree faerie—and lived to quack about it for years.

"It's good we finally found something in common, even if it is a shared fear," Madame Monfort said as she followed him down the center aisle.

"I never said I was afraid," he snapped. "Fear is for the power-less. The weak-willed."

"No need to bark," she replied. "I only—"

Ansgar lifted a hand to command her to silence. With each step he took closer to the altar, the pilgrims' song echoed louder. Their harmonies were sloppy, their phrasing stilted, but he tried to memorize the song. He might need it for something later.

Madame Monfort's humming drifted to his ears. She must

have had the same thought he did about learning the music. Perhaps she was not as vacant-headed as he'd believed. Perhaps she *would* reach the Seven Ovens alive. For a moment, he almost pitied the widow. The journey would only get more difficult, and in the end, she'd have nothing to show for it but scars and a story.

Six

As the pilgrims' song faded, Josephine trailed Monsieur Steuben through a torch-lit corridor identical to one they'd walked before. She thought about the poem she'd found in the garden; its suggestion that a fond memory should be spoken as the cakes were added to the oven.

She stepped over a broken floor tile, and the jerking motion made the cat yowl within the basket. "Hush," she whispered. Confinement in a feline body had done nothing to improve her husband's personality. Every five minutes, he meowed complainingly about something. She was glad she couldn't translate his feline rants. No doubt they were full of curse words and condemnation.

Eyes fixed on the back of the man she was following, she sifted through her memories of Thierry, searching for a moment of joy or delight to use as the poem instructed. He'd surprised her with the gift of a ruby brooch one Christmas. Would that be a fond enough remembrance to bake with? It worried her to think that it might not be—and saddened her that she had nothing else to offer in the way of happy memories from their thirteen-year marriage.

She watched Monsieur Steuben duck and lean to avoid a

spider web. Did he share a treasure trove of glorious memories with a happy wife? That seemed unlikely. He had the air of a roving bachelor who collected insipid lovers in every town and broke hearts for fun. She scolded herself for the uncharitable thought. The German was abrasive and unpleasant, but that did not mean he was deeply cruel or completely immoral. In truth, they barely knew each other. It would make sense for them to learn a bit about one another, to form a bond like fellow soldiers would so they'd feel united when battling side by side. Because if Monsieur Steuben was correct and this place was magic-tainted, they would surely face harder challenges than sore feet, uneven paths, and repeated settings.

They came to a long, straight section of candlelit corridor. The walking pilgrims came into view ahead of them. Monsieur Steuben stopped and crouched in the shadows. They'd wait until the pilgrims moved just out of sight, she knew. For once, she wished the chosen ones would move a little faster. Crouching and holding still made her muscles burn.

"Do you have a wife or sweetheart waiting for you?" Josephine whispered as she knelt close to Monsieur Steuben. She set Thierry's basket on the floor. The cat made no complaint, which meant he'd fallen asleep. It was as good a time as any to make inquiries of her traveling companion. To perhaps start to build a scaffolding for a friendship, however shaky.

Monsieur Steuben glared at her. "Quiet. You'll draw attention."

"I think you do have someone," Josephine said with a small smile. "I think you're making the journey for her."

"Will you cease your chattering if I say that is the case? If so, then yes, I'm risking life, limb, and sanity for the sake of true love."

"I knew it. How many years have you been together? Ten? Twenty?"

"Hush."

"A long time, then. Am I correct? I imagine you married quite young, after a fiery courtship. Her father objected. There was an elopement." Her imagination took flight, as it often did when she was overtired, and she allowed it to soar.

"Be quiet, woman."

"Not until you tell me how you met and married."

"Fine. She was the town apothecary. A most remarkable woman. I was her apprentice for a week before we became betrothed. We married soon after. She was the most terrible and wonderful thing to ever happen to me. Now, close your mouth and keep it closed."

"Fine." She imagined him young and dashing, a little shy before growing fully into manhood. Scholarly in bearing, with a white lab coat and ink smudges on his hands. In her daydream, stripped of his haughty airs, he was rather handsome. Curiosity twinkled in his blue eyes as he watched a tall, beautiful woman with a neat, golden chignon concoct medicine in a glass beaker. A look passed between them. A longing look. The apothecary took hold of his lapels and drew him close. His eyes widened and his breaths quickened. A smile spread across his face as she leaned in and...

"Madame? Are you asleep or have you become deaf? I said we must go."

She startled. "Sorry." Embarrassment heated her cheeks.

He shook his head and stood. "If we live through this, it will be a wonder. If I survive with even a shred of my sanity, it will be an absolute miracle."

Still in the pleasant haze of her daydream, Josephine said, "I am hoping for both. My *grand-mère* always said that a hopeful heart can make the roughest road a pleasant lane."

He grunted. "Gods above, I detest homely proverbs. Are you coming along, or have you decided to adhere yourself to the floor there like a patch of mildew?"

Her imaginings had softened her. That was the danger of daydreaming, of making people behave in impossible ways with one's imagination. Because of this, when she should have expected and been prepared to withstand his retort, the cruel edge of his words stung like a paper cut to the heart. "That was both unkind and unnecessary, Monsieur."

No apology came from his lips. He simply shouldered his bag and set off after the pilgrims. She picked up the cat's basket and whispered to Thierry, "What a bitter pill that man is. You warned me, though, didn't you, *mon chéri*? With your growling and hissing when first we met him? I should have listened to you. But we will endure it until the contest. We are strong enough to do that, at least."

The cat meowed in reply.

On feet that silently cried out for mercy, Josephine trudged behind Monsieur Steuben. She revised her earlier fantasy of him, the one in which she'd pictured him as a bright-eyed student. Young Ansgar Steuben was surely grim and gruff, with a snarling lip and cold gaze. Perhaps he had tricked his wife into marriage, luring her into his trap with plagiarized love poems and flowers plucked from neighbors' gardens.

Wait—was this apothecary the same woman he'd mentioned as a formidable witch-queen? That marriage would make sense. Two wicked people making a wicked life together, terrorizing children and ruining the reputation of whatever town they called home.

She would never know for certain, because she would never ask him. Besides, as *Grand-mère* used to say, expecting the devil to tell the truth is like expecting a goat to give a good Sunday sermon.

A sharp, left-hand turn in the corridor emptied them into an octagonal room perhaps twenty feet across. Brick walls soared to form a tower, windowless until just below its peaked roof. Deep shadows lurked like fog, barely touched by moonlight that trickled in the high windows.

"Keep moving," Monsieur Steuben said. "If you insist on stopping to gawk at every doorpost and beam, be sure that I will leave you behind without bidding you farewell."

Josephine opened her mouth to reply, but forgot to speak when the shadows shifted and deepened. A strange breeze ruffled the loose locks of her hair. The air smelled odd, like decaying leaves and burning feathers. Goose bumps rose along her arms. Thierry growled a warning.

She looked up. Something swooped in circles overhead. Something big and darker than the shadows. She held her breath, stood still, and squinted to make out its form, although her instinct demanded that she run: broad wings that looked too large for its body, blue-black feathers. Pointed talons, long as fingers, flexing as it flew. Eyes like glowing coals.

Monsieur Steuben collided with her, sidestepped, and ran back the way they'd come. "The door is gone!" he shouted. "Rouse yourself, woman! Find an exit!"

The creature descended, circling slowly, slowly, yet there was nothing gentle about its approach. As it grew closer, Josephine smelled blood. Rot.

"Madame!" the German shouted again. Still, she did not move. The straps of the cat basket slipped off her shoulders and the carrier hit the ground with a dull thud. Without thinking, she shrugged out of her pack and let it fall as well.

And then she remembered. In her childhood, on the full moon after the harvest was in, the farmwives and the children would gather for a bonfire-lit night of tales. With hands sticky and mouths sweet from celebratory pastries, she'd listened until dawn to stories of heroic women, strange faeries, and unusual creatures.

She knew this beast.

This monster had haunted her girlhood dreams for an entire winter, thanks to her great-aunt's wild-eyed descriptions of its flesh-tearing and bone-crunching. This was the *hibouchauris*, an owl-bat that the young shepherdess, Alphonsine, accidentally released from the goblin-hole in the hills near her home. She'd defeated it by...by...

Monsieur Steuben shoved her off her feet. She hit the ground hard and inhaled dirt as he pinned her down with his body. Nearby, Thierry hissed inside his overturned carrier.

"There is no way out," Monsieur Steuben said, his mouth brushing her ear. "Lie still. Pray. I will do what I can."

"You'll do what you can?" She almost laughed. What could a spoiled, overdressed, former student-wizard do to defeat such a mighty predator?

His chanted whispers tickled her earlobe. His body tensed, heavy as a boulder upon her back and legs. Strangely, the contact brought to mind a love scene in her favorite novel, in which the hero saved the damsel from a dragon by concealing her with his body. She blushed from head to foot as she remembered the kiss that had ensued. Two full paragraphs of kissing. Would the German try to kiss her if they lived?

Heavens, her mind was ridiculous, wandering to that when they could die at any second.

She had to think. Yes. There was something in the bonfire tale...*The shepherdess. The owl-bat.*

Tante Clothilde's voice echoed in her mind: *The hot breath of the beast washed over the little shepherdess, drying her sweat, burning her eyes. What weapons did she have? She'd lost her crook in a deep ravine that morning, clumsy girl. She'd lent her knife to her brother. All she had was the cloth sack she wore across her chest which held a skin of water, a crust of bread, a ball of wool half-knitted into a scarf, and the pair of silver knitting needles she'd recently purchased from a traveling peddler. After they traded coins for wares, the old fellow had jabbed her in the shoulder with his elbow and said, "Purl you shall, and knit as well, and banish your troubles to the pit of hell."*

The wee shepherdess had smiled indulgently at the madly grinning peddler and gone on her way. And here she was, not three days later, facing the worst troubles of her life. The hibouchauris had already gobbled up a lamb. She reached into her little sack, and...

With all her strength, Josephine pushed up from the ground,

twisting to dislodge the German from her back. He cursed and grabbed for her, but she dove for the pack she'd dropped. She tore it open and yanked out her knitting. Above her, within arm's length, the beast circled. Its long neck flexed. Its ember-gaze was on Thierry's basket. In its next rounding, the thing would surely snatch the cat's carrier with its talons.

Josephine stepped closer to the basket. The needles felt cold in her grip. She fought to keep herself from throwing up. Thierry yowled. Circling again, the hibouchauris approached in the swirling dimness. When the beast swooped low, she jumped to stab it in the belly. The needles slid in deep. Josephine released them and fell onto her knees.

The beast shrieked and convulsed in the air, with five inches of Josephine's unfinished pink wool shawl dangling from its bleeding gut and the rest of the ball of wool unfurling downward. Wings gone limp, it crashed to the ground inches away from a stunned-looking Monsieur Steuben. His mouth gaped like a beached trout's.

Josephine watched the hibouchauris exhale its last breath, and then, knees shaking, she went to retrieve her knitting. Greenish-red blood saturated the wool. She pulled the needles free of the beast's black-furred abdomen and bent to wipe them clean on the ground. When she was done, she stood up straight as a conquering queen and looked her traveling companion in the eye. Her heart-beat raced dangerously, but she had never felt stronger.

She looked away from the gruesome scene as nausea rolled around in her stomach. No, she would not be sick, nor would she allow herself to feel sorry for the dead creature. The hibouchauris had attacked them without provocation. It was time for her victory speech, and she would let nothing spoil the moment. "*Tante* Clothilde taught me to never leave home without my knitting," she said, holding the needles high. "Silver needles. Passed down from Clothilde's grandmother to her, and then to me. Only silver can kill a hibouchauris."

"Great gods." He shook his head. "You are a madwoman. And I thank you."

"You are welcome." She gathered her belongings, except for the bloodied knitting project, and returned her pack and the cat basket onto her back. Thierry whined, but she would deal with him later. As they stood there in the tower room, the pilgrims were gaining ground. "I see the door now," she said, pointing to a black rectangle. "There. We should go."

"Quite right," he agreed.

Josephine led the way, knees still shaking but wearing a proud smile on her face. "What do you think of me now, husband?" she whispered over her shoulder to Thierry.

The cat didn't respond.

As her head was turned, she noticed something astounding: the beast's remains had disappeared and left not a drop of blood behind. Had the thing been real or a very convincing illusion created by magic? It had felt real when she'd stabbed it.

"You know," Monsieur Steuben said grumpily as he followed her, "I'm starting to wonder what kind of religion this Sainte Yvette professes. This pilgrimage is certainly not like any I read of before we began."

She didn't reply, although she, too, had started to wonder about the nature of the saint and her pilgrimage. The thrill of defeating the hibouchauris faded. If meeting the monster had been a trial, worse trials were sure to come. Would she be equal to them?

Upon passing through the door out of the tower, Ansgar stepped around Madame Monfort to take the lead. If this was rude behavior, he did not give a fig. It was quite possible that he was out of proverbial figs. Perhaps for the duration of this mad journey.

In the long hallway lit by hanging lanterns, he tried to adopt an energetic stride but soon abandoned that idea. Perhaps in her own weariness, the Frenchwoman would not notice his. The last thing he wanted was to appear weak, especially after the incident with the flying monster.

His pulse had yet to settle down, and his entire body felt feverish with unexpressed anger. He could scarce believe that Madame Monfort had shown off so impulsively when the creature attacked. It was not that he cared much if she lived or died. What boiled his blood was that because of her rash behavior, he'd wasted a good deal of his limited magical strength. Almost all of it, in truth.

With great effort, and not a little pain, he'd gathered his magic into an invisible ball as they'd lain on the floor, forming a weapon to hurl at the beast. And then she'd leapt up and bested the monster before he did—*with her knitting needles*. What a waste! If only she would have obeyed him and stayed still for another half-minute, he could have obliterated the battish owl with a grand burst of magic. The thing had not been all that large, judging by what he could see of it in the oddly shifting darkness.

Perhaps just as disturbing was the image of Josephine Monfort which had imprinted itself on his mind; the widow lunging at the swooping terror, wild-eyed and brandishing the thin rapiers of her innocent pastime. How fierce she'd looked.

How unexpectedly beguiling.

He brushed dirt off his sleeve as he tried to brush off the memory, feeling sullied by both.

"I'd never actually seen a hibouchauris before today," the Frenchwoman said as they walked past a few alcoves containing small statues of saintly-looking figures. She sounded far too cheerful for someone who'd recently been a breath away from being shredded by talons and teeth. She continued, saying, "It looked so much different than the drawings I've seen in books. Those broad shiny wings and tufted ears! It was almost beautiful, was it not? Aside from its terrible claws and the murderous gleam in its eyes, of course."

"I found nothing appealing in the beast's appearance," Ansgar said, walking faster to distance himself from her. The only good thing about her chattering was that it pulverized the brief attraction he'd felt for her. "Now, if you could stop speaking so that I might listen for the others..."

"Of course." She lowered her voice to a whisper. "But I must ask, do you think we will meet another hibouchauris? Are they like dogs, fond of living in packs? Should I keep my needles in hand, perhaps?"

"If it pleases you." Ansgar rushed around a turn and Martel's voice met his ear, faint yet unmistakable. Thank the gods. He'd been certain that the brief encounter with the monster had allowed the pilgrims to pass beyond traceability. These halls were full of forked paths and closed doors that often blended in with the walls—so many opportunities for the eight travelers to choose a different path.

"This way," Ansgar said, indicating a spiral staircase almost hidden by a high wooden panel carved with the faces of birds. "Mind your footsteps. Silence is safety." He'd created that adage on the spot. Fond as Josephine Monfort was of homely sayings, she'd likely spout it one day to some rowdy and unfortunate grandchild—if she lived that long. The thought of his words plaguing her grandchildren brought an impish smile to his face.

Up and up wound the narrow stairs, into fog-like shadows and swaths of incense-scented air. Window slits pierced the walls, giving glimpses of a sprinkling of stars. Ansgar reckoned the time to be between midnight and dawn. The second day of the pilgrimage had begun without fanfare. Which was good, for the drama with the beast had provided enough blood-stirring excitement to last him for a year. His heart, at the moment, was not young. He hated to test its limits.

Finally, they stepped onto a landing. A sort of elevated loft, lit dimly by a golden glow that seeped through cracks underfoot and cutouts in the walls. Ansgar's ear caught the sound of voices.

Quietly, he set his pack on the wide oak floorboards and squatted beside it. Madame followed his example without being told.

Through a flower-shaped hole in a waist-high wooden wall, Ansgar peered down on the pilgrims as they settled into a large, open room heated by an enormous fireplace. In spite of the enormity of the space, they congregated near its center, unfurling their bedrolls close together, removing their boots or coats. A few conversed quietly while the others rubbed sore feet or folded themselves into their blankets to sleep.

Madame Monfort crawled close enough that he could feel the warmth radiating from her body. She still wore the cat carrier on her back. The blasted cat's proximity caused his eyes to itch and seep. He leaned away, as if it might help, and whispered, "They're bedding down for the night. We'll sleep here. Stay low to avoid being seen."

"I'm not stupid, you know." She said it without venom, as if informing him of the weather.

"My apologies," he said tersely. "It was not my intention to imply that you are less than stunningly clever."

Now she glared at him. She rose but remained bent double as she moved a few feet away. Back to him, she slipped the basket's straps from her shoulders and lowered it to the floor. The cat growled for no apparent reason. From the way the woman huffed and muttered as she unrolled her blanket along the wall, Ansgar deduced that he'd actually offended her.

Such verbal sparring had been one of the delights of his marriage to Truda. But Truda had never been one to walk away from an insult. She would have cast one back at him, or thrown a dish in his direction in lieu of words. The fight would have escalated until they found themselves overcome by a fit of laughter or a passionate embrace.

He imagined that kissing an angry Madame Monfort would be akin to kissing a prickly eel, the kind that squealed and flopped about before one dropped it into the cooking pot. Or would it?

Perhaps she would melt against him, tamed by his attentions, rendered docile as a milk-drunken kitten. He sneezed into his sleeve. Great gods, he hated felines. Even imaginary ones. But at least the sneeze had served to interrupt his thoughts of kissing the Frenchwoman.

Now, to keep his exhausted brain from wandering back to that subject...Food. Yes, he could think about food. He dug his hand into his bag and fished around until he found a pear. If anyone had been watching, he would have taken small, mannerly nibbles. Alone and famished, he devoured the fruit in a few wolfish bites. Once finished, he wiped the juice from his chin and went back to acting like the elegant gentleman he was.

The room darkened by degrees as someone doused the candles and lanterns in the chamber below. Ansgar settled onto the floor with a groan. Sleeping on the floor was torture. He liked a thick mattress, soft blankets, and fat pillows. He liked a carafe of spring water on his nightstand. To fall asleep reading something scandalous so as to keep himself from missing Truda's arm draped across his chest and her toes poking his ankle.

Truda.

While he favored the lavish bedroom in his Loire Valley chateau, with its ceiling painted with darting swallows and its gold bed posts carved with chubby cherubs, Truda would have hated it. His wife had loved the simplicity of her bedchamber in the gingerbread cottage, with its plain, timber-framed beds and whitewashed walls. Her tastes had baffled him, as had many things about her. She was as inscrutable as time and as uncontrollable as the wind. And he'd never find her equal, not even if he lived another century.

A century? He'd not live out the year unless he obtained the wish. He might be a rotting corpse before Christmastide. His bones commenced a chorus of aching to remind him that with every passing hour, he was aging by leaps and bounds.

Worry settled over him like a scratchy coverlet. This entire journey might be nothing but a farce. A drawn-out mistake fraught with the discomforts of sleeping on floors, supping on nasty dried venison and bruised fruit, and tolerating a travel companion who babbled like a senile grandmother. And to make matters worse, there was the stupid cat, making him sniffle and sneeze.

He rolled onto his side in an attempt to lessen his pain. His gaze fell upon his traveling companion. Overtaken by sleep, she was far less offensive to his senses. No one would have called her breathtaking, but she was pretty in the way of a meadow buttercup or a roadside daisy. Her mouth had a pleasant shape now that it was still. Her eyebrows were a bit unruly, as was her madly coiling hair, but they suited her. In spite of her obvious domesticity and tendency to prattle, she was not a fragile, needy girl, but a woman brave enough to risk body and soul to save someone she loved. Courageous enough to stab a monster to protect someone she hardly knew. No matter how she vexed him, he had to admire the woman's courage.

Ansgar closed his eyes. Merciful, black unconsciousness consumed him. After a while, he felt his wife's sharp, familiar elbow gouging his shoulder. He smiled and murmured her name.

"Monsieur?" The voice in his ear was not Truda's. Another poke, from a jabbing fingertip.

"Wake up. The pilgrims are leaving," Madame Monfort urged.

His eyes sprang open. The woman was kneeling beside him with her hair a mass of unbound frizzy curls. The pink imprint of her hand marred her left cheek. Her shirt was rumpled and untucked from her trousers. The sudden desire to pull her into his arms was strong and loathsome. He cursed in German and sat up. "You say they're leaving?"

"Yes, by now the last of them has exited the great hall."

He raked his hands through his hair. "You should have woken me before."

She stood and glared down at him, hands on hips. "I have been trying to wake you for ages. You sleep like a hibernating bear! I should have kicked you, I suppose."

"I'm surprised you didn't, you harpy!"

Her face turned crimson. She huffed and spun away from him.

Ansgar wished she would have said what she was thinking. He wanted her to say words so rude that far off in her chapel, Sainte Yvette would sense them and shudder. Swearing made him feel better, and judging by her lobster-like color, the woman needed some release. But he knew Josephine Monfort would not curse or call him names. She was simply too wholesome.

Groaning, he stood and stuffed his blanket into his pack. His limbs ached worse than before he'd slept, and his mouth tasted foul. Both his eyes burned and watered. He cursed once more, specifically targeting the cat this time.

Without acknowledging his presence, the Frenchwoman lifted her pack and basket and took the lead, down the stairs and then through the empty great hall. As they walked, he watched her hands weave her hair into a long, bumpy braid which she twisted into a knot at the back of her skull. The quick movements of her fingers and the manner in which she secured the knot by stabbing it through with a pair of short knitting needles bespoke her simmering anger. No matter what she did with her hair, she would not look tidy. He doubted a square inch of her could be deemed clean.

His own appearance likely paralleled hers after all the trudging, traipsing, and floor-sleeping. But someday soon, fortified by the wish, he'd head home to his enormous bathtub and his rabbit-fur slippers. A five-course meal. Coffee with fresh cream. Champagne and cake. Sheets scented with rosewater and ironed smooth.

"I've lost sight of them." Madame Monfort stopped and glanced over her shoulder at him. Her complexion had faded from scarlet to rose-pink. "They had to turn here, obviously, but which way?"

"Grand." He brushed past her, grumbling. "We must examine the floor for footprints, I suppose."

"Do not act as if I failed you somehow. You were the one who lay there snoring and refusing to awaken. Should I have left you there?"

"Were you always this churlish with your husband, madame? If so, perhaps he would prefer to remain a cat forever."

She gasped in shock at his jab, but offered no reply. He pried a torch free from an iron bracket and directed its light onto the brown-and-white tiled floor.

"No sign of which route they chose," Ansgar said. "We will simply have to take our chances."

"Left," Madame Monfort said just as he said, "Right."

"Fine," she said. "We'll go right, as you say. At least you will not be able to fault me if the choice proves unwise."

Torch held high, Ansgar hastened along the corridor and attempted to exude confidence he did not quite feel. Was the magic in this place affecting him or was his self-assurance simply fading with his vitality? This rapid aging was beyond cruel.

Cold, damp air skimmed along his exposed skin like an unwelcome phantom. Nearby, water plip-plopped with an uneven rhythm. As he advanced, the neat stone walls became rough and craggy. The tiled floor ended, replaced by bare earth that slanted downward. With Madame at his heels, he trudged for a mile or more. There was no sign of the pilgrims. No echo of voices. Not one footprint.

Had he chosen the wrong route? Was it possible to choose the wrong route? As much as he detested being robbed of autonomy, he hoped his wizardly intuition was correct in this case, and that they were being ushered along the pilgrimage route by magic in an "all roads lead to Rome" sort of scenario.

The torch in his hand sputtered and dimmed. If not for the glow coming from small oil lamps set into nooks in the walls, the place would have been dark as midnight. He suspected they were underground, wandering a warren of endless tunnels. He squinted to see the sloped path ahead. Madame Monfort grabbed at his coat and yanked him backward. The torch fell from his grasp and plummeted into a gaping chasm inches ahead of his toes. Equilibrium lost, he landed firmly on his posterior.

Inches from his body, the ground gave way to a black chasm. He swallowed down his body's inclination to vomit.

Madame Monfort crouched beside him, wide-eyed and panting as if she'd been the one to almost tumble to her doom. Her hand cupped his shoulder. "Are you all right?"

"Of course I am," he grumbled, annoyed that he'd almost died a fool's death. "You made me lose my footing, grabbing me as you did."

"Pardon me for saving your life." Her expression hardened. She stood and adjusted the straps of her cat basket. "If you would prefer not to be rescued, do say so. I'll gladly comply with your wishes next time you're imperiled."

Ansgar swore and got to his feet. "I said nothing of the kind, madame. No need for dramatics."

She turned away to pluck a clay oil lamp from a cranny in the wall. "You're one to talk about dramatics. *Mes étoiles*, I have never met such a spoiled, self-centered man." The cat meowed as if to agree.

He gaped at her as she hurried away. Did his ears deceive him or had she just insulted him? What would she do next to astound him? Breathe fire?

"Coming?" she asked without stopping.

Quickly, he snatched an oil lamp and followed her. The path slanted upward now, and all he could think of was the pain it aggravated in his legs and hips. Pain could be a blessing after all, for it left no room in his mind for Josephine Monfort.

After she'd been silent for a quarter hour—possibly the longest she'd kept quiet since they'd met—the path flattened and he found himself bored. An inclination to provoke her proved too tempting to resist. In a superior tone he asked, "Do you miss sitting by the parlor fire with your needlework, madame? Or is it taking tea with the gossiping spinsters of the parish that you most pine for?"

"Knitting in the garden while the birds sing above me in the apple tree. That's what I miss," she replied softly, as if she'd not noticed the mockery in his voice. "I detest embroidery, I loathe quilting clubs, and I cannot abide gossip. If anything blackens one's soul, it is spreading rumors about one's neighbor."

Ansgar bit his tongue, barely resisting the urge to describe a dozen more effective ways by which she might blacken her soul. If she'd had an inkling of how he and his witch-queen had lived, the ways they'd amused themselves at the expense of forest wanderers, simpleminded animals, and each other... Even he cringed when he recalled some of their vilest deeds. No one would say that Truda had brought out the best in him—unless one was measuring with the devil's yardstick.

"It's quite relaxing, knitting," she continued. "The rhythmic click of the needles, the softness of the wool in your hands. I could teach you next time we stop to rest."

"I'm sure that won't be necessary," he answered brusquely.

"If you change your mind, do let me know."

His oil lamp sputtered, providing a convenient reason to stop at a wall nook to exchange it for another. Let the woman move a few more paces ahead without him. He had meant to instigate a fight for the sake of entertainment. Instead of snapping up the bait, she'd dizzied him with simple sincerity, almost disarming him.

Great, unmerciful gods. Was he beginning to soften toward her? Did she perhaps possess some magic of her own, a tiny but effectual spark he'd failed to notice before? Or perhaps he was losing his mind inside this infernal enchanted landscape.

There had to be some explanation for the ease with which Josephine Monfort had put a dent—several dents—in his heart of cold, black iron.

Seven

Josephine bit her lower lip to keep from moaning in pain as she led Monsieur Steuben down a set of jagged stone stairs, through a door, and onto a garden path. She was loath to admit that her toes felt as if they were about to fall off inside her boots. Her companion would only mock her for the cheapness of the leather or taunt her for not training before the journey. Her shoulders throbbed, too, where the straps of the cat's basket had worn grooves into her skin. To remedy this, her companion would undoubtedly recommend leaving the cat to die. Not a chance.

The sky stretched overhead, purplish black veiled with deep gray swaths of cloud. A hedge of thick bramble bushes kept her from wandering off the path. A half-moon peeked through the haze now and then as if spying upon her and the German. Although they'd walked miles and had yet to discern any new sign of the chosen pilgrims, she clung to the hope that she'd see them soon. She could cling to hope like a barnacle sticking to the hull of a ship. It was one of her best talents—along with knitting, memorizing poetry, and baking. None of these skills were worth much— and certainly not in the estimation of her worldly, snobbish traveling companion.

Ansgar Steuben was a puzzle she could not seem to solve. He brooded almost constantly, hated to accept help or a kind word, gave out insults like a rat determined to spread a plague, and yet when he spoke of his wife, his devotion to the woman could not be disputed. If he'd loved her truly, some goodness must exist within him. Well, Josephine would not be the one to excavate that particular buried treasure. It would be enough of a miracle if she could figure out how to unearth the affection of her own husband.

Josephine's body grew heavy with fatigue. How could one's arms and legs weigh so much? If she were to stop for but a moment, she would fall asleep on her feet. She glanced over her shoulder at Monsieur Steuben. He looked as tired as she felt. His face was the color of the spying moon, an unhealthy grayish white. How long had it been since they'd eaten? If he fell ill and had to quit the journey, she would have to continue alone, and the thought filled her with alarm.

"We should stop and eat," she said firmly. "Here. We can rest on these boulders and avoid sitting on the damp ground."

"I could eat, I suppose," said her companion—without his usual belligerence. She watched him settle onto a throne-shaped rock and rifle through the contents of his bag, captivated by the odd gracefulness of his motions. After a moment, he drew out a cloth-wrapped loaf of bread and what appeared to be a small pot of butter. From an inner pocket of his coat, he took a folded knife. A flick of the wrist revealed a short blade. "Is there something amiss with my face, or are you simply enthralled by my handsomeness?"

Josephine's face heated as she stole her gaze away from him to eye the dirt at her feet. Had she not been so weary, she never would have allowed herself to fall into a trance observing the man. "I didn't mean to stare. I was just looking...around."

"I see." His blue eyes accused her of lying, and his devilish smile implied that he found it quite amusing.

The hot blush spread from her face to her neck. She tore into her own bag and made a show of searching for food, wishing he would start a conversation about the weather or the bread. About anything but the fact that she had been watching him, however innocently.

She felt his lingering gaze but tried to ignore it as she opened a tin of sardines and placed it inside the cat's basket. Much as she dreaded it, the cat would have to be leashed and allowed to perform his bodily functions after the meal. Thierry hated being leashed. She already had several deep scratches to prove it.

Monsieur Steuben swore and waved one of his long hands in front of his nose. "That smell! Like something died!"

"Fish died, of course. The cat must eat." She braced herself for another verbal battle over the cat, but Monsieur Steuben had turned his attention to slicing cheese and arranging it atop a buttered slice of brown bread. Her mouth watered at the sight.

He lifted the bread to his mouth, then paused. "I thought you were hungry, madame. Do not tell me you only brought food for the animal?"

"I have food." She took out a rather squashed roll and a dented apple and displayed them like newly won prizes. "See?"

Frowning, he shook his head. "That creature could have waited to be fed. You look about to faint from hunger. There is nothing wrong with seeing to your own needs first sometimes, Madame."

His concerned scolding might have come from her mother's mouth. But he was not her mother. They were not even friends. How dare he tell her how to live?

She tore into the roll with her teeth. Monsieur Steuben was right, and it was infuriating. As a dutiful daughter and a doting wife, she was used to putting others first even when it cost her dearly. Never once had she complained aloud about doing every-thing possible to serve and to please Thierry. She'd eaten Thierry's favorite foods and worn his favorite colors. She'd entertained his friends and stayed home without complaint while he attended parties. She'd found solace in quiet hobbies that didn't disturb Thierry's precious peace. Her only vice was living vicariously through the heroines of the novels she read while Thierry snored the night away.

The cat mewed plaintively. With a sigh, Josephine set aside her apple and took out a bundle of thin rope to attach to the cat's collar. She was doing it again, putting others first and setting aside her own basic needs. She felt Monsieur Steuben's judgmental stare as she squatted to open the basket.

"Allow me to walk the cat," he said.

Now she couldn't tell if he was being kind or making fun of her. "He's my problem," she said. Immediately she regretted her choice of words. Thierry was not a *problem*; he was her husband. She'd sworn vows before heaven to care for him in sickness and in health, for better and for worse. This part was the "worse."

Or was it?

As much as her feet ached, and her everything-else hurt, there was something thrilling about being on this adventure, free of the rules and schedules of her ordinary life. Maybe Thierry's temporary "worse" was actually part of her "better."

The cat pulled her along a narrow path that branched off from the one by which she and the German had arrived. As the animal pawed the ground and prepared to do his business, she averted her eyes.

While her dearest hope was that Thierry would be a changed man when he returned to being a man, what if the pilgrimage transformed her, too? The situation felt dangerous all of a sudden. Because she definitely *had* changed since setting out on the journey. Now that she'd spread her wings and flown through wild places, how would it feel to return to a life hedged in by Thierry's expectations and society's traditions?

Only one wish would be awarded at the end of the pilgrimage. Perhaps the wish would be powerful enough to provide a happy future for both her husband and herself, but what if she had to choose?

She refused to entertain the question further as she tugged the growling cat back toward his basket.

Eight

A dark, hedge-walled path, seemingly miles long, had recently given way to an enormous courtyard. Sudden rays of golden sunlight assaulted Ansgar's eyes. He squinted at his surroundings but kept walking. Before him spread a wild meadow of tall grasses and wildflowers. Although he'd always preferred dusk's subtlety, today he welcomed the bright scene. After so much time in dim places, this setting lifted his spirits. Thus, he was able to tolerate Madame Monfort's chirpy soliloquy on the benefits of morning walks with barely a grunt.

He, Madame Monfort, and the devil-spawn cat had spent the previous night in a shed they'd happened upon soon after nightfall. The building had housed only an assortment of shovels, rakes, and spiders, but nonetheless had lacked room enough for them to lie down to sleep. The cat had purred loudly on the French-woman's lap all night, as if bragging of its comfortable position. How he hated that cat! Fed and coddled, carried about like a prince —and still given to yowling complaints every hour of the day. In his magic-sensitive bones, Ansgar knew the creature did not contain a human spirit, and yet there was something unusual about it. Something un-catlike and unnatural. Perhaps the thing had a hint of faerie-cat blood. Regardless, he still planned to toss the thing into a river or crevasse whenever the opportunity arose.

He stepped over a fallen branch. A blurry-edged memory appeared in his mind. At some point in the night, when he'd lingered between sleep and wakefulness with eyes shut, he'd felt his blanket pulled up and tucked behind his shoulders. The recollection of his companion's simple gesture of kindness alleviated his foul mood—slightly. He still despised the cat. He would never *not* despise the beast.

A blackbird caught his eye as it swayed atop a tall weed. A few paces in front of Ansgar, Madame Monfort brushed her fingertips over the heads of a dozen daisies. How elegant her splayed fingers were—never mind that they were smudged with dirt and inscribed with scratches.

"So many flowers," she said with a contented sigh. "This place must not know it is almost autumn. Look! I've never seen blue tulips before, have you? And the size of those roses!" She practically skipped along the pebbled pathway. "Oh, foxgloves. I do love foxgloves!"

Ansgar sneezed thrice and lost every vestige of his good humor. The landscape he'd been thankful for had quickly become his enemy. He wiped his nose with his rapidly deteriorating handkerchief. "Delightful. As if the cat were not enough of an assault upon my physical wellbeing."

She glanced over her shoulder at him. "Does everything make you sneeze?"

"Only cats and certain flowers. Unfortunately, I have not yet found a pill or potion to permanently cure me of the annoyance." He rubbed his inflamed eyes and hastened down the central path. "Come. We cannot afford to stop and sniff every buttercup. It is imperative that we find the others."

To their left stood a whimsical statue of a rabbit wearing a crown. Madame Monfort patted its head as she passed. "Do you think there's a clue here, as there was in the other courtyard?"

"It is possible. I propose a quick search followed by a hasty exit from this disagreeable landscape." He sneezed, and sneezed again.

"I believe you'd find fault with the Garden of Eden, *monsieur*."

"No doubt I would, if it irked me as much as this half-acre of weeds."

She laughed and waved a long-stemmed daisy at him. "You are determined to hate everything, but I will not let you spoil my enjoyment of this place."

He harrumphed in reply. They separated, each searching among the plants and paths for a clue. Bees hummed in the grass and sipped from the blossoms. A field mouse scurried over the toe of Ansgar's boot and he winced. *Incorrigible vermin.*

"Over there," Madame Monfort said. From where she stood on a path parallel to his, she pointed to a hollow tree trunk in a far corner of the garden, protruding through a circular gap in a granite-tiled terrace. "Is that a beehive? The poem from before spoke of 'honey wild from among the stones.'"

"So it did," Ansgar said. "Have you any experience harvesting honey?" He would not volunteer to be a human pincushion. A clogged nose and itchy eyes were plagues enough for one man.

"No. Have you?"

"I sometimes observed as my wife gathered honey in the forest, but she held dominion over the wild creatures there. It made for an altogether different situation, I suspect. The bees swarmed about her head like a halo and never once stung her. She sang to them, and they to her."

"We will have to make the best of it, then. I'll do what I can, unless you'd rather...?"

"By all means, go ahead." He felt a little cowardly, but not enough to plunge a limb into a nest of insects.

They followed separate paths until they converged not far from the hive. Madame Monfort set her bag down and then shrugged off the cat carrier. Ansgar dropped his bag as well, and then opened it to retrieve a small glass jar. He pulled the cork and emptied salt onto the ground. "We can use this to carry the honey," he said. "If we're lucky, it will hold enough to satisfy the requirements of the poem."

From her bag, Madame Monfort withdrew a woolen scarf and gloves. She would be overly warm, but the garments would offer her some protection from stings.

Slowly, they waded through tasseled, waist high grass to reach the hive. Ansgar tried to recall the words of Truda's song, for he knew there was enchantment in them. If he could calm the bees and ward off an attack, he would willingly use his terrible singing voice to do so. Now was not the time to dwell on Truda's harsh assessments of his off-key serenades. If he sounded like a dying cow, so be it.

"I confess that I researched beekeeping a few years ago," Madame Monfort said as a grasshopper zipped past her head. "I had a whim to establish a hive in our garden, but Thierry objected. He hates insects, and prefers sugar to honey."

"Your husband sounds like an absolute delight," Ansgar said wryly.

She slid her hands into gloves and flexed her fingers. "Not all of life is a delight. Surely you and your wife did not agree upon every occasion."

"We did not. But she made disagreeing delightful." A smile lifted the corners of his mouth.

"You are a most confusing man." Still moving forward, she wrapped her scarf around her head, face, and neck, leaving only a narrow gap to peer through.

"Confusing, am I?" Ansgar replied. "I prefer the term 'mysterious.' Or perhaps 'enigmatic.'"

They stopped a few feet from the hollow tree. Bees darted in and out, hurrying about their business, their tiny, furred bodies oddly iridescent in the sunlight. Madame Monfort clutched a short knife in her hand—the one she'd threatened him with when he'd tried to free the cat on their first day together. Where had she pulled that from? She was proving trickier than a town-square magician.

The bees buzzed louder, as if to warn their brethren of imminent danger. Ansgar's heartbeat raced. As part of a magic-influenced environment, these bees might be deadlier than regular bees. He whispered, "Take care, madame, they—" But then a fat bee flew past close enough to graze the tip of his nose and startled him speechless.

"I will," she said, her voice muffled by her scarf. She left him, taking slow steps toward the hive. One step, two steps, three...Only a few more, and she would be able to touch it.

He cleared his throat, preparing to sing Truda's song. Part of him wanted to stop the Frenchwoman from taking such a dreadful risk, but they needed this honey. It might give them a great advantage over the other bakers. If the pilgrims had come this way, they'd obviously not disturbed this hive, and how many other hives could there be along the route?

"I'm going to sing what I can remember," he announced. "It might soothe the bees. But I confess I am no choir boy."

"If you sing like a sick hound and it helps, I won't mind." Her voice trembled, as did her body. Wrapped in layers and shaking, she reminded him of a young girl left out in the snow for too long.

"I will do my best," he said, tempted once more to bid her to abandon the task.

"Sing now, before I lose my courage," she said, one footstep from the hive.

"Are you sure you want to—"

"Yes," she said. "And no. Just sing."

Again he cleared his throat. Madame Monfort nodded, her hands lifted and poised to reach into the oozing bole. Ansgar began to sing. The words were nonsensical and he botched the melody, but the bees appeared to take solace in music. Their movements became less frenzied; their humming grew quieter.

Madame Monfort shifted so her back was to him. Her shoulders lifted as she drew in a deep breath. With both hands, she reached into the dark opening. Ansgar stopped singing, gripped by nervous anticipation. Fear. Seconds passed, each one eternal.

She toppled onto her backside, then held up a golden brown, fist-sized chunk of honeycomb. "*Voilà!*" she shouted through the scarf, and then she laughed.

Happiness overwhelmed him as he swatted a bee on the back of his neck. "Well done!"

What was this sudden sinking in his stomach, this sharp longing in his breast? He wanted to rush at her and kiss her hard enough that she'd drop the honeycomb and grab onto his sleeves. He'd not felt so smitten since he'd first fallen for Truda. Was he ill? Had he lost his mind?

A sharp nip at his cheek refocused his attention.

The bees.

The bees surrounded them both. With alarm, he noticed their number had tripled, and they were not merrily bobbing on the breeze. Their movements were quick, agitated.

The volume of the buzzing swelled to deafening as Madame Monfort rose to her feet. Above their heads, a roiling gray cloud of angry insects formed and reformed. His gut clenched with guilt. This was his fault. Enraptured and afraid, he'd stopped singing. He resumed the song as her eyes widened in terror.

Ansgar dove toward her, grabbing her hand and yanking her toward the small pond he'd noticed in the center of the garden, singing at the top of his voice. Screaming the words. They stumbled and ran as he sang, crushing patches of herbs, crashing through rose bushes. Through the sound of his own voice, he could hear her gasping for air. The desperate crushing of her fingers rearranged the bones of his hand. Into the water they plunged.

The pond was cool but not deep. Through the murky water, he watched the slow, graceful sweep of Madame Monfort's free arm as she worked to stay submerged. The hand he'd grabbed still clutched his. The honeycomb was gone from her other hand. Her scarf, now encircling only her throat, floated like a long frond of seaweed.

Their eyes met. His lungs burned, but her gaze strengthened him. When she shook her head, signaling that she could no longer hold her breath, they stood up in the chest-deep water.

"You can let go now," she said as they waded past cattails, but he kept his fingers laced with hers. They tripped, slipped, and coughed until they collapsed onto their knees in the grass.

"My hand?" she said, peering at him through a curtain of dripping curls.

Ansgar let go. "Pardon me," he said. He started to shiver, as if she'd been the only thing keeping him warm in an icy land. Why was he so cold with the sun beating down on him? Had the touch of her hand bewitched him? He stared at her. Her too-dark eyes. Her sodden shirt sticking to the delicate curves of her shoulders. Her pendant lying crooked on her collarbone. His chest tightened as if he'd inhaled water, as if he were drowning on dry ground.

"Your face," she said, worry wrinkling her forehead. "It's swollen. I think you were stung."

His already quick heartbeat doubled as his hands flew to his cheeks. His throat constricted.

She swore—which would have been amusing if he'd been able to take even half a breath. "In my pack," he wheezed. "Green bottle."

And then his world went black.

"You can't die. You can't die," Josephine chanted as she tore into Monsieur Steuben's pack and tossed its contents onto the grass. Socks, a journal, food, a pouch of coins, a wooden spoon, baking supplies, silk undergarments! *Good heavens! Silk?* At the bottom, finally, she touched glass. A bottle. When she pulled it free of the bag, it gleamed green as an emerald.

She bounded back to his side, working the cork free with her fingernails as she ran. She knelt and tipped his head back so she could pour the bottle's contents into his slack mouth. His lips were blue, his skin a sickly gray. He did mean for her to put the medicine into his mouth and not on the wounds, didn't he? It was too late to ask. Praying fervently, she dumped it down his throat. When not a drop remained in the bottle, she let it fall into the grass.

"Please don't die," she said again as she cradled his head in her hands. What if he did? Could she continue the journey without him? He looked so dead.

She didn't even have a shovel to dig a hole for his body.

His eyes flashed open. He sucked in air. Startled, she jerked away from him. His head hit the ground with a thump as she stood.

"Blast," he said in a raspy voice. "Are you trying to crack open my skull, woman?" The swelling in his face rapidly subsided, and his breathing became regular. Nothing but magic or a miracle could have accomplished such a feat.

Josephine stared down at him in awe. "Sorry. You startled me. I thought you were dead."

"As did I. You used the potion?" He propped himself up on his elbows and blinked wonderingly, as if seeing the world for the first time.

She bent to grab the bottle. "What was in this?"

"Dashed if I know. I bought it in a Parisian back-alley shop last year on a whim. The proprietress called it a 'rescue tonic,' and claimed it would reverse the effects of most venoms and poisons. I paid an outrageous sum for it, but she was not the sort of person one could refuse without fear of consequence. I feared she'd turn my liver to mush or cause all my hair to fall out at the next full moon. One must be careful not to provoke the wrath of witches, you know. And if you do not know, I will tell you presently, and from bitter experience, that the price of enraging a witch could involve years of growing feathers and supping on grubs. Believe me, grubs are not something you'd enjoy. The way they pop and ooze when you snap your bill shut." He shivered dramatically. "Your mouth I should say, as you would be unfamiliar with the experience of possessing a bill." With a shake of his head, he added, "Whatever is wrong with my mouth? Why this sudden loquaciousness? Have I been transformed by the stings of magical bees? Made a blathering ninny by a *dummkopf* amateur herbalist? Great gods, am I ruined?"

Josephine covered her mouth with her hands to stifle a giggle. The potion had loosened Monsieur Steuben's tongue as effectively as the pond had saturated his garments. Freed of starch and airs, he was much more tolerable. Almost likable.

Unfortunately, as he got to his feet and attempted to brush muck and leaves from his clothes with vigorous swipes of his hands, his old scowl and surliness returned. "You laugh, Madame? I fail to find the humor in any of this. Nature itself seems bent on humiliating me. Cursed bees! Wretched mud! My poor suit!"

His outburst sobered her. She couldn't help but pity him a little, disheveled and dismayed as he was. She said gently, "The bees have flown off, thank heaven. And I do not think that all of nature is against you. I aggravated the bees by trespassing where I should not have. I'm very sorry you were the one to suffer for it."

His angry expression faded into one of mild annoyance. He brushed a lock of fair hair off his forehead, leaving a smudge of mud behind. "I accept your apology, although in truth, I am largely to blame for the incident. I became distracted and stopped singing. It was then that the bees went mad."

For a moment, she was stricken speechless by his near-humility. She made a thorough examination of him, from his wet hair to his soggy boots. His formerly sallow skin now had a healthy glow. His posture had straightened. The backstreet witch's concoction had done more than counteracting the stings and making him babble. She said, "You look different now."

"I feel different. Stronger, in fact," he said. "Ready to resume pursuit of the pilgrims, if you are."

Josephine had dozens of questions, but she'd save most of them for later. "Yes," she said. "We should move on, but what about the honey?" She picked up the chunk of honeycomb from where she'd dropped it. "How do we—?"

"Allow me," Ansgar said. He took the honeycomb from her and used his knife to shear off a layer of wax. She found the jar he'd prepared earlier and held it as he drizzled the dark amber honey into it.

After she corked the jar, she placed it in the pocket of her trousers. It strained the fabric and pressed against her thigh, but she felt compelled to keep it close. Never again did she want to raid a beehive.

"Now we go," Ansgar announced.

Thierry growled long and low as Josephine lifted his basket. "I'll let you out to stretch your legs later," she whispered to the cat. "You'll find all your suffering was worth it in the end, *mon chéri.*"

"This way," Monsieur Steuben said. He walked swiftly toward the door set into the wall of the courtyard-garden. Without a doubt, the potion had done wonders for him. His gait was longer, his step more purposeful. He had the air of a young man setting out to slay dragons.

Bonté divine, she hoped they would not meet any dragons along the way to the Seven Ovens. Or any more angry bees.

The German glanced over his shoulder at her. "Are you coming, or have you decided to plant yourself there like a tree?"

"Of course I'm coming." She rushed to catch up with him, moving into the long shadow cast by his body. Her legs ached. If only she could have borrowed some of his newfound strength...

"You know, Madame, if you would free that blasted cat and set aside its cumbersome basket, you could maintain a faster pace. The saint will not delay the contest on our account. Especially since we were not among Martel's chosen."

His potion-induced good humor had not lasted long, but she was almost relieved that he'd returned to his former grumpiness. It was something predictable in an unpredictable world. "I am well aware that we must hurry, *monsieur*, but where I go, Thierry goes. If I win the contest, I need him with me so I can use the wish to help him."

Upon reaching the garden wall, he brushed a hanging vine out of the way and pulled open a green wooden door. Its hinges creaked as if no one had disturbed them in decades. Without facing her, he said, "Fine. I only hope you do not regret your choice later."

"Rest assured I will not," she said with more conviction than she actually possessed. Every time he suggested abandoning the cat —her husband—contrary feelings arose within her: a fierce, protective determination to save Thierry from spending the rest of his days in feline form, and the sheer, cold dread that as her traveling companion insisted, the cat was just an ordinary cat. The second possibility always sent a shiver up her spine.

Josephine followed Monsieur Steuben through the door. The moment she set foot over the threshold, she heard someone cough behind her. She shivered again. They were being followed.

"Monsieur Steuben?" Her voice squeaked as fear coursed through her. They were in what looked like a three-foot-wide, covered alley between the garden wall and a building. Practically trapped, as the building's windows were high off the ground and hardly more than slits. Her shaky right hand fumbled under her shirt to unsheathe the short knife from the scabbard belted to her ribs. Not a convenient arrangement, but what did she know of carrying weapons? Her heartbeat thundered in her ears as she held the knife against her stomach. "Monsieur?"

He kept plodding forward at a steady pace, his bag bouncing lightly against his backbone, no matter how hard she prayed he'd stop. "What is it now? A pebble in your stocking? Your cat's ear requires scratching?"

"I was just wondering if...perhaps...could you loan me your handkerchief?" She wanted to make him face her, to draw his gaze toward their stalker without alerting the person that she knew of their presence. "I think my nose is bleeding?"

Monsieur Steuben stopped. "Great gods, woman. You *think* your nose is bleeding? Does one not *know* if one's nose is bleeding? There are clues to such an event, such as some amount of blood leaking from the nostrils." Finally, he spun and whipped a damp handkerchief out of his breast pocket. "Here."

"Thank you." She pressed the handkerchief to her nose and made a small gesture with her head, up and back, to invite him to look behind her.

He squinted at her. "Are you feverish? You seem to have developed a twitch."

"Hello there," said a male voice.

As Josephine spun to face the stranger, her fingers lost their grip on the knife. It bounced off her boot and landed on the path. She cursed, stumbled backward, and collided with Monsieur Steuben's chest. His hands gripped her shoulders protectively. She was grateful for his firm hold, because the stalker was no stranger to her, and the sight of him made her knees feel as sturdy as jelly.

"Who are you, and what are you doing here?" Monsieur Steuben demanded.

"I might ask you the same," came the man's smug reply. "Or would you rather provide the explanation, *chère* Josephine?"

Nine

Still gripping Madame Monfort's shoulders, Ansgar took a step backward. Her body moved with his, offering no resistance. One of his arms slid down to wrap around her middle. With his free hand, he yanked the puny knife from the sheath at his hip. Would that he had been allowed to bring a dagger on the pilgrimage, but the list had forbidden it.

The stranger, a brown-haired, average-sized man dressed all in darkest green, raised his empty hands. In the dimness, his age was difficult to discern, but judging by the shape of his body and his confident posture, the man was no weakling. "Hold on now," the stranger said, eyes focused on the blade. "No need to become aggressive."

"In my opinion, this seems to be the perfect time to show aggression," Ansgar said.

The stranger offered a wide grin, like a crocodile attempting to look congenial. "Tell him we're family, Josephine."

"No, we are not," she said. "Not anymore, and never again." She wriggled out of Ansgar's hold, and he immediately put himself between her and the stranger, still wielding the knife.

The man's smile faded. "See it as you will. I'm here for the necklace. The one our dear Thierry left me in his will."

"You followed her here for a necklace?"Ansgar sensed there was more to the story. No one would have endured the endless tunnels and passageways of the pilgrimage for a mere trinket. No one sane, anyway.

The stranger shrugged. "What can I say? I want what is mine, and she ran off with it. I've been tracking her since she left home, the poor, muddled, grieving woman, forever muttering about wishes and cakes. She verges on madness, I fear." His gaze lowered to Josephine's face. "Hand it over, Jo, and I'll leave you to your silly, wish-seeking adventure. And when it's done, and you're battered and penniless, you'll regret refusing my earlier offer of marriage."

"As I have said before, I will never marry you. And neither will I give you the necklace. It's a family heirloom worth less than a day's wages, and it's all I have left of my grandmother."

The stranger shook his head. "All that was yours became Thierry's when you married. That is the law. And Thierry's legal will names me as heir to everything he owned, including the necklace. You know this, Jo."

"Leave this woman alone and go home," Ansgar said. "Is it not enough that she lost her husband? Must you take her only family keepsake?"

The stranger scoffed. "What makes this your business? Are you her lover, sir?"

"No," Josephine said, sounding offended.

But Ansgar said more loudly, "Yes." He reached back and pulled her to him, and she did not put up a fight—probably because she did not expect it. Now that he felt her trembling against him, his anger multiplied. "The lady asked you to go, sir," he said. "And now I insist upon it. Unless you care to fight me. I warn you, though, I will not hesitate to use magic against you." He concentrated and cobbled together enough power to make the knife glow in his grasp. Thank the gods he'd recently imbibed that healing potion.

Jacques retreated by several steps. "Fine, fine. You do know she's penniless and barren? Nothing but the daughter of an illiterate cabbage farmer."

"She is worth more than ten of you." Ansgar scrounged up another bit of power to make the blade hum ominously. The effort made his head throb, but he persevered. "Shall we fight? I believe I would enjoy listening to the sound of your blood sizzling beneath my blade."

"I shall take my leave," Jacques said, nostrils flaring. "But do not think you've seen the last of me, Jo." He bowed, then walked back the way he'd come.

"Should I go after him and wring his dirty neck?" Ansgar asked.

Madame Monfort stepped out of his hold and turned to face him. Embarrassment stained her cheeks rose-pink. "No, but thank you for defending me. That man, Jacques, is Thierry's brother. He thinks Thierry is dead, and so..."

He placed a hand on her shoulder and gave her a reassuring smile. She trembled harder now that the fiend had gone. "We need not speak of it."

Quietly, she thanked him again, and Ansgar watched her bend to retrieve the bag and basket that had slipped from her shoulder during the confrontation. Through the window in the basket, he noted that the cat was asleep. It had probably slept through the entire incident. *Worthless creature.*

"Let's move on," she said, and he allowed her to take the lead. As they proceeded through the narrow alley of stone, Ansgar vowed to be more vigilant. It should not have been possible for Jacques to follow them undetected. What if the man had abducted Josephine as he'd slept, or when the bees' stings had rendered him nearly lifeless?

She'd saved him from death several times. He owed her a debt.

Until the day of the contest, he'd do all he could to ensure her safety because he was beholden to her. It had nothing to do with the feelings that washed over him in waves as he watched her stride along in those ridiculous trousers: respect and amazement, adoration and desire.

What was wrong with him? This was no time to become sentimental and starry-eyed. Madame Monfort had proven to be stronger and braver than she appeared, but she was still a cat-toting chatterbox. Nothing compared to Truda.

He blew out a breath and tried to shake free of his longing for the Frenchwoman. Perhaps the feelings were a side effect of the healing potion or the magic-tainted bees' stings, in which case they'd likely dissipate soon. Yes, that must be the case.

A sharp turn erased his companion from view for a moment. Did he miss her in so brief an absence, as a besotted lover would? Of course not. But Jacques's words about her had stirred his imagination. As the corridor darkened around them, he pictured Josephine Monfort as a young farm girl, running barefoot through her family's cabbage fields, chasing butterflies and moths, her hair flying out behind her like a dark cloud.

"I have always thought the cabbage an admirable vegetable," he said quietly, impulsively. Knowing it was a mistake to speak one word to her while in his current state of nonsensical pining.

"Ha. I hate the stuff, and so would you if you had to eat it every day for over twenty-five years," she replied.

"I will never offer you a single leaf of it, then. I will take an oath, if it pleases you." He delivered the words dramatically, like an actor playing an overzealous knight. And then he whispered to himself, in a voice too low for her to hear, "You fool, Ansgar."

"Oaths will not be necessary. In fact, I must confess that I'm hungry enough to gobble up an entire pot of the stuff, were it suddenly to appear before me."

"Anything could happen," he replied. Magic had taught him as much. Believing it had always brought him comfort—until now.

What if the "anything" meant he could lose everything—the wish, his power, his identity, and his traitorous heart—and all because of a woman he'd met days ago in a colorless graveyard?

He was starting to think he should have found another way to save his life.

The passageway widened, and Josephine allowed Monsieur Steuben to slip past her. The walls featured large rectangular window openings edged in carvings of vines and fruits. A light breeze slid through the corridor, sending a dry leaf skittering across her path. Beyond the windows, she glimpsed a row of trees. Oaks, she thought, like the ones her family's spotted pigs had grazed beneath when she was small. She'd been in charge of carrying buckets of water to their troughs in the woods. They'd been fond of her, smart as dogs. It had been ages since she'd thought about that part of her life.

She trudged forward on legs gone mostly numb. She wished she could loosen her corset strings, for ever since Jacques had stepped out of the shadows, she'd been struggling to breathe properly. If only she'd been sensible enough to forego the confining garment when she'd chosen trousers over skirts for the pilgrimage. How ignorant she'd been.

Ignorant, too, to think she could escape Jacques Monfort. In the past, she'd thought Thierry's tales of his brother's hunting skills had been exaggerated. Now she believed them, and she hated the idea of being his prey. But why had he gone from desperately wanting her to become his wife to wanting only the necklace?

Thierry, too, had always been intensely interested in the pendant. More than once, he'd interrogated her about its history. Who made it? he'd asked. What was the name of the silver-speckled black stone in its center?

All she knew was that it had been passed down by the women

in her family for a few generations. And that she would not willingly relinquish it—which was funny, since she had no fondness for jewelry. She rarely wore earrings, brooches, or hair ornaments. Perhaps it was foolish of her not to hand it over to Jacques, because she knew he'd attempt to weasel it away from her again. She would have to arm herself in preparation. A man like him, with more brawn than brains but not much of either, would only withhold violence for so long.

What would have become of her if Ansgar Steuben had not stood up for her? What if he'd been devoid of magic and Jacques had stabbed him or whacked him with a stone? He'd just come back from the brink of death, for heaven's sake.

When Monsieur Steuben had gathered her close to his body, holding her firmly to chest, she'd almost gone limp with shock. No man, not even her husband, had ever made her feel so protected and cherished. Thierry was not an affectionate man. As a cat, he'd become even more aloof.

Inside the basket, Thierry yowled plaintively. He was probably hungry again, and she was almost out of canned fish. She hushed him, and he growled in reply.

Over her shoulder, she addressed the cat. "Did you even notice that your scoundrel of a brother paid us a visit? Or were you too busy napping in the comfort of your basket?"

"Madame? Did you say something?" Monsieur Steuben asked, slowing his footsteps.

"Only to the cat." She waited for him to mock her, but he said nothing. Was it her imagination or was the gentleman softening around the edges?

A few minutes passed before he said, "Another door."

She peered past him. How tired she was becoming of doors and corridors. Stone walls and dimness. The packing list had prepared her to brave cold mountainsides, to be harassed by squalls of wind, and to traipse over miles of rough terrain. Such a difficult journey might have killed her, but at least it would have been an expected end. The fulfillment of a promise.

She sighed. Since her wedding day, nothing had been as she'd expected. She gave herself permission to mope for a few seconds, then straightened her backbone and followed the German—who was also not who she'd expected him to be. She'd disliked Ansgar Steuben at first sight, but gradually she'd become rather attached to the curmudgeon. He cursed too often, grumbled at every inconvenience, and spent too much time trying to wipe dirt off his fine clothes, but there was something oddly charming about him.

When he'd taken her side against Jacques, he'd confirmed her suspicion: Ansgar Steuben was not a truly wicked man. Somewhere deep inside him, under layers of armor and cobwebs, some goodness lived.

Her hands wandered to her necklace, to rub the stone for comfort and courage as she walked. On her deathbed, *Grand-mère* had made her swear to never give it to anyone but her own daughter. She'd exhaled her last breath before Josephine could ask why.

When her own feet tripped her, Josephine tugged at the pendant. The chain snapped. She sighed, and then swung her bag off her shoulder. As she traipsed onward, she wrapped the necklace in a piece of silken cloth she'd brought to hem into a handkerchief as a gift for the saint. She tucked it deep into her bag, missing the weight of the stone on her breastbone but thanking heaven that she still had it close.

Never, never would Jacques Monfort pry it from her hands.

They were inside the church again.

Ansgar was not one bit surprised. This was a different section of the ever-shifting building, but most certainly the same structure of stone, mortar, wood, and glass. With his magic sharpened by the healing potion, he could sense it.

He grabbed a flaming torch from the wall without breaking his stride and led Madame Monfort up a flight of winding stone stairs. The steps were steep yet his breathing remained even. Every ache and pain had vanished from his body when he'd swallowed the potion after the bee stings. He felt as fit as a twenty-year-old. Best of all, the potion had revived his magical gift. It was good that Madame could not see his face, for he was grinning like a child who'd been given the keys to a confectionary shop.

Few people understood the ways of magic, but Truda had instructed him well. While it was true that some ordinary folk could conjure a simple trick, brew a potion to cure a simple ailment, or undo a low-level curse, only those born with the gift imbedded in their marrow could excel in the magical arts. He had been so lucky. But with rapidly advancing age weakening his bones and sapping his strength, and separated from his witch-queen wife, his magic had dwindled to almost nothing. After the bee sting incident, the healing potion had stimulated his bones to produce magic again. He could almost feel the tiny sparks of it leaping within him, popping like champagne bubbles.

By the time they reached the Seven Ovens, there was a good chance he'd have magic to spare to incorporate into the baking—if that wasn't forbidden by the saint. The gods knew he needed help to bake anything edible. Currently, he planned to convince or pay Madame M to teach him the secrets of baking before the contest, but how much better would it be to be able to win without a struggle?

Fate might be smiling on him. Finally.

He felt so, so good. Like he could flap his arms and fly higher than the duck he'd been, or scale a mountain in a few bounds. Like he could enchant the cat into leaping off the next cliff they came upon. His fingers tightened around the torch's handle. How he hated that cat, and not just because it made his nose stuffy and caused him to sneeze every five minutes. The animal had a glint in its eyes. Something suspicious and too knowing for an ordinary feline. Something that reminded him of the part-faerie cats he'd encountered a few times in his travels. Cats were not to be trusted, whether they contained the souls of men or no soul at all, and regardless of their bloodlines.

Behind him, the Frenchwoman muttered something to herself. Earlier in their journey, he would have snapped at her and demanded silence. Now, in the otherwise quiet stairway, her murmurings bothered him no more than rain pattering on a roof or wind rattling leaves.

He strained to decipher her whispers but failed. He ought not to care what she was saying, but an odd curiosity gripped him. When he could no longer hold back, he asked, "Are you reciting a poem, Madame?"

"A recipe. I apologize. I have a habit of thinking aloud. It drives Thierry mad. When I was a child, my father made me sleep in the barn more than once for 'mumbling foolishness.'"

Ansgar winced.

The embarrassment in her voice etched a hairline crack into his crusty old heart. "Your father was an unkind man," he said evenly, but his mind blazed with a dozen curse words.

"Papa was a practical man who taught me practical things. If I had tried harder to learn the lessons he taught of silence, piety, and obedience, perhaps I would have been a better wife."

Ansgar swore and almost dropped the torch. "You must be joking, Madame!" He spun to face her. Three steps below him, she wore an expression of surprise. There was a light sheen of sweat on her forehead, and the carnation-pink stain of exertion on her cheeks. Ringlets of damp hair framed her face. His heart pounded painfully as he noted the sad shape of her mouth. "Pardon my rough language. But your father was wrong to teach you that a woman should be nothing but meek and mild. My Truda could have burned down the world singlehandedly. She could have swiped every bird from the sky with a word. The touch of her fingertips could green a garden or blacken stone. And I do not doubt that you are every bit as powerful in your own way, Josephine Monfort."

Her mouth gaped open. Twin images of the torch flame danced in her eyes.

"Josephine." He said her name again, because he wanted to. Needed to. He was done with the formalities. They'd been alone together for days, and no one was around to enforce the usual customs of propriety. "Listen, please. You must know that you are not merely an ornament for some gentleman's parlor, or a brood mare to supply offspring."

The pink of her cheeks shifted to scarlet. "I'm a simple country girl, born and raised. I do not expect to be more than that, in the end. This will be my one adventure, and then I shall be content to return to an ordinary life."

He shook his head soberly. "It saddens me that you believe such untruths, Josephine. May I call you Josephine?" He should have asked before, not for the sake of manners but as a sign of respect. This woman had been shown too little respect. He himself was guilty of disrespecting her.

"I suppose there would be no harm in it," Josephine said. She looked at the floor. Within its wicker cage on her back, the cat hissed like a tea kettle on the boil.

"You must call me Ansgar, then."

The corners of her mouth lifted by a degree, subduing her frown and adding another fissure to his hard heart. "Ansgar," she said. "Should we not continue onward?"

Thunder rumbled outside the church and reverberated through the stone. To turn away from her took great effort, even though Ansgar knew full well the urgency with which they needed to travel. He drew in a deep breath and pivoted.

The image of her nearly-smiling face stuck with him as he continued to climb, step after step, as if someone had branded it onto his mind in vibrant color. He tried to replace the picture in his mind with other images: Truda on their wedding day, illuminated by golden rays of sunset; Truda casting a saucy glance his direction as she stirred a potion over the fire in the gingerbread cottage.

None of these images erased the one of Josephine in the stairwell, with her unruly curls and cat-scratched throat, her eyes dark as finest onyx in the dimness. Or the sensation of her tugging the blanket to his shoulders, caring for him with unearned tenderness. Or the vision of her standing victorious beside the hibouchauris, knitting needles raised high.

He was in trouble. Terrible trouble.

It had comforted him to blame the healing potion or beestings for his growing feelings, but he could no longer.

Desire flooded him, but not the crude desire he'd often entertained in the last few years. He wanted Josephine as he wanted breath in his lungs or a draught of cold water on a summer's afternoon. He wanted her like the earth longed to be carpeted with tiny stars of greenest moss, or the sky desired to be draped in white swaths of wooly cloud.

Never in a thousand ages would he have imagined yearning this fervently for anyone but Truda. His past infidelity with the larch tree faerie had been skin deep; this temptation, if he surrendered to it, would consume him utterly, crashing over him like a tidal wave and then sucking him into the churning depths of the sea.

He wanted to spend his days working at the puzzle that was Josephine, knowing he'd never quite solve the mystery she would always be. She was sweet but strong, ridiculous but wise, modestly pretty but arrestingly beautiful.

Passing the torch from his left hand to his right, he ascended to a landing, a rectangle of red-tiled floor stamped with the images of blackbirds. Ahead, two more steps led up to the next section of the building. Probably another long corridor. He was starting to feel like a rat stuck in an interminable maze for the amusement of a cruel owner. What was the point of all these hallways and passages? Had any pilgrimage ever been so ridiculous? Although he doubted they could stray from the true path, the constraints of time remained. If they reached the Seven Ovens after the contest, the entire journey would be for naught. But then, drifting from afar, a faint murmur of voices found his ears. Breath held, he stilled his body to listen. Josephine stopped beside him and cocked her head as if she, too, heard the sound.

Their eyes met. A stupid grin took over Ansgar's face, but he made no effort to quench it. They had a reason to rejoice. They'd found the pilgrims again. He nodded to Josephine, and then they took off running in the direction of the voices, both of them landing lightly on their feet as they hurried, mindful of keeping their approach as quiet as possible.

After a few minutes, Josephine's breathing became labored. He turned his head to look at her, slowing his pace. When he noticed how pale she'd become, he stopped.

"I must rest," she said, leaning hard against the wall with one hand on her heaving chest. She let the cat's basket slip off her shoulders and descend slowly to the floor. It landed crookedly, causing the cat to yowl in dismay.

"We cannot afford to stop for long," Ansgar said. The pilgrims' song was fading by degrees with every passing second.

"Go without me, then. I'll catch up soon."

He could not imagine leaving her. What if Jacques returned, or some monster materialized in the corridor to challenge her? He lifted the cat basket and slid the straps onto his own shoulders. In an instant, his eyes itched doubly and his nose swelled, but he ignored his discomfort and leaned to offer his hand to Josephine. "Come. Allow me to tow you along. The pilgrims seem to be moving at a brisk pace. If they make a turn or fall silent, we might never find them again."

She blew out a breath. "Fine." As she took hold of his hand, she added, "I imagine I will regret this."

He smiled. "My dear, if you do not have a mile-long list of regrets at your age, you truly have never lived." His long fingers closed around her hand. He was keenly aware of the places where his skin met hers. Those fractions of his body felt more alive than the rest of him, more sacred.

It should have disgusted him to want sweet, guileless Josephine. Had he not devoted his life to scorning sentimentality? But this was no time to pause for self-examination.

Ansgar ran, hand in hand with Josephine, down the corridor, around a corner, up a creaky set of wooden stairs; through a passageway lined with blue glass, and along another passage lit by a hundred small, yellow candles. Every second, he was conscious of her hand clenching his. A dozen times, he was tempted to halt and draw her into a long kiss, pilgrims be hanged. She'd never been kissed well, of that he was sure. A man who hated the sound of his wife's voice would never have taken the time to kiss her until she all but melted.

The voices grew louder. Ansgar tugged Josephine into a niche. The pilgrims were close. In the next chamber. He listened as he tried to catch his breath. Guide Martel suggested a meal to be followed by resting for the night. Ansgar thanked the gods that he and Josephine would be able to rest and eat, too. She needed feeding. He did not like the hollows that had formed in her cheeks or the bruise-like shadows under her eyes.

When Josephine pulled her hand free of his, Ansgar almost snatched it back. Instead, he shook his arm to restore the feeling in fingers that had held hers too tightly.

Back pressed to the wall, Josephine slid to the floor. Her chest rose and fell fast as she shut her eyes and rested her head against the wall. Her hair was an explosion of curls, jostled completely free from the confines of twists and knitting needles by their running. His fingers itched to delve into the tangles.

Ansgar crossed his arms tightly over his chest. Control and focus were what he needed. His legs throbbed after all the galloping and stair-climbing, but he would not lower his body to fit next to hers in the narrow alcove. If he did, his hip would touch hers. His shoulder would graze hers. Her dark storm cloud of hair would tickle his cheek. He would lose his mind. Possibly his soul, if he had one.

He closed his eyes and remembered the scorn and disappointment he'd seen in Truda's face the moment before she transformed him into a duck to punish him for unfaithfulness. After so many years, the memory of that terrible look could still bring him to his proverbial knees. He groaned both from past regret and the present pains in his legs.

"Are you all right?" Josephine whispered.

He opened his eyes and assumed his usual cool demeanor. "Well enough," he said coolly. "We should find a more hidden place to rest, in case any of the pilgrims come wandering."

"I agree, although I hate to move. I feel as if I've been run over by a herd of horses."

"Indeed. Stay here, if it pleases you. I will search for somewhere suitable to spend the night." He set his bag next to hers and then slunk along the wall until he found a door that led to a small chamber. The room contained nothing but a single bed covered with gray woolen blankets. It would suffice, for they could not both sleep and risk being left behind again by the pilgrims. They'd rest in shifts.

Ansgar eyed the bed like a starving man regarding a three-course dinner. The urge to throw himself onto the mattress was almost irresistible—but he overcame the impulse and closed the door. He was proud of himself for resisting so many impulses in one hour. *Blast that woman, this pilgrimage.*

He returned to Josephine hesitantly. The journey could not end soon enough. These unrefined yearnings, these reckless cravings...they were not Ansgar Steuben. Since leaving life as a duck behind, he'd become a man who did nothing on a whim. Even his crimes and vices were carefully orchestrated. He would not permit himself to fall under the spell of a sad, middle-aged widow, no matter that she was also brave, kind, and bright.

In a matter of days, after he'd won the wish, he would put Josephine behind him and resume life as the Ansgar Steuben he'd been and loved. In the meantime, he would do his best to resist the Frenchwoman. He'd remind himself that nothing in an enchanted place could be trusted, especially not one's emotions.

His bones tingled as his magic grew by another degree. Power was something he could trust. He needed no one and nothing other than his own magic. It would see him through this pilgrimage like an invisible friend. His magic had dwindled in the past, but it had never betrayed him or utterly deserted him. It would not grow weary of his company or prefer the company of a mad cat. It would not scowl at him for doing something wicked.

There now. He'd straightened himself out.

"There's a bedchamber just that way," he said to Josephine, pointing. He did not look into her eyes as he spoke. It was too soon to test his new resolve. "Go to sleep. I'll take a turn after you."

"I could take the second shift—"

"No," he insisted. "Go."

If she cringed a little at his harsh tone, he only noticed from the corner of his eye.

Once she'd left him, taking her cat basket, he slumped to the floor outside the bedchamber door. He listened to the pilgrims settling down for the night and fought to stay awake. For not the first time, he envied the cat. The animal would undoubtedly be sharing its mistress's pillow.

Ten

In the small bedchamber, Josephine rolled onto her back and sighed. She had never felt more tired in her life, yet sleep eluded her. Of course Thierry, temporarily freed from his basket, purred loudly as he slumbered close to her ankles.

An assortment of wool blankets weighed down her fully-clothed body as she stared at the ceiling—or toward where the ceiling ought to be, for the room was black as pitch. Her thoughts weighed on her almost as heavily. They'd arrive at the Seven Ovens soon, and she'd face the baking contest that meant life or death for her marriage. And life or death for her comfortable existence. When she considered losing her cozy home, her beloved books, and her evenings knitting in the well-cushioned armchair by the hearth, tears welled in her eyes.

Was it wrong of her not to regret the possible loss of Thierry himself? If she were a good wife, that would have been her first thought. Heavens, she was a mess. A disgrace.

She swiped her tears away and covered her eyes with her hands. Fretting wouldn't help. She needed a plan. More than that, she needed a recipe.

Of course she'd memorized a good recipe for little gingerbread cakes before setting out. She'd baked at least twenty different kinds before settling on the simple recipe *Grand-mère* had taught her long ago. The palm-sized cake had a crisp bottom and a soft top—but not too soft—and was spiced with cinnamon, nutmeg, cardamom, and cloves. She'd used clover honey at home, but the wild honey she'd harvested would provide the sweetness when she baked at the Seven Ovens. Her recipe was sound. She was a skilled baker, and had a good hand for decorating with icing. So why did she feel unsettled?

In her heart, she feared her recipe was too rustic to enrapture the taste buds of the saint. Would the special honey make enough of a difference to help her win the wish? What if it didn't? What if she trudged home from the contest with the cat still in his basket and no hope left?

Monsieur Steuben—Ansgar—must have brought along a recipe he believed in. She could hardly imagine him elbow deep in sticky dough, but he exuded such confidence that she thought he could convince birds and mice to do the work for him—although the saint would likely frown upon anyone enlisting the aid of wild animals.

A cricket chirped underneath the bed, shrilly, loudly. *Wonderful.* Now she'd never fall asleep. She nibbled a thumbnail and thought about changes she could make to her recipe. Should she put in more cinnamon and less nutmeg? Or omit the cloves and double the nutmeg? Add a little more honey, perhaps? Would it help to add another egg?

She groaned and covered her eyes with one arm. She was doomed. She'd spend the rest of her years living in a cramped room over a shop in a slum, talking to her persnickety cat-husband after days of working her fingers to the bone making thread in the mill or scaling smelly fish by the docks.

For not the first time in her life, she wished she were smarter. If only she had known what made recipes work or fail, she might have created a new and better one. She was good at many things and excellent at nothing, that was her problem. She could knit, sew, and play a few tunes on the flute. She could make decent soups, bake a nice enough loaf, and knew enough steps to participate in village dances. She was passably pretty, passably able to function as a housewife. And she was getting older by the minute, as Thierry had liked to remind her daily. According to her husband, her smooth skin and nimble fingers would soon betray her, and then she'd have only his grace to rely upon. The bitter icing on the disappointing cake of her life was the fact that she'd failed to conceive even one child. Would Thierry have loved her if she'd given him a son? It was a question she'd never dared to utter.

If she excelled at anything, it was her loyalty to Thierry. From the first day of the marriage her father had arranged, she'd been devoted to her spouse. Thierry was aloof and demanding, but she'd vowed before heaven to cherish him, and so she had. When he cursed her for talking too much, or smashed dishes when she over-salted the fish, or tore all the blankets from her and left her shivering in the night; when he belittled her in front of his friends, she made an effort to love him more. She tried harder to please him and to obey him. She kept her unruly hair tamed under a scarf and wore his favorite color. She cooked his favorite meals and put on the demure smile he demanded. Surely, once she proved her worth by freeing him from feline form, he would see the vastness of her love and realize the error of his ways. He would sink to his knees and call her his jewel, his darling. Finally, they would be happy. Getting him out of the cat, she hoped, would be the one grand act that opened his eyes and heart to her.

A knock silenced the cricket. She sat up as the door swung open.

"Josephine," Ansgar said from the doorway. His torch had burned down to a pale, meager flame, but daylight leaked in from a window high above the bed to illuminate his face. The man had never come to take his turn in the bed, yet he didn't look much wearier than before. Perhaps he'd nodded off while on watch. "Time to rise," he said.

She yawned as her feet touched the cold tiles of the floor. How would she walk another ten or more miles today when she had not slept for one minute? Thierry meowed from the end of the bed where he'd been slumbering, and the answer came to her swiftly: she would do whatever she had to do, weary or not, to save her husband. If it meant walking to the ends of the earth, she would somehow find the strength.

The cat hissed as she coerced him back into the wicker cage. He swatted her with sharp claws and drew blood on her wrist. Still, she spoke soothingly to him. "I know you dislike the basket, *mon cher*, but soon you'll be back in your own body again. You'll—"

"Are you talking to that cat again?" Ansgar asked with a frown. "Such a waste of time."

She picked up the basket and retorted, "That is my business, not yours."

His frown turned into a teasing grin that annoyed her twice as much. "Impertinent this morning, are we?" he said. "And after I so generously allowed you to occupy the bedchamber all night."

"I didn't sleep, and your mockery does not bring out the best in me, *monsieur*," she answered, stepping past him and into the passageway.

"Blame me for your foul mood if you must. But I have news that should brighten your outlook."

Josephine raised her brows and waited for him to continue.

"I crept over to spy on the pilgrims. The old woman with the limp is no longer part of the group. Martel must have sent her home—or buried her. The sickly gentleman is still with them, but he's grown thinner, and as yellow as a cheap onion. Bad luck for them, but our good fortune."

"There will be enough ovens for us to bake on the saint's day," she said. She almost leapt for joy. For a moment, she felt guilty for rejoicing, then she shoved the feeling aside. The pilgrims' troubles had not been her fault. Her eyes welled with happy tears. "We really will have a chance to win the wish."

"As we have planned all along. Come now. Let us fetch our bags and prepare to follow the others. They will set out again soon, no doubt."

"Of course." Cat basket in hand, she hurried after Ansgar. "Did you hear that, husband? I'll have an oven. I'm going to save you."

The cat did not reply.

Ansgar kicked his ravaged leather pack and swore. He threw his hands in the air and swore again, more loudly. On the floor of the alcove where they'd left their bags, his belongings lay tangled with Josephine's. Socks, journals, undergarments, matches, trousers— spread out as if attacked by a wild beast sometime during the few hours that he'd kept watch by the bedchamber door while Josephine rested.

Because they *had* been attacked, he could see that plainly. The cloths that had wrapped their foodstuffs were strewn across the tiles and covered with crumbs. Something, or perhaps someone, had dragged off or consumed everything edible. Spare garments were riddled with filth and tears. Their bags of flour had been torn apart, their spice jars shattered.

He swore again.

"It will be all right," Josephine said as she set the cat basket down and surveyed the damage. Her optimistic words did nothing to alleviate the anger that roiled in his gut. She added, "You will see, Ansgar. We'll cross another courtyard with fruit growing in it, or happen upon a well-stocked kitchen. The saint will feed and clothe us. What kind of saint would she be if she did not?" There was a slight wavering in her voice, as if she were holding back tears. It wore away the sharpest edges of his rage—which annoyed him in an altogether different way. He would have rather been consumed by anger than weakened by pitying the woman.

Pacing, he raked his hands through his hair. "We cannot bake without flour and spices, and neither of us will win the contest if we do not bake. No baking, no wish."

"I do still have the honey. Thank heaven I tucked the jar into my pocket."

"Thank heaven? I doubt that any deity is looking on us with favor, or has since we began this accursed journey." He kicked a crumpled sock hard enough to send it sailing across the room.

Josephine's stomach growled loudly. He imagined the woman was unused to skipping a meal. Her usual life of quiet domesticity surely featured regular dining times and hearty fare, probably delivered to the table by a plump old cook who'd been put out to pasture by a wealthier family years ago.

Ansgar watched her swipe a single tear from her cheek. Silently, she crouched to pluck her belongings from amid the mess. He heaved a sigh and followed suit, glancing in her direction from time to time. When she untangled a pair of his silk underdrawers from a coiled rope, her face glowed scarlet—as if she'd never beheld a man's personal garments. He snatched them from her hands. "I'll just take those," he said, promptly stuffing them into his torn pack. He grieved the fact that every other item of spare clothing he'd brought had been ruined beyond saving. The sight of his Flemish linen shirt in tatters almost brought a tear to his own cheek.

A few minutes later, they stood and shouldered their dirt-stained baggage. Flour and crumbs, spices and nibbled wrappings littered the ground at their feet. Josephine's nose and right cheek were smeared with flour, and if he'd been in the mood to act either more or less chivalrous, he would have alerted her to its presence. As it was, he took secret amusement from the sight. Other women adorned themselves with face powder, wigs, and corsets so tight they could hardly speak a sentence without becoming out of breath. Josephine was unembellished by cosmetics, had hair as wild as a bramble bush, and was currently dressed like a middle-class gentleman who'd fallen on hard times, and yet his eyes could not get enough of the sight of her.

Why, in the name of whatever gods dwelled on high, did he continue to yearn to embrace her? Was she some kind of witch in disguise, bespelling him so skillfully that he never noticed? Had he missed some clue about her identity that he should have seen on day one?

Or was something tangible to blame? Her necklace, perhaps?

That would maybe explain why Jacques had made such a great effort to take ownership of a small piece of jewelry. Come to think of it, there was something peculiar about the black stone. He'd have to lay his hands on it to find out what, but...

Josephine's shrill scream made his hair stand on end. He spun to face her. Pale as a snowdrift, she shook her head and wrung her hands. "He's gone," she said. "Thierry has escaped. The basket must not have been latched properly. I must find him. I can't help him if he's not with me, can I?"

He resisted the urge to comfort her with an embrace. "I confess I do not know the limitations of the wish magic," he said. "It might require proximity, but it would not be unheard of for it to affect the cat in spite of a great distance."

Tears dripped from her eyes and nose. He hugged himself harder. Where was the crusty wizard he'd once been? The irascible white duck? His magic had been bubbling and growing since the bee incident, yet *this*. These tender, horrid feelings. "Crying won't help," he said flatly. "And neither will standing here bemoaning the situation. We must search for the animal before it has a chance to venture far."

What had he just said? Great Odin and mighty Thor, had he just volunteered to look for the fur-covered nuisance? He wanted to smack himself. With a brick.

She nodded and dabbed her tears with her sleeve. "You are right, of course."

He pointed to a wall of shelves that held dusty books and a pair of glowing, ancient-looking lamps. "Take one of those lamps. I'll go this way, and you go in that direction. Mind you, we cannot spend long searching or we'll risk being late for the contest."

Again, she nodded, and then they separated.

"Here, cat," Ansgar said—not too loudly, mindful that his voice could alert the pilgrims to his presence. He did not know how Monsieur Martel would react to finding out that he and Josephine had been following the chosen on their sacred quest, but he strongly suspected the guide would respond with the violence of a self-righteous crusader. Ansgar hated hand-to-hand combat and all manner of dueling, and he didn't want to waste his small store of magic on defeating Martel. Again, he whispered, "Here kitty-kitty."

The light from his torch fell upon a faint, floury row of feline paw prints. Ansgar followed them to the edge of a little puddle made by water that dripped steadily from a crack overhead. The water must have washed the cat's paws clean, for the prints did not continue on the far side of the puddle. Nevertheless, he continued his hunt down the stone-walled passageway. *Five minutes*, he told himself. After that, cat or no cat, he'd turn back.

Josephine really ought to abandon the animal. He had repeatedly informed her that the thing did not, in fact, contain the spirit of her lost husband. Even when he'd had almost no magic at his disposal, he'd been dead certain of that. Why did Josephine need the husband, anyway? She'd had nothing good to say of him—only that they were bound by the cords of marriage. Sacred vows, *blah blah blah*. If Thierry were dead, those bonds were loosed. A wife became free of all obligations to her husband in such circumstances. Even a heathen such as he knew that.

Finding the cat would help no one. Losing the cat would help everyone. Obviously, the creature wanted to be free. Josephine needed to be liberated from the physical and mental burden of it, and he'd very much enjoy not sneezing all day long.

Ansgar turned back. He would not mention the footprints and risk her running off to follow them.

Once he returned to their scattered belongings, he gave the wreckage one more going-over to make sure nothing of value remained on the flour-and-spice-dusted dirt. He toed a scrap of silken fabric and it unfurled to reveal a dark stone set in silver. Josephine's coveted necklace. It gleamed although the torchlight barely touched it. The chain appeared to have broken.

What luck! The discovery saved him the trouble of figuring out how to remove the necklace from the Frenchwoman's neck without her knowledge. The challenge would have been entertaining, but the less he thought about her smooth, white neck, the better.

Ansgar bent to pick it up. His magic sensed the magic inside the stone, a pulse as faint as the voice of a falling snowflake. As a tool or weapon, the thing would be almost worthless. But sometimes, combined with something else—another stone, a certain word, the rays of the moon, or the like—an almost harmless thing could become extremely powerful. He needed more time to properly assess the piece.

Josephine's footsteps and sniffling alerted him of her approach, and he quickly pocketed his find.

"You had no luck either?" she said.

He shook his head. "But do not despair. It will come back when it is ready, as cats are wont to. Their sense of smell is exemplary, if I'm not mistaken. If it is truly your husband in feline form, the creature will want to return to you all the more."

She nodded somberly. "I wasn't feeding him enough, and that's why he escaped. To go hunting."

"Of course! Now, dry your eyes and take up your bag. We must hurry after the others." He shouldered his own pack and the cat's basket. Anything to get her moving again. "For when the cat returns," he said kindly. Smiling as sweetly as he could and hoping he didn't look like a madman.

She sniffed as she trailed behind him, and then said, "Thank you for looking for Thierry, and for helping me not to despair. I did not expect we could become friends, but I see now that I was wrong."

The passageway turned, and Ansgar stopped to exchange his almost spent torch for one that blazed brightly in its bracket. "Well," he said, turning to face her, "we are compatriots now, but remember that once we reach the Seven Ovens, we will be competitors. Rivals."

"Perhaps we can be both. There is no law that says friends cannot compete and remain cordial. I think we can support one another even as we compete."

"Time will tell." He led her down a sloped walkway lined with windows of stained glass. Colored rays of morning light spilled across the path. Friendship was out of the question. In fact, he needed to focus on becoming her enemy. He needed to desire to ruin her. To want to drag her into his darkness and boil her perfect sweetness until it distilled into sharp crystals. He'd failed at his last attempt to coerce a good woman to embrace the power of wickedness, when Gretel had chosen to rule as a benevolent witch-queen. He was wiser now.

The path leveled out and gave way to a windowless corridor. Ansgar slid a hand into his pocket and touched the shard of mirror. An idea formed in his mind. As Truda had molded his crooked heart, could he not mold Josephine's? How satisfying it would be to lead her down the shadowed paths he'd always preferred. She was so full of hope and gentleness. Watching her change would be like witnessing the transformation of a brightly colored caterpillar into a dark-winged, destructive moth. His lips curved into a thin smile. His spine tingled with magic eager to be spent.

If he could drive all goodness from her, they would be equals. Worthy of one another. He could love her with every bit of his cold, black heart.

Behind him, Josephine babbled softly about growing up as the daughter of a hardworking farmer along the banks of a temperamental river. Of tending swine and living simply. *Ha!* How many fairy tales featured such a lass becoming an unexpected version of herself when met with challenges and foes? This was a narrative he could bend to his liking.

She tugged his sleeve. "Ansgar? Did you hear my question?"

"I apologize. I confess that my mind drifted for a moment. I was considering ways we might lure your cat back to us." The lie warmed his belly like a hearty serving of spring lamb stew. He felt more like himself than he had in ages.

Although the day had begun with chaos, he'd found purpose in its midst. His yearning for this mouse of a woman would not lead to his undoing, but to her remaking. Finally, after suffering as a weakling duck and then as a man nearly stripped of magic, the best version of Ansgar Steuben was about to take the stage.

Eleven

Josephine slipped on a patch of mud and collided with a wall. A bruise would blossom on her shoulder, no doubt. She said nothing of it and kept following Ansgar through the damp, low-ceilinged passageway they'd been traveling for hours.

She was not one to complain over small matters. At least not out loud.

As a child, any complaints had earned her more chores or the sting of a switch. Her father had been stern in his piety; his children would learn righteousness through industry or pain, and therefore avoid the fires of hell. What he lacked in accurate theology, he surely made up for in zeal.

Josephine would not complain now that her feet were more blister than skin, or that her mind raced with fear that Thierry had fallen into a crevasse or been snatched by a monster. She would not grumble that Ansgar's behavior—grumpy one second and helpful the next—vexed the life out of her, or that she was almost hungry enough to eat the moss that grew in the cracks between the stones. She simply let out a long sigh and set one painful foot in front of the other, following her mercurial companion and clutching the last vestiges of her dwindling hope.

Would she ever find her lost cat? Husband. Cat-husband? She sighed again at the absurdity of it all.

The corridor narrowed. Dry red brick replaced the weeping, mossy, stone walls. Here, dozens of small torches hung, arranged in geometric patterns as if by an artist. For a few minutes, she gloried in the warmth, but with every footstep, Josephine felt the temperature rising sharply. Sweat beaded on her brow. Ahead of her, Ansgar shed his jacket and tied it around his waist. She copied him as the air became almost too hot to breathe. Not a whiff of smoke hung in the air, so what was causing such heat to flood the passageway?

"Should we turn around?" she asked. Nervousness drove her to touch the pendant at the base of her neck for comfort, but her fingers found only damp skin. She'd put the cloth-wrapped necklace back into her bag after her belongings had been ransacked, hadn't she? Her memory was murky. That concern would have to wait, though, as she couldn't very well pause to look for jewelry in the midst of the current emergency.

"Not yet," Ansgar replied. "I suspect there's a turn soon. A route away from this invisible inferno."

Josephine's throat felt raw. Her dry tongue found nothing to swallow. With all her being, she longed for a drink. Unfortunately, her bottle of water had spilled when the packs were raided. Her vision darkened at the edges. She steadied herself with one hand against the wall. Her knees felt like melting wax. She was going to faint.

But then she heard the sound of a cat mewling.

"Ansgar! It's him!" she exclaimed. "Thierry! Thierry, I'm here! Come to me!" Just a few words, but they'd used all her breath. She panted, one hand pressed to her pounding heart. How could anywhere on earth be so hot? Would the very stones soon liquefy?

"Impossible." Ansgar's voice sounded far away although he stood just steps from her.

The mewling repeated. Josephine tried to run, but her legs

folded beneath her. She pitched forward like a cut tree. Strong arms caught her and lowered her to the floor.

"Are you all right?" Ansgar asked. His hand cradled the back of her head as she lay flat on the ground.

"Find Thierry," she said. "Please."

"Woman, have you no concern for yourself? This heat will kill you. We must go back the way we came."

Of course he was right. Never had she felt so weak. It took all of her remaining strength to grab his shirt and beg, "Please. Find him."

Ansgar slid his hand from beneath her head. With nimble fingers and a mumbled apology, he opened the buttons of her blouse. "To cool you," he said. She should have objected, but modesty mattered little to her now. Ansgar had to find Thierry before the cat eluded them again.

"Go," she said.

"I'll look for five minutes, that's all. We need to get you out of this wretched heat. Lie still now. Breathe. Think about snow and ice."

She closed her eyes and tried to obey him. She imagined Christmas and frosted windowpanes. A horse-drawn sleigh ride through a snow-dusted village just before sunset, with December tinting the sky pale orange and pink. Skating on the river and laughing with her friends until her teeth felt cold as the ice skimming under her blades.

It was no use. The heat pressed down on her, settling onto her prone body like a giant made of embers and charcoal. Her consciousness faded. Her last thought was not of her cat-husband but of the man who'd left her to search for the cat.

Where was Ansgar? Had he, too, fallen victim to the heat? What a sorrow it was, that they would die within the selfsame hour yet separately, after all they'd endured together.

Ansgar heard the cat meowing somewhere nearby—unless the perceived proximity was an illusion created by the magic-infused walls. The animal sounded miserable. Good. It deserved to be miserable, for all the trouble it had caused.

He was miserable, too. Hotter than he'd ever been in his life, and he'd often stood close to Truda's strong, magic-driven fires as she melted strange things into potions and medicines. He let the torch slip from his sweaty hand. Surrounded by an orange glow, he didn't need it.

Why was he looking for the stupid, runaway cat? Ah, yes. Because *she* had pleaded with him to do so. Blast Josephine! More though, blast the useless fleabag!

If Josephine perished while he was searching for Thierry, he'd make sure it paid in blood.

The cat uttered a horrid, screeching-yowling noise. Ansgar reached an intersection and turned toward the sound. A blast of scorching air blew his hair back from his forehead. Great gods, how could anything be hotter than the air he'd already been trudging through? Perspiration dripped from his clothes. His eyes, as dry and scratchy as desert sand, could hardly blink. Was this actual hell?

Almost blind, he stumbled through an open doorway. The rooftops of the church sprawled before him, glossy black slate under a somber gray sky. Lightning flashed above steeply pitched rows of shingles and a pointed steeple. Thunder rattled his bones. Not far off, a spire jutted upward, its base surrounded with a squared ledge of stone. And it was there that the cat sat, its ears flattened in fury, its dirty orange fur blown into disarray by the ceaseless, searing wind. When it saw him, it howled.

Ansgar swore, cursed, and blasphemed. He detested heights almost as much as he hated cats. Now that he was in the situation, though, he would not retreat. He made his way across a narrow walkway of blackened stone, arms extended at his sides for balance. The wind shoved him, and he faltered. Bent awkwardly at the waist, he flailed his arms until he regained equilibrium.

Never in all his days as man and duck would Ansgar have imagined that one day he'd risk his life to save a cat.

The beast hissed at him from the ledge. Another burst of wind pummeled them both. The cat flinched. One wrong move and it would plummet to certain death.

"Be careful!" Josephine shouted from behind him. Not a brilliant thing to say, but of course she meant well. *Devil take the woman.* She always meant well. And what was she thinking, following him when he'd clearly told her to remain still?

It was a relief to know she was still alive, but now was not the time to think of anything but inching along a thin shelf of stone toward a hostile cat. And breathing. Neither task was easy in the current hellish climate.

"Don't move," Ansgar said to the cat when only inches separated them. It arched its back and hissed. But the animal had nowhere to hide now. The creature could choose life or death, surrender or doom.

In a swift motion, Ansgar leaned forward to scoop up the cat. In his arms, it growled but didn't fight. When he stood straight again, a wave of dizziness struck. He threw one arm out to his side to steady himself. Josephine's gasp seemed to echo over the rooftops as he regained his footing, turned, and shuffled along the ledge.

The stone beneath his feet quaked. Cracks formed in front of him, and then a row of fiery tulips slid up from the fissures, crimson and orange blossoms of flame supported by thin black stems. The flowers crackled and hissed as they grew. They were ankle high, and then seconds later, knee high. Another row popped up close beside the first. Ansgar wanted to curse, but he didn't know a word strong enough to suit the situation. The cat struggled in his arms, claws flying, obviously alarmed by the threatening sounds of the unnatural garden.

"Hurry!" Josephine urged. "The flames are growing!"

"Am I blind, woman?" he shouted in reply, yet he did not leap into action. If he ran through the blazing tulips, he might be utterly consumed. Even if his sweat-soaked clothes provided some protection, the flames would sear any exposed skin. Burns caused the worst sort of pain, and pain was something he'd always dodge if possible.

"Ansgar!" Her voice was shrill with panic. The fire-flowers stood waist high.

He clutched the cat closer and stepped forward. His wet trouser legs sizzled at the touch of the flaming petals. His boots felt like twin saunas. Another step. The cat had gone still, perhaps unconscious. The air singed his throat. Another step as the flames leapt toward his waist. Thunder rumbled, shaking everything. He heard stone cracking, crumbling. He dared not look down to check the state of the path he had to take.

There was no way he was going to survive this.

"Keep your eyes on me and don't stop moving," Josephine said, but he could hardly see anything through his desiccated eyes. Pain tore into his bare elbows as his skin burned and blistered. He gritted his teeth and took another step.

The fire lapped at his legs like a demon dog. The hems of his pants were aflame. Dizziness threatened to send him reeling over the edge. A quick death beckoned through the haze of relentless pain. One step to the side, and his suffering would end.

Lightning flashed, blinding him for a moment. Thunder roared like an angry deity. If only the skies would open and pour forth rain to douse the flames.

Rain.

As a duck, all but stripped of his power, Ansgar had possessed enough magic to pull rain or snow from the heavens. The power he had now, although limited, ought to be enough to conjure a brief shower.

Ansgar closed his eyes and called out to the clouds with his magic. Lightning carved a silver scar across the dark sky. Thunder rumbled through his frame. A few drops tapped him on the head. And then, *oh blessed rain*! Water slid from the heavens in sheets. All around him, fires hissed and transformed into wisps of vapor. The air cooled.

Embracing the cat, he fell to his knees, almost unaware of the agony of blistered skin meeting stone as he laughed and cried. Tears and rain mingled on his face. In his arms, the cat stirred, but Ansgar kept a firm hold on the beast until he felt soft hands prying at his fingers.

"Let me take him," Josephine said as she knelt before him. Ansgar relaxed his grip and she took the cat. It meowed weakly as she pressed it to her chest.

"You walked through fire for me, and I will not forget it," she said. "Thank you." Gingerly, she leaned forward to rest her head against his shoulder. It hurt. He must have been burned there, burned almost everywhere, but he gritted his teeth and bore the pain rather than pushing her away. She said, "I have never seen anyone behave so bravely. It was terrifying."

When she broke into sobs, he wrapped his arms around her, ignoring his pain and the presence of the wet cat. The rain ceased, but thunder continued to roll through the landscape. She smelled of smoke and salt, mud and sweat, and faintly, remarkably, of lavender soap. It was a miracle to breathe deeply of rain-freshened air, and a wonder to be alive. Astounding to be holding her close. His fingers tangled in her long ringlets. He felt a thousand things at once, raw and wild. Who was he now, and who was she to him?

That was a mystery for later. In this moment, all he wanted was to hold her. He pulled her closer, and she did not resist.

Sharp claws punctured his shoulder. He jerked backward, fell onto his behind, and clutched at the fresh wounds.

"Thierry, how naughty!" Josephine scolded the cat in her arms. "Ansgar risked his life to save you, and this is how you thank him? Your rudeness is abominable." She stood, still clutching the cat, and looked down at Ansgar. "I'm sorry. I'll put Thierry in his basket, and then I'll come back and attend to your injuries. I have salve, I think. Wait there."

"I'll see to myself, thank you," he said to her retreating form. With a loud groan and a few strong curses, he got to his feet. Every limb objected strongly, having been bruised, burned, or scraped—or punctured by that hellspawn cat. The brush of clothing against scorched skin was enough to make him want to bawl like a baby.

Disgust rose in his belly as he hobbled forward. He hated himself for reuniting Josephine with the poison she craved: the terrible cat she worshiped as the incarnation of her horrible husband. And what of holding her like a lover and *crying*?

The day had been one disaster after another. How Truda would have mocked him for display after display of indiscretion. Pursuing a cat through hellish fires to please a silly widow! Offering the Frenchwoman comfort after she'd all but caused him to combust!

A breeze pressed at his back. Steam rolled around his ankles like fog used to billow off the lake he'd once called home. Even as a duck, he'd stayed true to himself and his plans. Who was he now? A few feet from the door into the church, he tipped his head to the sky and made a solemn vow to keep his eyes on the proverbial prize and to abandon all notions of transforming Josephine into his wicked mistress. The sooner they parted, the better. She'd been nothing but trouble, like tempting sweets that melt quickly and leave holes in one's molars.

Exhausted, he sat against the door jamb to wait for Josephine to return with treatment for his wounds—if any was to be found among their remaining provisions. He'd undertaken this pilgrimage to save his *own* life, he'd do well to remember after this. To fall in love with any version of Josephine could be to invite death to take him before the week ended. Look what bodily harm she'd caused already.

She'd return soon. It would be a mistake to let her hands roam over his injured skin with salve, to allow her to wrap his body with bandages as she babbled words of gratitude. The very thought of submitting to her ministrations made his heartbeat falter.

He forced himself to his feet. As he stumbled his way back into the church, dripping and cold and limping with pain, he started to compose a mental list of reasons to hate her.

Twelve

Thierry lunged to bite Josephine's hand as she shoved him into the wicker cage. Fortunately, his jaws nipped only the air. She latched the door fast, and he glared at her through the little barred window.

"What has gotten into you, *mon cher*? Running away, biting, scratching like a wild beast. If you don't behave better, I swear I'll keep this basket shut tight until after the baking competition."

The cat tucked his head under his puffed-out tail as if he could not have cared less what she said. *Rude animal.* He bore hardly a speck of soot and none of his fur appeared to be scorched. If only poor Ansgar had fared as well. Everything he wore would have to be thrown into a rubbish pit. Not a stitch of his once fine suit had escaped being singed, torn, or stained. It was all Thierry's fault, and obviously Thierry wasn't grateful in the least.

Gratitude had never been a habit of her husband.

If Josephine was honest, the cat version of Thierry remained true to Thierry's human character. Her husband was an impatient, impulsive man, used to having his way and all the freedom in the world. He did as he pleased, regardless of the consequences others suffered.

She checked to make sure the latch held firm. For the rest of his time as a cat, Thierry was going nowhere without a leash. His little jaunt had almost left Ansgar fried to a crisp.

Poor Ansgar.

The memory of his embrace sent a shiver through her. It was a moment she would not soon forget. She'd been so relieved that he'd rescued Thierry, and more relieved that he'd lived through the fire. He'd sobbed like a child as he'd held her tightly, and she'd clung to him as if she'd been the one saved. She could hardly imagine the pain he was suffering after his heroic exploits.

Josephine crouched and rummaged frantically through her bag in search of something to ease Ansgar's pain or treat his injuries. Her mind whirled. She had little memory of what she'd salvaged from the mess. Her fingers grazed a tiny object wrapped in cloth as she dug deep, most likely her necklace—and thank heaven for that. She would have rejoiced if she'd had time. She kept digging instead. At the bottom of her bag, she found a small tin labeled "blister curative," one of the things she'd bought in compliance with the supply list. She turned her attention to Ansgar's pack and fished out a similar tin of salve and a small bottle of Doctor's Best Headache Powders. Neither of these promised a magical instant cure, but she would offer them to him. She stood and rushed through the corridor that now hung with wisps of smoke. Her boots sloshed through shallow puddles.

Ansgar appeared in the doorway before she reached it, a gray and black phantom moving stiffly toward her, hissing through his teeth. The fire-ravaged man could have stepped out of a nightmare, but the sight of him filled her with more pity than fear.

"How can I help?" she asked. "I brought these, but..." She showed him the bottles and tins, but he shook his head in refusal.

"They're not strong enough. You must aid me in making a potion for my injuries. Hurry back to the last courtyard garden we passed through, the one with the beds of herbs. Will you be able to find the place?"

She wasn't at all sure, but said, "Yes. Tell me what you need."

An hour later, she returned with one hand full of fragrant leaves and twigs and the other clutching a torch she'd snatched along the way for light. She'd stuffed her pockets with plants he'd requested. Heaven above, she hoped she'd remembered everything. Ansgar lay on the floor of the corridor, right where she'd left him. Had he not been shivering hard, she might have taken him for dead.

"Fetch my pack," he said through chattering teeth. "You'll need...the small silver bowl."

She set the herbs on the ground and ran to get his bag. When she returned, she inserted the torch into a metal bracket. With her back to Ansgar, she crouched to sort through the contents of his bag again. As she dug, her fingers caught onto a leather-bound book. A journal. The perfect place to hide a recipe. How had she missed it earlier? If her pockets had been larger, she might have— *would have*—stolen it to examine later. The wickedness of such a thought made her blush. But could not so little a sin be excused if it was done to save the husband she'd vowed to honor and cherish?

A glint of silver caught her eye and she let go of the journal. She pulled out a shallow bowl the size of her open hand.

"Have you found it?" Ansgar asked feebly.

"I have." She brought the bowl and the herbs to his side. "What should I do?"

He directed her well, telling her which leaves to crush, and how many petals of which flowers to add to the vessel. Finally, he sent her to find rainwater to add to the concoction. When she came back, he sat up and took the bowl in his quaking hands. She sat on her heels and watched him utter foreign words over the mixture. She couldn't tell if he spoke German or gibberish, and it didn't matter, for his words did their work. The air around Ansgar's body shimmered faintly. The bowl glowed and its contents swirled like water circling a drain. When he stopped speaking, the potion stilled. He shut his eyes and brought the bowl to his lips. Slowly, he sipped until it was empty, then set the bowl down.

Hardly daring to breathe, she waited. He sat so still. So quiet. Was that good or bad? She knew little of magic—but enough to know it was dangerous. She watched his face in the flickering torch light. The lines etched by suffering faded, and where it could be seen through the soot, the color of his complexion shifted from pallid to a healthy peach tone. The oozing cat scratches near his exposed collarbone dried up. He inhaled deeply and released a sigh.

Ansgar had saved himself with magic.

Who was this man? He'd mentioned that he'd been a student of magic as a youth, but she'd assumed that had come to naught—otherwise would he not have bragged continually about being a great wizard? He was not a humble man. Yet, half dead, he'd just expertly directed her to craft a healing potion.

Why on earth would he need the saint's wish when he already had access to such magic?

A chill washed over her and left unease in its wake. She'd be wise not to trust Ansgar, no matter how many times he saved her cat.

The contest and their subsequent parting could not come soon enough, for she knew her own weakness. If he showed her kindness, she'd forgive and forget with hardly a second thought. Like a malnourished mongrel, she had a history of overlooking almost any kind of deceit or meanness in exchange for a few words of praise or apology.

Ansgar opened his eyes and smiled.

"Feeling better?" she asked. "We can rest here for a while. For as long as you need."

"Some of the worst burns linger, but the pain is mostly gone." He stood easily and offered his hand. "Come. The cat has cost us much time. If we find the pilgrims again, it will be a miracle."

She shook her head to refuse his aid, and used her own tired muscles to rise to her feet. He would need whatever strength he had for the journey. "Thank you for rescuing Thierry," she said. "I'm sorry his mischief caused you injury. That you might have died—"

"You cannot be blamed for the actions of a senseless animal." He shouldered his bag, grimacing as if it pressed upon one of his less healed burns. He took the torch from the wall. "Where is the cat now? Well secured, I hope."

"He's in his basket. I checked the latch several times. And trust me, I reprimanded Thierry for his behavior."

A bitter laugh fell from his mouth. "I don't believe cats are capable of remorse, Madame. And I know, I know. In your estimation, the creature is not merely a cat, but your husband. But tell me truly. If he stood here as a man, would he regret causing either one of us to suffer? Because I suspect that he was the kind of man who cared only for his own interests and pleasure."

She opened her mouth to protest, but then shut it. She had no legitimate argument to offer, for Ansgar wasn't wrong. If she said Thierry was generous or self-sacrificing, she'd only encumber her own soul with lies. Besides, she was a terrible liar. He'd never believe her.

"Your silence speaks volumes." He walked away, toward where they'd been before they'd heard the cat's cries.

Although his smug tone riled her, she followed him. "All right. Thierry isn't perfect, but who is? Not you, certainly."

His laughter started soft as a sigh, but grew into a loud chortle.

"I fail to see what's so amusing," she said when he stopped laughing to gasp for breath. "And shouldn't you be trying to stay calm as you recuperate?"

He glanced over his shoulder at her. "Your concern is touching, but you need not worry. The potion continues to work. With every footstep, I feel my strength returning."

"Well, I'm becoming more exhausted by the minute, if that's possible. Perhaps I should drink a potion, too."

"Potions are not to be trifled with."

"I was exaggerating, *monsieur*. I'd rather avoid dealings with magic. *Grand-mère* always cautioned against it. Her uncle went mad after trying to cure himself of warts with a spell." She wasn't lying, but she *was* steering the conversation so that he might spill some hints about the extent of his magical abilities.

He stopped beside her bag and bent to grab it. "You're joking, surely."

"Well, Father said the man was never quite right in the head to begin with, so..." She took the bag from his hands and slid its strap onto her shoulder. Next, she picked up Thierry's basket. The sleeping cat made no sound.

"Madness and magic ought not to be mixed," Ansgar said.

"Now you sound like *Grand-mère*."

"I confess I'm beginning to find the woman interesting," Ansgar said, but she didn't like his snobbish tone, so made no effort to continue the conversation.

Again, they started to walk. She let him lead. Weariness numbed her legs, and then her arms, but she kept her suffering secret. She envied Ansgar. Covered in ash and tatters, he walked with perfect posture and the long stride of someone just beginning a journey. And he'd already almost died twice on this pilgrimage. Three times if she counted the hibouchauris attack.

If anyone had been keeping score of heroic acts, she would have been ahead. Ansgar had saved Thierry, but she had saved Ansgar from the hibouchauris, the bee stings, and his burns. The potions had done their part, yes, but if she had not administered them, he would have been doomed. And look at the German now, sauntering through the corridors like he had not a single blister or ache—because the magic-infused medicine had healed him utterly.

The corridor split, but the route to the left was blocked by a crudely built wall. They turned right. Walked on and on. A bolt of pain shot through her shoulders, so she adjusted Thierry's basket straps.

Ansgar halted and lifted a hand. "Do you hear voices?"

"I do not."

"It was only an animal, I suppose." He started walking again.

Impulsively, Josephine said, "The others must be far ahead by now. Do you think...would it be possible for you to locate the pilgrims with magic?" She wanted him to say no because it gave her the shivers, but yes because they needed to find the others as soon as possible. And because the situation they were in seemed increasingly dire. Hunger cramped her stomach, and she felt faint. The halls kept turning and twisting endlessly. She didn't even know what day it was anymore. What if they never reached the Seven Ovens at all?

"I could not," he said flatly. Did he mean he could not or would prefer not to?

She dropped the subject and fell silent as they traversed a long, straight passageway and then climbed a set of creaky, rickety wooden stairs. But she was far from finished trying to learn more about Ansgar's abilities. If he meant to use magic to win the baking competition, she needed to be prepared to somehow foil him. She needed to weasel out his weaknesses so she could use them against him...no matter how wrong it felt after all they'd been through together.

In an effort to avoid feeling guilty, she imagined herself as the heroine from one of the novels she'd kept hidden from Thierry: bold, brave, and ready to do whatever it took to rescue someone she loved.

Ansgar marveled at the pines towering above him.

Not five minutes had passed since he'd led Josephine through a cavern of jagged gray rock with a charcoal-filled fire pit at its center. About three minutes ago, they'd crossed the tiled floor of a small, gilded chapel, and approximately one minute ago, they'd moved through an arched doorway. Ansgar had expected to enter another garden or stone-paved courtyard, as the journey had proved to be one of repetition. Instead, he'd set foot in a grove of towering evergreens. A pang of homesickness for the Igelwald penetrated his heart, a sentiment so strong that it stole his breath. He'd never thought he'd miss that forest after all he'd endured there as a duck. Indeed, he'd sworn never to return there.

These pines had undoubtedly seen two hundred years of starlight and sunbeams. Their knobby trunks held forth sparse, bare limbs at their lower heights. Overhead, they bore branches so dense with needles that they blocked most of the daylight. The fresh evergreen scent was almost intoxicating. Too long had he and Josephine traversed damp alleys of mildewed stone. And he was all too glad to smell something pleasant rather than his personal charred-cloth-and-rank-sweat stench. He took a deep breath, and then sneezed three times in succession. The stupid cat was several feet away, yet it continued to vex him with its foul miasma.

The trail widened and Josephine fell into step alongside him. Her dying torch sputtered out as a mild breeze swept through the forest, but it mattered not, for his eyes had grown accustomed to dim places.

Best of all, there were footprints in the pine needles. Ansgar was certain the pilgrims had gone this way. Soon, he and Josephine would catch up with them. He said nothing to her about his discovery, hoarding the joy of it for himself. If she was too flighty to take note of the evidence, it was not his fault.

"This is beautiful," Josephine said with quiet awe, as if she did not hear her blasted cat yowling inside its basket. "It reminds me of a place my father took me one summer, high in the mountains outside Valerienne. We stayed three nights there. I hardly slept because all I wanted to do was lie in a patch of soft ferns and gaze at the stars that sparkled over the treetops. The woods were full of owls, too. My father thought their eerie calls would frighten me, but I found the sound soothing and beautiful. Forests are such peaceful places, don't you agree?"

"Peaceful implies lack of noise," Ansgar replied. "Your cat's ceaseless bellowing surely annoys even the trees."

"Thierry is angry with me. He wants out of the cage."

Ansgar smirked. "You speak the language of cats?"

"Of course not, but I know this one well enough to guess what his cries signify."

When he glared at her in disbelief, she blushed scarlet. With his attraction for her held firmly in check, he could enjoy making her squirm. He relished the power he had to bring color to her cheeks. He decided to make a game of it. He'd count the number of times she blushed because of his words or actions between this moment and their arrival at the Seven Ovens. The game would make the miles seem shorter. He'd start right away. With a superior air, he said, "Know that if you release the creature and it runs off, I will not risk my life again to retrieve it."

"I do wish you would refer to Thierry as 'he' rather than 'it.'"

As he'd hoped, the pink in her cheeks darkened a shade. He said, "You know without a doubt that the cat is a male, then. You checked its...accouterments?"

Josephine gave him what might have been a scathing look if another woman had thrown it his way. Her innate sweetness interfered. As a result, her expression was one of charming annoyance. He looked away to avoid being charmed.

She kicked a pine cone off the path and caused a spray of brown needles. "I'm absolutely certain the cat is male. Not that it matters whether the cat is a tom or not. My husband's presence within the cat is what's important here. The indwelling of Thierry's soul."

Blazes, it was difficult not to hoot with laughter when she played into his hands. "Tell me, as I am neither a philosopher nor a theologian: can souls be classified as male or female, or is such a distinction purely biological, a constraint cast upon one's immortal essence only when housed by human flesh?"

Her silence bespoke her befuddlement. He stole a glance. The same color continued to stain her cheekbones. Would it be fair to add another mark to his mental tally board for the blush's remarkable duration?

When she finally spoke, the words gushed out. "I know you are mocking me, Monsieur Steuben. I am not a scholar. I am not even a clever woman, and I would never pretend to be. I only know what I know, what I feel, and who I am. I know that Thierry is stuck inside the body of a cat because I feel his presence there. I know that I pledged before heaven to be my husband's helpmeet until death, and I know that I am a kind and loyal person who keeps her promises. So mock me if you must, if it pleases you in some sick way, but your barbs will not pierce me and your poison will not leak into my veins."

Stunned, Ansgar gripped the straps of his bag. And as his shock faded, it gave way to wonderment. Josephine's appearance gave the impression of a soft, sweet bun spiced with a daring dash of cinnamon, but inside all that goodness lay a core of granite one could break their teeth on. He'd been the fool, believing her simple and malleable.

Josephine Monfort was nothing short of astounding.

He could hardly draw a breath. Never in all his days had he been more attracted to a woman—and a woman of good character at that. By no means would he ever have guessed that he'd betray himself so thoroughly—with *feelings*.

"Are you in pain again?" Her tone was one of genuine concern, in spite of her recent biting comments.

"You might say so," he mumbled toward the ground, not daring to look at her.

"I know we cannot afford to stop for long, but we could watch for plants along the trail that might help you. Some leaf or root you could chew as we walk? Willow bark is good for headaches. Perhaps—"

"I have not seen a single willow since we set out on this insufferable quest," he interrupted gruffly. "Besides, no tree on earth can mitigate my suffering."

"There must be something. *Grand-mère* always said the woods were nature's apothecary shop. She made a tea from red hare nettles that would have cured you of your sneezing in no time. They only grow along rivers, of course. What about that plant there, with the pink berries? Is that asterpenny? Aren't the berries used in cough syrups? Might they help you?"

It was on the tip of his tongue to inform her that his sneezing could be easily cured by tossing the cat off the next cliff, but instead he said, "In my country, we call that plant 'death berry.' I would not recommend touching any part of it." He wanted to be rid of her, but not responsible for her death. If he were to play a role in her demise, she'd probably haunt him forever, floating above his bed spouting endless nonsense every night. Hovering just out of reach, like a ripe plum taunting a starving man.

She grabbed his arm and pointed. Something like the squeal of a young pig preceded her giddy exclamation, "Mushrooms! So many mushrooms! Over there. Do you see them?"

Growing at the foot of a copse of hazel trees were dozens of small brown mushrooms with black speckles, curled at their edges like fancy little parasols. Before he could speak, she snatched up his hand with hers and pulled him toward them.

The fact that she was running did not stop Josephine from talking. "I've never cared for the flavor of mushrooms, but I'm hungry enough to eat a boiled shoe." They left the path to dash over pine needles and leaf litter. "You must be starving as well. Especially after all you've been through. I'm sure almost dying would leave me ravenous. Of course, Thierry always said I could out-eat a whale."

When they reached the patch of mushrooms, she released his hand, dropped to her knees, and shrugged free of her baggage. She plucked one of the small, umbrella-shaped fungi and held it between her finger and thumb. "Are these safe to eat?"

He knelt beside her, miscalculating where his knees would fall in the pine needles and cursing internally when his exposed shin brushed against her trouser-covered leg. Blast the flames for eating away the fabric of his clothes. And blast his blood for surging at the merest hint of contact.

It was foolish to consider using his almost exhausted supply of magic in an attempt to end his yearning for her, especially since he doubted his magic could quench it. But he felt a hair's breadth from being undone by her—and it was driving him mad. He needed to focus on winning the contest, and that alone. If he surrendered to his emotions, he'd soon be nothing but her groveling servant, good for only penning sappy poetry, fetching her cups of tea, and untangling her (undoubtedly endless) stockpile of yarn.

And he'd be dead in a year.

He clenched his eyes shut and called upon what remained of his magic after conjuring the rainstorm and helping to activate the healing potion. It answered with the weak buzz of a housefly languishing on a windowsill. *Drat.* With such a tiny portion, he probably couldn't startle a flea into jumping. He'd have to use his self-control instead. Gods help him.

When he opened his eyes, he found her peering at him expectantly. "Well? Are they good to eat or not?"

He cleared his throat and took the mushroom from her hand. Red mushrooms were definitely dangerous to eat, but this specimen was dull brown. Its gills were closed; was that good or bad? He sniffed it. The mushroom smelled only of earth and the forest.

The scent awoke memories. Long, long ago, when they were newlyweds, Truda had tried to teach him about the flora and fauna of the Igelwald. He'd been a terrible student of nature, too fixated on his bride to care about ferns or hedgehogs. But he remembered this particular mushroom. He could picture it cupped in his wife's fair hand as birds trilled in the treetops. She'd given him the name of it. If only he could remember...

Clutching its stem between his thumb and forefinger, he held the mushroom up and rotated it slowly. The name came to mind, and he smiled. Not all Truda's efforts at instruction had been futile. He might have thanked her now, if he'd been able to speak to the dead—or not. Expressions of gratitude had always made Truda peevish.

"These are trolls' ear mushrooms," Ansgar announced. "They're edible. If I recall rightly, their flavor has notes of smoke and thyme."

Josephine turned her face to him. One fuzzy ringlet of silvered brown hair slid over the wrinkle of concern on her forehead. "You're sure enough to eat them yourself?"

He nodded, suddenly ravenous in a way that had little to do with food. He leaned away from her. "Indeed, I am."

Before another second passed, Josephine plucked several mushrooms from the earth. Ansgar joined her in frenzied picking. They tossed the fungi into one pile. Josephine had almost popped a mushroom into her mouth when Ansgar grabbed her wrist. "Wait. They must be boiled. There's something bitter in them that must be cooked out before they're palatable."

She yanked her arm free. "You might have said so before."

"I only just remembered. Besides, you didn't ask for a recipe, did you?"

"I suppose I did not," she replied tersely.

He expected her to apologize, but she didn't. Hunger was not improving her mood. Did he mind, or did her insolence made his heart beat faster with longing?

She gathered the harvest into her arms and said, "If they must be cooked, I guess we should go back to the cavern we passed through with the fire pit and cauldron. Thank heaven it won't take long to reach." A few mushrooms tumbled to the ground as she got to her feet. "Come on, and bring my things, if you would. Or am I the only one who's famished?"

"You have quite a mouth on you when you're hungry," Ansgar

remarked wryly, taking her bag and basket in hand. He allowed for some distance to form between them as she rushed back the way they'd come.

That mouth of hers. Why was it so blasted hard not to think about what it would be like to kiss it? And how wishy-washy he'd become, unable to conform to his own plans to resist the woman in thought and deed.

He would have kicked himself if he could have.

Thirteen

The rich scent of simmering mushrooms almost drove Josephine wild. She stirred the cauldron with a stick and prayed for patience. She was no expert in wild mushrooms. Ansgar would tell her when he deemed them done. He sat on the opposite side of the fire pit whittling a branch with his short knife, coaxing the rough shape of a spoon from wood they'd found stacked in the corner. If he was as desperate to eat as she was, he gave no sign. From his expression, she might have guessed he was bored halfway to sleep.

They'd been in the cavern less than an hour, but to Josephine, it seemed like half a week had passed. During that time, Ansgar had collected water from an adjoining cavern while she poked and blew on the embers they'd found among the charcoal, embers probably left by the elusive pilgrims. After they'd dropped the mushrooms into the water-filled cauldron, there had been little to do but wait. And wait.

Her stomach growled more loudly than she'd known a stomach could, but she was too starved to be embarrassed.

"They should be ready to eat in a few more minutes, I believe," Ansgar said. She gazed over the yellow-orange flames at him. His blond hair looked as if a family of filthy squirrels had wrestled in it, and his once fine suit was blackened rags. There was a patch of bare skin on his sharp cheekbone—one of the few parts of his face not obscured by ash or grime. He could have gone onstage to portray an impoverished miner recently mauled by a lion.

"Is something wrong?" he asked. "Has a spider nested atop my head, perhaps?"

She returned her attention to the bubbling soup, stirring it more vigorously. "Nothing is wrong. But you are completely covered in filth. When we began this journey, dressed in your costly coat and new boots, I could not have imagined you in such a state."

"Pray do not mention my poor clothes," he said with a sigh. "After all the unimaginable things that have happened on this pilgrimage, the sorry state of my attire ought not to bother me half as much as it does." He sounded thoughtful rather than cranky, which surprised her. He tried to run his hand through his hair, but it became stuck and he pulled it free. "Our adventure will end soon. I imagine mere days remain until the baking competition, and only the gods know if we'll even make it to the Seven Ovens in time."

The cauldron's contents spattered her shirt, but she didn't care. Her clothes were almost as ruined as Ansgar's. The rich aroma of the soup was beguiling. Seductive. She wanted to put her face into the pot and suck up the contents, burns or no burns. Her hunger was growing by the second, transforming from an ill-tempered bear into a ferocious dragon.

"Shall we eat?" Ansgar surprised her by reaching across the pot to pass her the wooden spoon he'd made.

"You do not need this?"

"It's for you." He picked up the dented tin bowl and mug he'd pulled from his pack earlier and moved closer to the cauldron. With the mug, he scooped soup into the bowl. He handed the bowl to her and then filled the mug for himself.

Josephine sank to the floor, careful not to spill a drop. It took every ounce of restraint she had, but she made herself wait to avoid scalding her mouth. Ansgar reclaimed his seat on the rock and blew onto his mug. And then, with the drip of water and the bubbling of the cauldron echoing around them, they partook in unison—she, sipping from the spoon, and he, drinking from the mug.

The first taste warmed Josephine to her toes. The second sent a shiver of pleasure through her. Her tongue fell in love with the woodsy, slightly sweet flavor. How was it possible for anything to taste so good? How had she detested these delectable morsels from the forest floor all her life? She spooned the rest of the soup into her mouth with her eyes closed, relishing every bit.

Across from her, Ansgar chuckled. That was unexpected. The man only ever laughed when mocking her. But she could not fault him for laughing now. She felt the same giddy happiness.

Bowl emptied, she set it aside. A little dizzy, she lay back to rest on the cool ground. Above her head, she watched clouds of swirling colors drift just under the cavern's curved stone ceiling. Little butterflies darted in and out of the clouds, trailing ribbons of gold and silver sparkles.

From the corner of her eye, she saw Ansgar topple off the rock he'd been sitting on. Instead of trying to stand, he remained on his back, limbs splayed like a starfish's. Instead of cursing, he grunted. The grunt wasn't even laced with frustration. It resembled the sound a contented swine would make when settling into a bath of mud.

Josephine rolled onto her side. With nothing else to do, she watched Ansgar breathe. His chest rose and fell slowly. Breathing was an amazing thing, the way air slipped in and out of a person. Even a very dirty, exceptionally cantankerous person like Ansgar Steuben. He was better looking with his eyes and mouth closed. There was less haughtiness in his face. He wasn't her type, with his pointy cheekbones and all that floppy blond hair, but she guessed other women would find him quite attractive. That swoop of hair did invite caresses. From *other* women. Women who were not already married. To men or to cats, or whomever.

"I am going to beat you, you know," Ansgar said without opening his eyes. She watched his mouth move in profile. Mouths were strange, the way they opened and shut and formed words. "I do not mean physically, as with a switch. No, never that. I mean when we bake for the wish. There is absolutely no way you can win. And I'm not even a bakery, baker sort of person. I could burn a water pie. But not this time. This time, I shall triumph. I will be the champion. I am already the victor, because time itself is beneath my feet. Did I say time? I meant...Oh, hang it. Suffice it to say, I am the victorious champion of the future."

She sat up fast, which made the room spin. A giggle fell from her lips as she pressed both palms to the earth to steady herself. "You're a pompous old pig's behind, that is what you are, *monsieur*."

Still flat on his back, he opened his eyes and grinned. His too-white teeth hurt to look at. He turned his face toward her and said, "I don't mind being part of a pig's anatomy as long as I win. And win I shall, for I have a secret recipe for the best and most magical of gingerbread. This recipe built the home of the greatest witch-queen ever to reign. This recipe is priceless. Unmatchable. What do you have? Some flimsy piece of paper given to you by your grandmother with instructions for a boring old cinnamon biscuit, perhaps? You will never conquer the great wizard of wizards, the powerful Ansgar Helmut Steuben!"

She laughed hard enough to snort. Her stomach ached from laughing, but she couldn't stop. Helmut? What sort of name was that? She would not name a goldfish something so ridiculous.

"You do not believe me? Wait. I will show you." He struggled to his feet and stumbled to retrieve his pack. Mumbling to himself, he dug out a small book and waved it in the air. "*Voilà!* It's in this musty old journal, here in my glorious, magical hands. An old recipe for magic-infused gingerbread strong enough to withstand any storm, yet delicious enough to lead a saint to sin! Stolen, no less, from the very tall but very oblivious husband of the thankless brat, Gretel, who conquered my Truda."

Josephine could not seem to convince her body to stand, so she crawled to him. At his feet, she knelt and extended her hand. "Let me see this recipe, Ansgar Helmut. For all I know, you're telling tales and that book is nothing but the diary your grandfather scribbled while locked in prison."

"Silly girl, my grandfather was a righteous man. A pillar of the community. But he never wrote a word. Not even his name. Stupid as a cracked brick in that regard." He sat beside her, close enough that their thighs touched. The book fell open in his lap. "Look here."

This was the book she'd seen earlier, the one she'd hoped to steal. When she leaned over to peer at the page, she knew immediately that he was not lying about the recipe. She could read enough German to translate the list of ingredients and the simple instructions. There was a block of words, too, that seemed to be an accompanying incantation.

She plucked the book from his hands. He still reeked of smoke and singed hair, but she'd smelled worse things. She started to read. "*Mes étoiles!* This recipe would make a lot of cake. Enough to feed an army! Never in my life have I seen that amount of cinnamon. And how many hens would you need for so many eggs?"

"Your life before we met was small," he said dreamily. His shoulder bumped against hers in a convivial sort of way. The jolt made her lose her place in the recipe. He further distracted her by saying, "This journey has changed you. It has rendered you brave. Or perhaps, it has merely brought out the braveness hidden within you all along."

A new wave of dizziness and warmth washed over her. Her fingers held the book tightly, as if it were a life raft in a storm. After a moment of silence, she replied to him. "I am brave because I must be. I must free my husband from the cat." A tear leaked from her eye and she brushed it away as if it offended her. "Without Thierry, I shall be ruined."

"Look at me," Ansgar said, and she peered into his deadly serious countenance. His too-blue eyes. They were like the sky over the sea on a summer afternoon. He leaned closer to her and said, "Who lied to you and made you believe you are weak and incapable? You are one of the strongest women I have ever known, in spite of your cloying sweetness. It confounds me, you know. How you can be both honey and steel; the first gentle rays of morning and the raging ball of flame that is the sun itself."

His words. How pretty they were, even if false. She blushed so hard she felt the heat in her bones. Had there been butterflies in the soup? Moths, perhaps? She could feel their tiny wings fluttering in her belly. She sniffled, then wiped her nose with her sleeve —a rude act Thierry would have scolded her for—and answered feebly, "You are mistaken."

"I am almost never wrong," he declared.

A honk of laughter escaped her mouth. She met his gaze again. "*Almost* never, eh? Are you certain, oh great Ansgar Helmut, almighty lord of faraway lands of strudel and dumplings?"

The grin on his face could not have been wider. "Never, then, if you insist."

"Oh, I do insist. I insist very much." She leaned closer to him.

He poked her playfully in the shoulder. "I confess that I like your insistence."

"I confess that I like...I like...mushrooms. And I did like your fine suit of clothes. And I like you, sometimes. Not always, of course."

"Naturally. At times, I even dislike myself."

Josephine's pulse sped with giddy hope, and her vision focused and unfocused as she stared at the confusing man next to her. If his bragging had its roots in truth, and he really was a powerful wizard, perhaps he could save Thierry within the hour. Her mind was full of words, tumbling and dancing words, but she grabbed onto the ones she needed. "If we are friends, and you are a mighty wizard, could you please do me the favor of making Thierry a man again? Now, so we can go home?"

He shook his head, somehow managing to look regretful while maintaining a grin. "Alas, I do not have the kind of magic to make a cat become a man, my dear. That is beyond the scope of my power." He paused and seemed to take careful inventory of her features. "Now, now. Do not look so glum. We are on a grand adventure, you and I, and it does not have to end with the competition. Let me show you that life is worth living well. You were made for much more than drudgery and minding nasty cats."

The disappointment stung Josephine only for a moment. She was too warm-bellied with soup and Ansgar's pretty words to mope. Besides, she could still win the wish and help Thierry.

When Ansgar's smile faded and a look of intense longing took its place, she knew she was in trouble. She looked away, toward the steam wafting from the cauldron in pretty streamers of gray and white. She actually *did* like Ansgar in this hazy cavern, sitting next to her and speaking encouragements. His shoulder against hers, solid and warm, was a comfortable thing. In fact, ever since she'd eaten the soup, she'd felt more relaxed with the man. More fond of him in spite of his usual snobbishness. His fingers brushed her cheek as he tucked a lock of hair behind her ear. The intimate gesture made her breath catch, but she did not shrink from his touch. Her heart skipped and cavorted like a spring lamb in a sunny meadow.

"Josephine," Ansgar whispered. Goose pimples spread along her skin. He was a magnet and she was a metal trinket being drawn closer and closer. The journal tumbled from her hands as she leaned toward him.

What was happening to her? Her ability to reason had all but deserted her, and she hardly cared. Was this what it was like to fall in love as a young, impetuous person? Like every bit of bone and blood was singing the most beautiful song in the universe? She felt tipsy, but she'd not sipped wine in months. Had the air in the cavern poisoned her? Or had something she'd eaten caused inebriation?

The soup!

The diabolical soup! The mushroom concoction was surely to blame for her floaty head, the giggling, the telling of secrets, the pleasant looseness of her limbs, and her sudden affection for her traveling companion. She needed to inform him immediately of the danger they were in, but just blinking seemed to take an age.

She opened her mouth to speak, but words failed her. Ansgar's eyelids were half closed and his mouth wore the faintest smile. The hand he'd used to tenderly move her hair now cradled her cheek. His palm was warm and soft as he turned her face toward his. His breath brushed over her skin like a feather.

"I did not find you beautiful when first we met," he said. "But I see you now, Josephine. I see the tiny gold flecks in your brown eyes, the little scar above your right eyebrow, the way your nose wrinkles when you are angry. I see your good heart, and all the hope you harbor there. You make me want to be better. You make me want to care for you, to kiss you, and to have you by my side forever."

She froze, stunned by his words. Her heart pounded harder as his mouth approached hers. His eyelids fluttered shut.

The cat growled behind them. Hissed, then yowled. Scratched desperately at the basket walls.

"May I, Josephine?" Ansgar whispered.

She had never wanted to be kissed so badly. But it would be wrong. Did she care? How was *not caring* an option?

What was going on here?

Oh, yes, the mushrooms. The mushrooms!

"Stop! The soup!" she shouted. She clambered backward like a frightened crab.

"Soup?" He blinked, confusion wrinkling his brow.

"It inebriated us! Those mushrooms were not safe! You almost *kissed* me! I almost allowed it!"

Ansgar swore in German. He turned radish-red and leapt to his feet. "My apologies, Madame! I assure you I never would have made such advances had I not been compromised by that...foul fungus." He gestured toward the cauldron.

Miserable and nauseated, she sank onto her posterior and stared into the dying fire. "We were both overtaken. I apologize as well." Her head pounded. Already, she could not quite recall everything she'd said and done in the last hour, but she remembered enough to be mortified.

"We must remain here for as long as we feel any effects of the mushrooms," Ansgar said. "Were we to meet another hibouchauris, or something worse, while in such a compromised state, we'd not fare well."

"Agreed."

In silence, they moved to opposite sides of the fire pit. She stared at her shoes, the cat's basket, her fingernails. After a while, Ansgar snored softly. She glanced at him. Even outside the influence of the soup, she had to admit he was handsome. Almost the antithesis of Thierry, who'd been dark-haired, broad-shouldered, and on the edge of plumpness. Ansgar's fair hair, his slim but muscular build, his elegant way of moving...

Her pulse skittered as she remembered the near-kiss and the tender way Ansgar had spoken to her. The desire that had flared as he leaned close. *No!* What a thing to think about! A sin, considering that she was still married. Wed to a cat—for however long cats or ensorcelled husbands in cat form might live. A tide of guilt washed over her, and she folded her hands and prayed for the strength to adhere to her marital vows.

The cat purred almost as loudly as Ansgar snored. Sleep would be a mercy, but if she'd been any more awake, she might have jumped out of her own skin.

Josephine stood and tossed the last of the wood onto the fire.

She watched the flames for a moment, and then something caught her eye. The old journal. It lay on the floor near Ansgar's slumbering body, where it had fallen from her hands.

Now was her chance to take it. She needed that recipe, especially if all of Ansgar's boasting about it had been true.

She tiptoed across the floor and snatched the book without making a sound. With her back to Ansgar, she flipped through the pages to the recipe. The wicked thrill that coursed through her was unlike anything she'd ever felt. She almost giggled. *Drat those mushrooms.*

Ansgar snorted in his sleep, moaned, and rolled over. Her pulse fluttered with nervousness; shame turned her stomach. This was wrong. Theft. She'd never stolen anything in her life, save for a biscuit or two from her mother's secret tin. This was a hundred times worse. Who had she become? The old Josephine prided herself on honesty and integrity. She was the sort of person who always counted change in the marketplace twice, for the merchant's sake rather than her own. She felt guilty if her serving of dinner was a teaspoon larger than her husband's, even if she'd toiled all day in the garden and house while he'd lazed on a sailboat with his friends.

This new Josephine, the one who'd dared to leave her safe home to rescue her husband from confinement within a cat's body, the one who'd stabbed a flying monster, the one who'd saved a man from dying, would not stop at petty thievery. She'd do whatever had to be done, and to Hades with the rules of society. What was a little stealing or deception in the grand scheme of things, anyway? Why should others get everything they wanted while she stood by wallowing in heartbreak and lack?

She deserved to win as much as Ansgar Steuben did. Besides, even if he lost, he had magic on his side. He'd find a way to get what he wanted. If she failed this one time, she'd have nothing to her name but a petulant cat and the tattered clothes on her back. A second chance to save Thierry would probably never come her way.

The small book felt heavy in her hands, as if its importance was somehow expressed in its weight. She saw now that the recipe page was not connected to the binding. It was a separate piece of yellowed vellum that slid into her hand with barely a tug. Quickly, she folded the recipe and slipped it inside her clothes, between her chemise and her skin. She set the journal next to Ansgar, hoping he'd not notice the recipe's disappearance before she had a chance to copy it.

"*Liebling,*" Ansgar murmured. In sleep, he looked almost vulnerable, and much younger.

Liebling. A German term of endearment. No one but her mother had ever called her anything other than Josephine or Jo. She wondered how it would feel to be adored so much that one's name simply was not strong enough to bear the burden of the emotion connected to it.

If she freed Thierry from the cat, would he finally speak fondly to her?

She sank to the ground and drew her knees to her chest. She knew the truth, and she didn't like it. Thierry would never be a man who fussed over her. This was not a fairy tale in which a beast might transform into a kindly prince. The best she could hope for was the security he provided: the house she loved, food upon the table, firewood to keep her warm, clothes for her back and shoes for her feet. That was enough. It had to be enough.

This far along in life, with silver streaking her hair and aches in her knees, she could not wander off the sensible path she'd always trodden. She would not be the foolish woman the grandmothers gossiped about in the market square, one of those fallen wives who abandoned their families to chase after silly, late-hatching dreams of romance, only to slink home later in shame.

"No, Josephine," Ansgar grumbled. His eyes remained closed in sleep, but his brow furrowed. What had she done to annoy him in his dreams? Heaven knew she was good at annoying him when he was awake.

With a sharp inhalation, his eyes opened and he looked straight at her. "You're fine. Thank the gods," he said sleepily. "I dreamed..."

"Of course I'm fine." His gaze lingered, and she turned away, uneasy. "The mushrooms must still be affecting you. Go back to sleep."

A moment later, he snored. She was glad the journey would not last forever. She was tired of jumbled feelings, arguments, perils, and guilt. She craved a cup of tea, a fireplace, a book, and a great deal of comfortable silence. Really, what more could she need?

Josephine yawned, suddenly drowsy. Finally, a chance to escape her thoughts. She crept to the opposite side of the fire. There, she spread her blanket beside Thierry's cage, said goodnight to her cat-husband, and quickly slipped into the blessed unawareness of slumber.

Ansgar sat up fast and immediately regretted it. The room seemed to be tilting and swaying, as if he were trapped inside a storm-tossed ship. With clammy hands, he clutched his pounding head. His stomach lurched at his own stench: smoke, sweat, charred wool, cat.

He was no stranger to the aftereffects of a night of overindulgence, but this felt far direr. The headache and dry mouth were not the worst of it. The chills that shook him, he could endure. What rattled him to the soul were the stark memories of the words he'd spoken to Josephine and the emotions that had accompanied them.

He feared the mushrooms had done more than temporarily inebriate him. Because when he looked at the woman sleeping on the floor, the very sight of her almost moved him to tears. His fingers itched to swipe the piece of dried leaf off her cheek. The slight flare of her nostrils as she inhaled made it hard for him to catch his own breath. He felt the urge to write poetry about the bend of her elbow.

Ansgar had never been a tender man. Courtship and marriage with Truda had been anything but quiet and calm. Truda had been a fierce woman, and he'd risen to the occasion of her, matching her curse for curse, kiss for kiss. They'd been a pair of scrapping tigers, but he now felt reduced to—*great gods, not a kitten*—but perhaps a domesticated mongrel. One that would follow at Josephine's heels with tongue lolling. This was intolerable.

Shivering, he added wood to the low-burning fire. His dizziness had abated, but he felt far from well. He rubbed his hands together and watched the flames grow and dance. Thank the gods this was ordinary fire, not the horrid enchanted stuff from which he'd rescued the cat. What a nightmare that had been.

The Frenchwoman murmured incoherently, drawing his attention to where she slumbered on the dirt floor. He watched her tug her brown blanket to her neck. Her smooth, dust-smeared, pretty-as-a-lily neck. There was a tiny bruise at the edge of her jaw, the bluish-purple of dawn, or was it a smear of dirt? He imagined sliding a finger over her skin to see if it held or smudged. His pulse sped. *Darnation!* He took a step backward and turned away from her. What he needed was a long drink of cold water and a harsh dose of reality. He needed to remember why he'd come on this blasted journey: to save himself, not to lose his mind over a simple widow.

His thirst drove him to grab his tin cup. With the firelight behind him as the only illumination, he followed the sound of trickling water into the adjoining cavern. He fingered the shard of mirror in his pocket as he walked. His mind filled with the image of Truda's most severe scowl, which he most certainly deserved. Had she the ability to see how he'd recently behaved, Truda would have turned him back into a duck—and she would not have brooked the excuse that he'd fallen under the influence of bad mushrooms.

The shadows churned and thickened in front of him, but he kept moving. The effects of the two healing potions and the mushrooms were most certainly fading, because his legs and back felt a hundred years old. He had to ignore the pain. Soon, with the wish's help, he'd put all weakness and suffering behind him.

Under a dribbling stalactite, Ansgar held the tin cup steady until it was brim-full. He drank it dry, refilled it, and drank again. His head cleared a little. Once more, he allowed the cup to fill, this time for Josephine. *Blast it all.* Part of him insisted that he should let her fetch her own water, but the other part, the part that regretted offending her with mushroom-fueled amorous advances, wanted to bring her water as an apology. But did he really owe her an apology? She and that stupid cat had almost gotten him incinerated. He'd only indulged in a little morally questionable flirtation —questionable only because she believed herself married to a cat— and no one had come to any real harm.

The Frenchwoman might be the death of him. He'd accepted her partnership because he thought they'd have a greater chance of reaching the Seven Ovens together. But did he need her anymore, now that they were getting close to their destination? Should he leave her as she slept, and put trouble and temptation behind him?

Why was he arguing with himself? He would take the water to Josephine, and he would continue to travel with her. He still wanted to know the secrets of the pendant he'd snatched from among her belongings. And to prove to himself that he could resist the woman's saccharine charms. No one was going to ask him to justify his decisions, anyway. He was a free man, beholden only to himself.

Although he'd been standing still for five minutes or more, his aching knees insisted that he rest for a moment. He sat on a boulder and put the cup down. The steady drip-drip of water soothed him like music. As he bent to re-tie his sagging bootlaces, a great sigh escaped him. The answer to the question he'd recently posed to the universe was yes, he did need Josephine. Even with a magical recipe, the odds that he would win the contest were small. He couldn't bake bread without burning it. Josephine, however, had been taught to bake by her grandmother. She'd gone on and on about cake-making as they'd navigated one of yesterday's dim, infernally long corridors. In spite of his efforts to ignore her voice, he'd learned the importance of not over-mixing one's batter. If anyone could educate him sufficiently before the contest, it was she.

He rose and returned to their little camp beside the fire pit. One of his hands carried the cup of water while the other clutched the smooth piece of looking glass deep inside his pocket. The memory of Truda's face was becoming hard to conjure, dimmed by time and distraction. An arrow-sharp pang of grief lodged in his chest. His mood darkened.

"You're up," Josephine said around a yawn. She looked dazed, sitting there enrobed with blankets.

"As you should also be by now," he retorted. "We've wasted too much time here." She scowled, and he forced himself to look at the dark stone wall instead of the shape of her angry mouth. *Darnation, that mouth of hers.*

From the corner of his eye, he glimpsed Josephine stuffing her blanket into her bag rather aggressively. "You say that as if it's my fault alone. In case you have forgotten, you were the one who deemed the mushrooms safe to eat."

How he wanted to fight back. To make her seethe and snap at him. Instead, he mastered the impulse and said coolly, "Regardless, the pilgrims are surely far ahead of us. If we find them again, it will be a miracle." He approached her with the mug of water. "Here. Drink this to help your body rid itself of the soup."

"Thank you," she said politely. She still looked peeved.

"Do not mention it. We'll go as soon as you're ready." He relit the torch by dipping it into the fire pit's remaining embers. The torch's flame flickered weakly, but it would have to do until they found another portable light source.

The cat meowed when she lifted its basket, but for once, Josephine did not address the animal. She simply said to Ansgar, "I'm ready."

He cast one last glance at her and regretted it. The peevishness had left her face. Her expression now was one of sadness. And whether he was to blame for it or not, the sight hurt worse than being stung by a thousand bees.

Fourteen

Sober and quiet, with a dim, smoking torch in hand, Ansgar led Josephine away from their camp. A series of room-like caverns funneled them into a low-ceilinged passageway of wet stone. Trickles of water ran down the walls, and their feet splashed through shallow puddles. He waited for Josephine to comment about damp socks or the mildew-scented air, but she said nothing. Even the cat had ceased making noise. He ought to have been thanking the gods for the near-silence, but it only served to aggravate his crankiness.

Fortunately, crankiness felt like an old friend. He much preferred its company over that of senseless infatuation.

His mushroom-addled memories were hazy, but he knew he'd almost kissed Josephine. Did she remember the moment, or had the soup's inebriating effects erased it from her mind?

After an hour, they left the caverns, ducking through a low doorway to enter what looked like a typical cellar. The room smelled slightly of root vegetables, although none were to be seen. Ansgar's stomach grumbled. He would have committed murder for a roasted potato. Double murder for one slathered in butter.

"It just occurred to me that you've never mentioned what

you'll wish for if you win the contest," Josephine said behind him. Finally, her former cheerful loquaciousness seemed to have returned. In a strange way, he felt relieved. She had either forgotten the near-kiss or forgiven him. Not that she had seemed unwilling. He had seen longing on her face. His fingers had pressed the pulse point on her throat and felt the quick throb of her blood.

She shocked him back into the present by asking, "Does your quest have something to do with your wife?"

Ansgar tensed. Josephine had no business speaking of Truda. He held few things sacred, but he held Truda highest of them all.

He took a deep breath and gathered his wits. He would answer Josephine, but carefully. He would also use the conversation to manipulate her feelings. "Yes," he lied. "I need the wish in order to free my wife from the bonds of a spell." Let Josephine think they were alike: heartbroken spouses set on reuniting with their great loves. Even if comparing his love for his magnificent Truda to Josephine's love for her loathsome husband was akin to comparing the blazing sun to a flimsy matchstick.

"Ah, so our quests are much the same. You should have mentioned it before," she said, taking his bait like an eager young trout nipping at a dangling worm.

"They are surprisingly similar indeed," he said. "Now that we're discussing the contest, I do have a request." Before him appeared a black wooden door carved with cherubs and clouds. He opened it and allowed her to pass through first. She started to ascend a set of spiraling stairs. He climbed behind her, sliding his hand along the smooth metal railing.

"What is your request?" she asked. "After everything you went through to save Thierry form the fire, I am certainly in your debt."

He cleared his throat and then told the truth. Gods, he hated telling the truth. "You see, I have little aptitude for baking. I fear that no recipe, no matter how magical, would result in something delicious when mixed by my hands."

She glanced over her shoulder at him, eyes bright in the torchlight. "Truly? You're not joking, *monsieur*?"

"Truly." The confession made him feel small. Humbled. It was not a feeling he enjoyed. "I once tried to bake a simple loaf of bread. The result was inedible. I have tripped over softer boulders."

"I will teach you, then. It's only a matter of following instructions and knowing a few basic methods. You are more than clever enough to bake little cakes, I promise."

"Your faith in my intelligence is most encouraging," he said with a wry laugh.

"I didn't mean you are...What I meant was...I—"

Ansgar chuckled, genuinely amused by her flustered state. "Let us pretend you said nothing that could be construed as an insult." As they reached the top of the staircase, he said, "All is well, Josephine." Immediately, he regretted using her name. They should have never stopped addressing one another formally. To be so personal, so familiar with her...it felt like placing a foot on an unsteady stone. He needed to remain in control. No wrong steps.

Ansgar followed Josephine into a small chapel decorated with swooping garlands of holly, ivy, and evergreen. Hundreds of white votive candles flickered on tiered shelves. The aromas of warm wax and fresh pine filled the air.

Josephine clasped her hands over her heart. She turned slowly, eyes wide, smiling with unrestrained delight. "Just like Christmas. Have you ever seen anything so pretty?"

Oh, but he had. At this moment, he was seeing something very pretty indeed as she tipped her head back and pointed to a star-shaped, amber glass lantern. She was incandescent. A star in her own right.

She spun to face him, her countenance blissful. "When I was a little girl, this is exactly how I imagined the church would look on my wedding day. Isn't that strange? I'd forgotten it until now."

Under the scents of beeswax and greenery, he detected the bitter tang of active enchantment. It had been present in the air throughout their travels, but here it was much stronger. "You may blame the magic of this place for that. I believe it is capable of discerning things: memories, fears, hidden desires. We should be on guard, lest it leads us astray from the pilgrim path."

She shivered. "You think the magic read my mind and then made this to trick me? Well, that takes all the joy out of the place."

His words had extinguished her happiness, but he could not allow her to remain ignorant of the danger. "Alertness is essential. As we draw nearer to the Seven Ovens, we are sure to encounter more perils and tests. This place might well be one of them."

Josephine rushed down the side aisle as if anxious to escape, and Ansgar followed closely. They'd almost reached a doorway when he spied an alcove filled with cabinets and a small table. White candles of various lengths, many of them partially burned, lay scattered on the tabletop. One of the doors of a tall wooden cupboard stood ajar. "Wait," he said. When she turned toward him, he passed the torch into her hand.

The candles would be useful, but the thing that really drew Ansgar into the tiny room was a glimpse of clothes hanging inside the cupboard. The burnt rags he wore stank and itched. The extra clothing he'd brought had been plundered back when animals had raided their belongings, save for a single pair of silken underdrawers. With a change of attire, he'd feel like a new man.

"What are you doing?" Josephine asked, but he didn't reply as he approached the cupboard. He felt as elated as an explorer about to delve into a cave of treasure.

At least a dozen garments sagged from iron hooks. Dust furred their top edges. He fingered one article of clothing and then another, and soon came to the disappointing conclusion that everything in the cupboard had been the property of monks or priests. Gowns and robes with straight or bell-shaped sleeves—and not a single pair of trousers. Some of the vestments were highly embroidered with symbols and flowers, the shiny fabric stained with age but still beautiful. Others were crafted of rough, heavy material, fit to be worn as an act of penance.

Ansgar chose a plain brown woolen gown with wide sleeves. He would resemble a medieval peasant in the thing, but at least he'd reek less.

Quickly, he shrugged out of what was left of the shirt he'd put on the morning he'd set out for the pilgrimage. A Parisian tailor had charged him a shocking amount for the pure white linen shirt embellished with tiny tucks and pearl buttons, but it had been a thing of beauty. If only a roadside seer or back alley fortune teller would have warned Ansgar that the glorious garment would be soiled and singed beyond recognition, he would have left it at home.

He slid the drab gown over his head and found it softer than he'd expected. Its hem brushed his knees—both of which were currently exposed by his burnt and tattered trousers. For a moment, he considered continuing to wear the remnants of his trousers, but they'd soon disintegrate anyway. *Oh, how the mighty are fallen*, he thought as he let them drop to the floor.

As soon as this trial was over, he would call upon the best tailor in the land and forget this time of woeful degradation.

When he glanced up, Josephine was watching him with a strange expression. Like she'd bitten into a lemon when she'd expected an apple. "Have I offended you by my state of undress?" he asked, tempted to tease her. "I believed you had remained in the other room."

"I am not a prude, *monsieur*," she replied. "Only surprised by your choice. I would have guessed you'd take one of the finer robes."

"I am neither a high ranking clergyman nor incapable of practicality. This will serve until I obtain something more befitting my taste."

"Good. Can we go now? I don't like this chapel."

She turned and walked away, but he paused to fill his bag with candles before stepping over his discarded clothes to follow her. After a few steps, he stopped short. *Truda's looking glass and Josephine's pendant.* He'd almost left the shard and the necklace in the pocket of the trousers. Would losing the magic-touched items bring him bad luck—or *worse* luck? With trembling hands, he retrieved both cloth-wrapped tokens and placed them deep within his bag. He was angry at himself for almost forgetting them. Angrier still that he might forget Truda.

He had expected the pilgrimage to be a journey across difficult landscapes. High mountains, slippery pathways, frigid nights—all of these, he'd been prepared to endure. He had not thought he'd be forced to traverse an inner landscape of painful memories and cruel temptations.

A door creaked and Ansgar chased the sound to catch up with Josephine. He glimpsed her crossing a barren stretch of ground behind the church. Purple mist swirled around her feet. She looked like a painting done by some romantic fool. A hapless maiden strolling along moments before Zeus plunged to earth to vex her. Ah, to swoop from the heavens and dazzle Josephine like a god! To see her drop her baggage—cat and all—to run into his arms.

He pressed one hand against his traitorous heart and wished he could cast off his troublesome feelings as easily as he'd shrugged out of his ruined shirt.

What he required was fortitude. To focus on his dire need to take the prize. He had to remember that this was a life or death situation—death that would overtake him soon if anyone else won.

He'd been skilled at self-preservation in the past. But like the leaves of a mindless plant angled toward the sun, his eyes fixed on the perfect dark curl that danced along Josephine's backbone as she led him down yet another corridor. The tendril called out to be touched, to be rubbed softly between his dirty fingers. Great gods, was he still inebriated? He cursed all mushrooms, from Eden's first to those that would cling to the earth when its last day dawned.

Affected by mushrooms or not, he knew he'd never be able to

carry out any plan to seduce and betray Josephine. If ever she responded positively to his flirtations, he'd lose himself to her forever.

She stopped. He stumbled over nothing, almost colliding with her.

"Listen," she whispered.

Eyes closed, breath held, he cocked his head. The sound of pilgrims singing, faint as a whisper, drifted from somewhere ahead of them. Relief filled him for the briefest moment, until another sound came from behind to rattle his nerves: the echo of footsteps.

Josephine rushed toward the singing. The slapping of her boots against the ground all but masked the sweet sound of the pilgrims' voices. She wanted to listen to the music with a desire as strong as physical hunger. It almost hurt when her footfalls obliterated some of the notes. Nevertheless, she bounded ahead like a deer. A clumsy deer that almost tripped every few steps.

She ran and ran, hardly noticing when the stone-walled corridor gave way to one paneled with wood. She rushed through a courtyard full of rose bushes and a chapel lit by countless candles, and then descended into a tunnel that smelled of decay and mud. The torch she bore flickered weakly, threatening to go out. The voices swelled, a heavenly chorus drawing her forward. Forward.

Stairs lifted her into the daylight. She stumbled into an herb garden much like the one from which she'd plucked ingredients to save Ansgar after he'd been burned. Was it the same garden? The scents of sage and thyme filled her nostrils, clearing out the stink of the catacomb she'd just left. A hand grabbed her upper arm. She tugged in an effort to free herself. She had to keep moving toward the voices.

"Wait, Josephine," Ansgar urged. "Stop."

She spun to face him, annoyed and panting for breath. "Let go! They'll get away if we—"

"Let them. The song is not coming from the pilgrims." He paused to gasp for air. Sweat beaded his ashen brow. He continued, "It's a lure cast to lead us into danger. A siren song, as it were."

She scowled and wished she were the sort of person who'd punch someone without a second thought. How tired she was of the German's snobbery and know-it-all attitude. "This is your expert opinion, is it?"

He raised his chin. "Madame, as you well know, I have experience with enchantments. My ear is trained to detect magic cloaked in certain sounds. I don't mean to offend you, only to alert you of danger."

"Why did you not stop me sooner, then?" She believed him as much as she believed she could jump to the moon.

"I have been trying to catch up with you, but I believe you could outrun a champion racing horse." Somehow he smiled and looked grim at the same time. "Now, we must make haste to somewhere shielded from that sound."

Was he telling the truth about the song? Josephine cocked her head and listened as the singing grew louder and more beautiful. The voices rose in sweet harmony and her heart felt heavy in her chest, weighted with longing to join the company of choristers.

"Josephine," Ansgar said strongly. "We must get away from here." He offered his hand. "Please, come with me. I implore you."

She met his sober gaze and shook her head. "No. No, I think you're wrong. I want..."

He moved so fast she had no time to react. His arms swept her off her feet and he pulled her tight against his chest. The cat basket, dangling from her shoulder, banged against his body as he ran back the way they'd come. Thierry gave an earsplitting yowl.

"Put me down, you blackguard!" She wriggled, but his arms squeezed her like a vise. He ran as if death snatched at his heels.

When they reached an intersection, he turned to the left,

choosing a hallway lit by hanging lanterns of punched tin. His pace slowed; his chest heaved with breathlessness. His body was hot against hers. Still, his grip did not loosen.

"I can't hear them anymore," she said. "Put me down now." In the absence of the music, she recognized that he'd been right. There had been something sinister about the song, something too irresistible to be natural.

Ansgar halted. Before them stood a tall wooden door with an ornate brass handle. "I suppose the danger has passed." He set her on her feet gently.

She backed away from him and adjusted the straps of her pack and basket. Thierry growled as the basket shifted. How spoiled he was, being carried about, coddled, and protected—yet he dared to complain. But Thierry had been the same as a man, forever seeking his own comfort and entertainment. Was she a fool to think he'd be different after she changed him from cat to man with the wish?

Ansgar pushed the door open. In the middle of a dewy, grassy meadow stood a white cottage with a gray slate roof, like something out of a storybook. A high stone wall surrounded the property. Three sheep grazed lazily near a patch of blackberry bushes, unbothered by their sudden presence.

"We should go back and choose a different corridor," Josephine said as she examined the ground. "There are no footprints. The others could not have gone this way."

"Before we leave, I insist that we harvest some berries. We may not come upon another source of food before the competition, and no one functions well in a state of starvation."

"Fine." She could not deny that she was hungry. It seemed like a week since she'd eaten the unfortunate mushroom soup. Perhaps a few handfuls of berries would relieve her of the headache throbbing behind her left eye. She followed Ansgar across the squishy ground. The sheep ambled out of their way.

When she reached the bushes, she found them covered with countless dark purple berries, pretty as jewels.

"In the Igelwald, the forest in which I used to dwell, the berries grew twice this size," Ansgar said after sampling one. "These are good, though. Quite good."

Josephine plucked four at a time with one hand. On her tongue, they burst with flavor. A groan of pleasure escaped her before she could stop it.

"I'm going into the cottage to look for a basket," Ansgar said after a while. His hands and lips were stained with juice. "These are too good to leave for the birds."

Mouth stuffed full, she nodded in agreement.

Once Ansgar left her side, night fell hard. The branches in front of her face became dark shadows, and the cottage was barely visible. A cold wind tickled the back of her neck. She rummaged through her bag, searching for the candle and matchbox she'd salvaged from their scattered belongings and saved for such an occasion.

"Josephine!" Ansgar's shout cut through the blackness. "Wait there. I'm coming."

"Over here," she said, hoping he'd follow the sound of her voice. The darkness felt unnatural, as if someone had cast a black veil over the skies. Her trembling hands fumbled with one of the few remaining matches, but she managed to light the candle before Ansgar arrived at her side.

She stood as he lifted a small, square basket to show her. "Perhaps we should wait until daylight returns to fill this," he said.

"Or we should leave. Something about this place bothers me."

"Oh? I was about to suggest that we spend the night inside the cottage. I believe there was a bit of food there, although the darkness mostly obscured my vision. But if you wish it, we will go," he said amicably.

She'd expected an argument or snide comment. By candlelight she examined his face, searching for any hint of teasing. It was unlike him to be readily agreeable. "Do you mean that?"

"Yes, of course. We are partners, Josephine. You do have a voice in how we proceed."

"I want to go."

Side by side, they retraced the route they'd taken upon entering the garden. She held the candle high, but its flickering did little to dispel the darkness. Ansgar stumbled over a rock and swore. She slid across a patch of mud and almost lost her grip on the candle. Either the sharp drop in temperature or her unsettled nerves made her shiver. Why was it taking so long to reach the wall?

When the wall finally materialized before them, the door was nowhere to be seen.

"I thought we'd entered here," she said. "I'm almost certain of it."

"That was my belief as well. But perhaps we are mistaken. Come this way." Together, they inched along the wall, searching carefully until her candle burned down to a stub.

"Blast," Ansgar said as the candle sputtered out.

"There has to be a way out," Josephine said. "We could look for a place to climb over the wall. Somewhere with strong vines. Did you bring candles from the chapel?"

"I'll find one, but you're trembling with cold," Ansgar said. "And the darkness is only deepening. Might I suggest we shelter in the cottage until dawn? It has a fireplace and a well-stocked wood box, and whoever last lived there left it in a surprising state of cleanliness."

A minute later, sparks flashed as Ansgar lit a match. He handed her the candle and set the flame to its wick. The glow comforted her little.

"Are you sure the cottage is safe?" she asked. "You don't feel any dangerous magical stirrings?"

"I felt nothing ominous there, although since the door disappeared, we would be wise to remain wary. At least the cottage's four walls offer some protection. And the warmth of a fire would be most welcome."

With a sigh, she said, "I agree." Nearby bushes rustled as if something sizable was moving through them. Reflexively, she grabbed Ansgar's arm. "Let's hurry."

"This way."

Her hand remained on his arm until he turned to latch the cottage door shut behind them.

"There," Ansgar said. "Secure for the night." He used the candle to light others on shelves throughout the room. "Not luxurious accommodations, but snug."

Josephine's nerves calmed as she looked around the cottage. Someone had loved this place enough to make it welcoming and cozy. An armchair covered in floral fabric sat near a wall of full bookcases. The wide hearth boasted a wooden mantle topped with small, framed paintings of ferns and forest creatures. A green-painted cupboard held stacked plates and bowls. Mismatched teacups dangled from hooks. Next to a white washbasin draped with a folded towel, a blue glass jar held wooden spoons. A bouquet of dried strawflowers sat in the center of an oak table. An open door led to another room, probably a bedchamber, and someone had painted twining vines on the doorframe. "It's very pretty," she said finally.

"I'll start a fire to drive off the chill." Ansgar set his bag on the floor, and she followed suit. Thierry was silent. Probably asleep.

"Would it be wrong for me to check the cupboards for food? I feel as if we're trespassing in the home of someone's dear old *grand-mère*."

Ansgar squatted by the fireplace and took a handful of kindling from a wooden crate. "I'll leave the owner a few coins. Enough to convince them to forgive our trespassing."

"I'll look for tea, then," Josephine said, gripped with a sudden longing for a strong cup of her favorite drink. Perhaps it would uncloud her memory. Parts of the day seemed to be missing entirely, particularly the hours between cooking the mushrooms and arriving at the cottage, yet she had an unsettling feeling in her gut that she'd said or done something regrettable. If so, she hoped Ansgar's memory had been similarly impaired, to keep him from mocking her for whatever mistakes she'd made.

She found a row of small tins on a shelf, opened one, and breathed in the cheerful scent of dried mint. The simple fragrance brought back good childhood memories of spending time in her grandparents' kitchen. But her heart sank when she realized she had no water to brew a pot. As she opened her mouth to ask Ansgar if he'd noticed a well near the cottage, a knock sounded upon the door. She froze.

"Stay still," Ansgar whispered. "Perhaps they'll go away."

Josephine held her breath.

The visitor knocked again. Pounded harder and kicked the wood. Ansgar grabbed an iron fire poker and rose to his feet. The latch splintered and the door flew open.

"Josephine," Jacques Monfort said, tipping his hat and stepping inside with a casual air. He looked neat and fresh, as if he'd just wandered over to pay a call from next door. "And Steuben, was it? How good to see you again. And in such an interesting outfit, *monsieur*. Have you taken up religion, or is this the newest fashion?"

Josephine muttered a very bad word.

Fifteen

Ansgar swore, mostly at himself. This invasion should not have happened.

He'd heard someone following them earlier in the day, but he'd assumed they were being trailed by a hungry animal rather than a human.

Curse Jacques Monfort to the depths of Hades.

Brandishing the iron poker in his right hand, Ansgar rushed across the room to stand beside Josephine. He would not hesitate to whack Jacques if the fellow made one wrong move.

"I told you to go home," Josephine said. "I'm not giving you the necklace."

Ansgar wrapped his left arm around Josephine's shoulders. "Yes, I believe she was quite clear, Jacques." He spat out the man's name like an insult.

Jacques reached back to close the damaged door as much as the cracked planks would allow. He grinned. "I decided I'd continue to follow you, and it is good that I did. Regretfully, I became entangled in a patch of singing ivy for a time, and fell far enough behind to miss whatever antics you got up to after ingesting the inebriating mushrooms. Yes, I could recognize the smell of frilled callish mushroom soup half a mile away. But look at you two now, cowering in this little cabin, filthy and without a crumb to split for dinner." He slid his satchel off his shoulder and set it on the table. The bag had been stuffed so full that it rolled onto its side. His wide grin held, as if glued to his face. "I have almost too much food. I'd be willing to share, if you're willing to negotiate, Jo."

"I have no plans to change my mind about the necklace," Josephine said. "But I suppose you can stay the night, if you pay for your lodgings with food."

Ansgar frowned and said, "What? I say we keep the pack and shove him out the door."

Jacques pointed at him. "This one's funny, Jo, even if he looks dull as church."

Ansgar's left eyelid twitched as his rage mounted. Jacques Monfort deserved a sound thrashing. Or perhaps a magically-induced rash someplace tender. It would be worth the cost to his personal supply to see the man hopping about in agony. But for now, Ansgar chose to restrain himself. Coolly, he said, "Forgive me. It was not my intention to amuse you. Personally, I believe you should leave our company immediately, but if Josephine chooses to show you mercy tonight, I won't interfere. Once morning comes, however, I expect you to depart from us. Permanently."

"Is he your keeper now, Josephine? Your paramour? So soon after poor Thierry's passing?"

"Monsieur Steuben and I are traveling companions and nothing more," Josephine insisted. Something howled outside the walls. "Now, stop talking, Jacques. It isn't safe to make so much noise, even indoors."

"Could we talk privately, please?" Jacques whispered. His expression shifted from haughty to somber. "Just for a minute or two, Jo? Please."

"No," Ansgar said.

But she shocked him by saying, "Fine. For one minute. As long as you promise not to ask me for the necklace."

Ansgar swore under his breath and moved to the other side of the room to provide the pair a modicum of privacy. Josephine's niceness was going to be the death of her. And possibly of him.

"Well?" Josephine said to Jacques, crossing her arms over her chest.

Jacques was not an expert whisperer. Because of this, Ansgar caught enough of his speech to know that the fiend wanted Josephine to turn back with him from the dangerous journey. That he wanted to deliver her safely home, to honor his brother's memory. He loved her, and always would, and although he'd followed her partly for the necklace, he was more concerned with her survival, *blah blah blah.*

"Thank you for your concern, but I'm not going home with you," Josephine said firmly.

"Fine. We'll talk again in the morning," Jacques replied. He grabbed a blanket from a shelf and unfolded it. "I'll bed down by the fire, if that is agreeable to you. And you might want to block the door somehow, to keep out those wild things."

Ansgar stared at the man. He'd relented too easily. What was he up to?

But a minute later, Jacques had stretched out on the floor in the glow of the fire Ansgar had kindled. Almost immediately, he started to snore softly.

"Who is this loathsome man again, and why is he obsessed with your necklace?" Ansgar asked as he loosened his grip on the poker. He crossed the room to Josephine and stood almost toe to toe with her. The temptation to kiss her felt dangerous yet exhilarating. He hardly trusted himself to resist, even with the odious Jacques in the room.

"Surely you remember that he is my brother-in-law. And obviously, he is a nuisance."

"Yes, well. If only he were a cat like his brother. Containable. Easily tossed over a cliff."

"Monsieur Steuben," she scolded—yet she smiled. The mischief in that smile delighted him like an unexpected gift. "I hardly wish him dead. Just locked up somewhere far away."

Ansgar held back a laugh. The situation called for seriousness. Focus. "And what of the necklace? Why is he bent on possessing it?"

"I don't know precisely. Thierry was also obsessed with it for a time. He insisted on taking the pendant to his workshop one night soon after we married, but returned it the next day. He looked battered and unsettled, but refused to tell me what had taken place. After that, he never asked to borrow it again."

"You mentioned you inherited it from your grandmother. Had she given you its history, or apprised you of any lore attached to the piece?"

"She only said that I must always keep it close and never sell it. She promised there would be a letter with it when it came to me as an inheritance, but she died so suddenly that..."

Jacques snorted and rolled over.

"I detest that man," Josephine said. "I know it is wrong to hate, but he is so very hateable."

Her guilty face was one of the most adorable things he'd seen in his life, like a pile of kittens atop a pile of freshly washed babies in a field of daisies. He grinned.

"Are you ill?" she asked. "You look...odd."

Now that she'd mentioned it, he noticed that he did not feel as strong as he had. The effects of the healing potion were fading, yes, but what if the hint of nausea and vertigo were also related to his possession of the pendant he'd stolen and hidden in his pocket?

"I am as well as one could hope to be after all we have endured. Now, help me move this cupboard, if you please. I hate to be in accord with our unwanted visitor, but I believe we should take precautions."

He laid the poker atop the table near Jacques's pack, and then together, he and Josephine shoved the cupboard until it blocked the door. It did not weigh much, but the brief exertion left him breathless.

"Now you look worse," Josephine said. "Like death in his ditch-digging clothes, *Grand-mère* would say. Sit before you collapse. We might as well help ourselves to some of that food Jacques said he has too much of."

"Yes, it must be a burden to carry so much food," Ansgar said as he sat at the table. Josephine stayed on her feet and wrenched open Jacques's satchel. She drew out clothes, a wedge of cheese wrapped in cloth, a neatly coiled rope, a tin of shortbread biscuits, and a candle. And then she said a very bad word for the second time that day.

"What is it?" Ansgar asked, trying hard to contain the sly grin her foul language had inspired. Clearly, he'd been a terrible influence on her.

"That snake." Frowning, she held up a pair of brown woolen stockings with red stripes. "These belong to me."

"Are you certain?"

"I knitted them myself. Do you know what this means? It wasn't an animal that tore into our bags and took our food. It was Jacques. I could strangle him." She threw the socks onto the table. Her nostrils flared and red splotches mottled her throat as she clenched her hands into fists at her sides. She looked as dangerous as a newborn rabbit.

"Take a breath, dear Josephine. Revenge is best delivered as an unexpected gift." He broke off a piece of cheese and offered it to her. "Sit. Eat. And then you and I shall devise the best possible plan of vengeance."

She slumped into a chair and nibbled the cheese. "I suppose you are correct, but I would feel better if I could punch that big liar."

"While I admire your pugilistic spirit, I promise our future retribution will be far more satisfying."

"I don't think I've ever been so angry in all my life."

"You should get angry more often, Josephine. See it as a strength. You must look out for your interests in this world. No one else can be relied upon to do so." Her dark mood had only made her prettier: adding shine to her eyes, a rosy stain to her cheekbones, and a slight pout to her mouth. Part of him wanted to start fights with her every day for as long as he lived.

Which might not be long if he kept losing focus and allowed her to beat him in the contest. He cleared his throat and said, "We should finish our meal and try to sleep. Who knows how long night will last here?"

"You sleep first, and I'll keep watch—with that poker in hand. I trust Jacques as much as I'd trust the devil himself." She reached for the poker and he passed it into her hand.

"I'll rest in the chair, close to our uninvited guest," Ansgar said, indicating an armchair by the fireplace. "You can wake me when you want me to take over the watch."

"Of course," she replied.

Once they'd eaten until their stomachs could hold no more, Ansgar settled into the chair. The fire crackled, and wind rattled the windows gently. He would only rest his eyes, not sleep. Jacques seemed the sort of brute who'd throw a woman over his shoulder and abscond with her, as if she were a sack of turnips with no say in the matter.

And that was exactly how his dream of Josephine's abduction began.

He awoke with a start. The room was cold, the fire dead. Sunlight streamed through the windows at an angle that suggested early afternoon. His heart pounded with dread until he saw Josephine slumped over the table with her cheek resting on her hand. No one had carried her off.

But Jacques was gone. He'd taken his satchel, but left the food they'd sampled. An odd kindness—or was it?

There had been something in that food. Something to induce sleep. The blackguard had played them well, sending them into dream land. But why?

Ansgar stood. "Josephine? Wake up." As he crossed the room and she drowsily lifted her head, he noticed several things. The door of the cat basket stood open, the cat was gone, and Jacques had dumped the contents of both their bags onto the floor, probably to look for the pendant he'd overlooked the last time he'd ransacked their belongings. Jacques was truly a nincompoop.

"Thierry!" Josephine shrieked. "He's gone!"

The chair toppled backward and crashed to the floor as Josephine rose to her feet. Dizzy with sleep and awash with panic, she gripped the edge of the table. Her stomach threatened to reject her last meal. All she could think of was Thierry.

"He must be here in the house. "I'll look under the furniture. Check the bedchamber, please," she said to Ansgar, who was rummaging through his strewn belongings. "Ansgar? Did you hear me? What on earth are you doing?"

He held up his journal. "I had to find this."

She glanced at him before dropping to her knees in front of a cabinet. "Thierry is more important than a silly book." Guilt reddened her face as she remembered stealing the recipe from the journal. That recipe was surely the reason Ansgar had been intent on finding the book. At least now he'd blame Jacques if he noticed the recipe's absence.

Under the cabinet, she discovered only dust. She scrambled to her feet and rushed to look under the cupboard Jacques had moved away from the door before he'd fled. "Help me, would you?"

"Fine. Although I think the cat went with Jacques. Possibly by choice."

"Why would he...? Never mind. Just check the bedchamber, please." She didn't want to waste a second imagining the dastardly plans the Monfort brothers might have concocted. The pair had a penchant for sharing illicit activities.

Mumbling curses, Ansgar obeyed and wandered into the bedchamber.

A few minutes later, their search of the little cottage ended without success. As she stood face to face with Ansgar near the emberless hearth, Josephine burst into tears. She either leaned forward into his embrace or was gathered close by his arms. It did not matter. Thierry was gone, and this time she had a feeling he would not be found.

Ansgar said nothing. One of his hands stroked her hair while the other pressed firmly against her back, holding her to his body. She appreciated his silence, that he did not whisper "hush" or implore her to stop crying. She clutched the thick wool of his monastic robe as she sobbed into his shoulder. Ansgar's embrace should have felt strange and awkward, for they were neither family nor lovers—and hardly friends. But in his arms, she felt secure and comforted.

There was something familiar about being held by him. Had they embraced back in the cavern, after eating the soup? She remembered so little about that day. Good heavens, had they *kissed*? No, she would remember that. Wouldn't she? No, they definitely had not kissed. If they had, he would probably still be gloating about it.

Why was she thinking about kissing Ansgar when Thierry was lost? She was a terrible wife.

She pushed away from the German and wiped her tears with her sleeve. "I'm sorry. It was childish of me to cry. Thierry would have sent me to my room for such behavior."

"Thierry is a fool." His tone brooked no argument, although

there was kindness in it. "Now, it's time to gather our belongings and leave. We'll watch for signs of Thierry and Jacques as we seek the pilgrims."

Josephine nodded. As she knelt to pack her things, shame weighed heavily on her. Finally, Ansgar was treating her like a friend, and she had stolen his prized recipe. What would he say if she confessed? Would he demand to have it back and then venture off in anger without her, leaving her to find her own way to the Seven Ovens?

She would make no confession. At least not now. The truth was she still needed to win the wish, and his recipe might be the key to victory. She clung to the tiny bit of faith she had that the saint's granted wish could restore Thierry no matter where he was in the world.

Ansgar stood, pack in hand. "Ready?"

"I am." The lightness of Thierry's empty cage brought new tears to her sore eyes, but she did her best not to let them fall. She shouldered her belongings and followed Ansgar out of the cottage and into the glaring sunlight.

Nodding flowers and trilling birds welcomed her back into the garden. The world was a strange and perplexing thing. How was it possible for sorrow and suffering to co-exist with so much beauty? How could she herself be willing to give her very life to honor her sacred vows to her husband but also be willing to betray her morals by committing theft?

She snapped a blossom from its tall stem as she lengthened her steps. There was no use in thinking and trying to make sense of things. She was tired, dirty, and starving, with no energy to spare for philosophizing. For now, she would walk and watch, as Ansgar had wisely recommended.

The flower fell from her hands to the trampled grass at her feet. The door in the wall, the one they'd sought in vain last night, stood wide open before them. They rushed toward it, ignoring the plump berries that had tempted them before. Who knew how long the door would stand open?

Only then did she wonder if her cloth-wrapped necklace had been among the things she'd hurriedly tossed back into her bag. Of course the pendant was what Jacques had been looking for when he'd emptied their belongings onto the floor. *I'm sure I saw it*, she told herself.

She would not make a fuss about it now, or even mention it to Ansgar. Finding Thierry was all that mattered.

Sixteen

Ansgar knew he should have been elated by the sight of the open door, but his feelings spun like a wagon wheel stuck in deep mud, forming a trench from which escape seemed impossible. Josephine was the hub of the wheel, of course. The center of every thought.

His current thought was a memory: holding Josephine close as she'd wept in the cottage. If he had yearned for her before that brief embrace, it had been but a shadow of yearning. All of his plans to resist her blew away like a puff of smoke exiting a chimney pot.

In the hallway of punched tin lanterns once more, he glanced over his shoulder to make sure she still followed him. No, that was a lie, for he could sense her presence behind him without looking. In truth, he'd turned his head because he longed to behold those serious eyes, that glorious riot of hair, that mouth from which words poured and poured until he could barely stop himself from kissing it quiet. She drove him mad with all her talking, and he wanted to be driven mad by her bright chatter every day for the rest of his mortal life.

Even confined to the form of a duck, he'd never felt more bewitched.

Did he still want to win the wish? Yes, more than ever, because his will to live had doubled. He wanted a long life so he could win Josephine's love, and thereafter spend the rest of his earthly existence striving to make her happy in every way.

"Ansgar?"

Her voice invaded his reverie. He'd left the hallway and stopped at an intersection of corridors, his mind too occupied to choose which way to go next.

"Should we turn left?" Josephine asked. "There are boot prints. No cat prints, but Jacques might be carrying Thierry."

"Yes, left," Ansgar said inanely. He started to walk again. Once, he would have longed for an herbal tonic or powerful potion with which he could cure himself of her, but not anymore. If she was the fever sent to plague him, he desired only to surrender, body and soul.

"Are you ill?" Josephine asked as if she'd read his mind. She came alongside him as the brick corridor gave way to walls of moldering yellow plaster. In the narrow passageway, inches separated her body from his.

He kept his gaze forward. "I am as well as one could hope to be after so many days of rough travel and malnourishment."

"The journey will soon be over," she said encouragingly. "You'll be home again in no time, wearing your own fine clothes, eating lavish meals, sleeping in a soft, clean bed. Do you know what I will eat first? Bread with berry jam. I have been dreaming of it every night. Isn't that an odd thing to crave, out of all of the food in the world?"

"Quite," he said as he pictured lifting a slice of jam-smeared bread to her lips.

"What will you eat first? Roast partridge? Cream of langoustine soup? Plum tart with apricot glaze? No, I suppose you would choose something from your homeland. A dozen sausages. A bowl of those heavy dumplings. I cannot remember the name of them, but—"

"Eggs," Ansgar said, interrupting her. "Fried crisp in butter and served on toast."

"You surprise me," she said.

"Do I?" he replied before she could start rambling again. "I had a simple childhood. My grandmother kept a dozen hens. Their eggs tasted better than any dish I have eaten in my adult life."

A fresh breeze brushed his hair back from his forehead. Ahead, rays of sunlight danced on the floor. An open door creaked on its hinges, pushed by the wind.

"Sunshine," Josephine said wonderingly. "We must have walked all night, although that doesn't seem possible."

"Thank the gods we're getting out of this dank passageway," he said. He reached for her hand, grasped it tightly, and pulled her toward the exit. As they ran, his intuition told him the next part of the journey would be different. His grip tightened around her fingers, and every inch of skin touching hers felt infused with starlight. His heart pounded with exertion and excitement. They ran hard, and the sound of her rapid breaths was better than music.

Together, they stumbled out of the passage and onto grass.

Before them loomed a great gray mountain partly furred with green moss. A swath of spindly spruce trees swept up its side like a ribbon sash. And from its peak, seven tendrils of silvery smoke drifted toward the heavens.

"The Seven Ovens," Josephine said, squeezing his hand. He felt her trembling ever-so-slightly with excitement or fear. Perhaps both.

A cold, evergreen-scented wind rushed over them, tousling his hair and whipping her curls into a frenzy. The sight of the mountain chilled him more than the wind, for its sides were steep and jagged—sure to delight wild goats but not rapidly aging gentle-men. The mossy parts were equally daunting, for they could be dangerously slippery. Nothing about the terrain suggested an easy ascent.

"I suppose all we must do is climb to the top, then," Josephine said, using her free hand to push her hair away from her face. "Have you climbed many mountains, Ansgar?"

"None like this. But fear not. We will conquer it together." He spoke with exaggerated confidence, but his words appeared to bolster her courage. She wore a brave smile as she stared at the peak.

"Together," she said, glancing at him and then the path in front of them. "Look there. More footprints. Let's hurry. But wait, your boot has come untied."

"Indeed." He released her hand, inwardly cursing his bootlace for forcing him to do so. His fingers ached as he crouched down to tie the offending strip of leather. In truth, it would have soon become awkward to keep holding her hand. They were barely friends, and besides, she believed herself married to the cat. She'd tolerated his touch when it meant adding speed to her steps. If she'd suspected a hint of impropriety, she no doubt would have yanked her sweet fingers away already.

Another breeze rolled off the mountain. Ansgar stood. "Ready?"

She nodded. "I can hardly believe we are almost there. Do you smell the smoke from the ovens? The saint is waiting for us up there. The wish is waiting."

He drew in a deep breath and detected the scent of burning wood. "We are almost there," he agreed. Her effervescent hopefulness both inspired and pained him. His heart beat unevenly. Was she to blame for the faulty rhythm, or was he simply destined to die before he reached the summit, the casualty of a moldering mortal frame?

Side by side, they took the path toward the foot of the mountain. She chattered about the varieties of plants brushing their ankles, but he only half listened, willing himself to stay alive long enough for her to discover that her husband no longer lived—long enough for him to kiss her like she'd never been kissed before.

"Is that a person?" She pointed to a shadowed area halfway up the mountain. "And look there. Is that Thierry?"

The pain in Ansgar's chest doubled as he uttered a silent and unholy prayer that Jacques and the cat would plummet to their deaths.

Josephine's legs ached, but she kept trudging forward, higher and higher. Sometimes scrambling over enormous boulders, sometimes jumping over wide cracks in the mountain. She had never known the world contained so many rocks.

Every inch of her body was bruised or scraped. Once, she'd fallen face first into a bed of moss so thick and sticky that she feared she'd never be able to wash its juices off her skin. Ansgar had pulled her out before she suffocated. He'd also caught her by the arm when she'd almost stumbled off a ledge. Another time, he'd grabbed her by the waist to prevent a fall. And once by the shoulder. Honestly, the man had touched her more today than she'd been touched in the last five years by anyone.

She'd saved Ansgar a few times, too, hauling him away from a cliff edge by grasping a handful of his woolen robe. By shouting to warn him against stepping into a crevice that would have trapped his foot forever. Guiding him by the arm when the wind blew grit into his eyes and rendered him blind for a time.

Ahead of her on a thickly wooded section of the trail, Ansgar huffed and puffed as he used the lowest branches of trees to pull himself up an incline. She reached for the same branches, following him closely. Her breaths were rapid gasps, and she wondered if she might faint. He could not catch her if he didn't see her collapsing. Nevertheless, she imagined the sensation of collapsing into his arms and being carried to the top of the mountain. Of drowsily resting her cheek against his collarbone as he whispered, "*Liebling, liebling.*"

She stopped, one hand gripping the bole of a young spruce. Obviously, she was not getting enough air to keep her mind in order. Such thoughts! Next she'd be imagining she could fly, or diving to catch faeries in the undergrowth. She closed her eyes and drew in deep breaths. The scents of wildflowers and ferns filled her nostrils.

Her bag slipped off her shoulder and fell to her feet, but she ignored it. It felt as if she'd been relieved of a hundred pounds although the bag contained little. Thank heaven she did not have to lug Thierry up the mountainside in his cumbersome basket. Did Jacques carry him now, or had he released his cat-brother and allowed him to walk?

"Are you hurt?" Ansgar asked.

Josephine opened her eyes and found Ansgar had come back down the trail for her. He stood within arm's length, looking more concerned than annoyed. "I just need to catch my breath," she said.

He sat on a tree root and patted the space beside him. "Sit. We have earned a few minutes of rest. We will rise stronger afterward."

She laughed and lowered herself to sit beside him—but not so close that their bodies touched. "You say the most unusual things sometimes, *monsieur.*"

"I meant to inspire perseverance not laughter," he said crossly, but then his face broke into a charming smile. "You are correct, of course. I do not expect that either of us will feel strong again until we've had a week of rest and hearty meals."

"Meals without mushrooms," she said, and immediately wished she hadn't made reference to their night of inebriation.

He cleared his throat. From the corner of her eye, she watched him pluck a burr from his dull brown robe. She tried not to notice the bareness of his shins, forcing her gaze into the treetops as he said, "I confess that I cannot remember much of that evening, but if I said or did anything to offend you, I beg your forgiveness."

"All is forgiven, although I also have little memory of it," she said. But suddenly, as if her memory had been struck by a bolt of clarifying lightning, she remembered everything in painful detail. Or enough of *everything* to inspire mortification. In her mind, she saw Ansgar lean close and heard him call her beautiful. She felt the tender touch of his fingertips along her jaw. His breath warmed her cheek as his mouth neared hers, and she'd wanted his kiss. Badly. Until she'd realized they'd been poisoned...

She swore a silent oath to eschew mushrooms until the day she died.

"Good. Forgetting is good sometimes. Let us never speak of it again." Ansgar stood with a groan and offered his hand. She allowed him to help her to her feet.

"Is that the smoke of the Seven Ovens on the breeze again?" she asked as she pulled her hand free of his.

"It could very well be. Perhaps the pilgrims have already arrived and are practicing their baking." He lifted his bag and waited for her to do the same. "Before we go...the baking lesson I asked you to provide after the incident with the fire. I realize it may be too late for me to acquire enough skill to win the saint's favor, but I would like to present her with something edible. Could you...might you be still willing to teach me, if fate offers enough time for a lesson?"

He sounded like a boy asking a girl to a village dance, half-shy and expecting rejection. Perhaps the thin air had affected him, too. Regardless, his demeanor charmed her.

"Of course," she said.

"You are most gracious, Josephine." He set out, using the tree as leverage to ascend the slope.

"We are friends, and friends help one another." She pulled up her sagging trousers and followed him, yearning for the day she could put on a clean dress that fit her properly. She almost regretted not changing into religious robes back when Ansgar had.

"I have not had many friends since I was a child," he said. He scrambled up a rock and then offered his hand to assist with her ascent. "Not one, to be honest. It means a great deal to me that you would call me yours," he said.

His words were polite and formal, but the way he spoke them made a blush spread across her cheekbones. If Thierry had been there, he surely would have hissed or yowled to remind everyone whose property she was. Her skin grew hotter as her anger flared. After all she had been through to save her husband and all she had learned about herself, she did not want to be anyone's property.

She was not a chair or a silver box. Marriage, she decided as they walked along a flat stretch of mossy rock, should be a partnership based on mutual respect. She intended to keep her vows when this adventure ended, of course, but she would no longer live like a caged pet who wanted nothing but scraps. She and Thierry were going to have to reinvent their relationship—and she knew him well enough to know that he was going to object to the idea. Well, he would simply have to get used to the new Josephine.

The sound of rushing water grew louder as Josephine and Ansgar took cautious steps across a ledge of stone hardly wide enough to accommodate a squirrel. Her fingers clutched a vine attached to the rock face, moving along its stem inch by inch. *Don't look down*, she told herself. Her foot slipped on a pebble.

She looked down. She shrieked and flipped around to face the wall of rock. With both hands, she gripped the ivy. Until now, she'd never known she was afraid of heights. It was an inconvenient revelation. Her knees went weak and perspiration dampened her forehead. She wanted to pray but words failed her.

"Josephine," Ansgar said calmly from nearby. Her forehead rested against the rock. Ivy leaves all but surrounded her head, obscuring any view she might have had of her companion—had her eyes been open rather than clenched shut. "I know you're frightened, but you cannot stay there."

"I think I can stay," she replied in a trembling voice. "Go on without me. Perhaps an eagle will swoop down and save me, or I'll simply become one with the vines."

"Josephine." He sounded closer now. "After all the terrors of this journey, do you mean to let a bit of height keep you from competing for the wish?" She felt his hand press against her spine. "I'm here. I have no fondness for heights, either, but we will do this together, yes? We will be brave because we must."

"I cannot. I'm sorry. Go without me."

"I would carry you, but the ledge is too narrow," he said in a thoughtful voice, as if he meant to work out the problem by verbalizing his options. "I don't have the right kind of magic to call upon eagles to rescue you, nor can I grant you wings."

Tears dripped from her eyes, splattering onto the leaves with the sound of fat raindrops. She inhaled the bitter scent of the vines. Numbness spread through her tightly clutching fingers. She wondered how long she'd be able to hold on. And if she collapsed with his arm around her, would she cause them both to plummet to their deaths?

"I refuse to leave you here. The very notion is insupportable. What of Thierry? Who will care for him if you remain on this rock until you decay into skeletal remains?"

"Since when do you care for him? Besides, you have insisted all along that Thierry is dead and the cat is only a cat. If he is a cat, he will survive as cats do. What are you doing?" One of his arms crossed the breadth of her shoulders and he'd extended a leg around hers in order to plant his foot on the ledge alongside hers. "Get off me! This is most improper!"

Ansgar's front pressed tightly against her back, as if they were a soup spoon and a teaspoon in a drawer. "It would be more improper to let you surrender to fear." One of his hands came to rest on her waist. A shiver ran through her, although her whole body felt aflame. "Now," he said firmly, "when I move, you will move. And before you consider struggling, I will remind you that to do so might send me toppling backward and earn you the title of murderess. While being rid of me might appeal to you, do think of the state of your soul, Josephine."

"I cannot think of my soul or anything else with you all over me," she said angrily.

He laughed, and his breath warmed the top of her head. "Ready? We slide to the right in three, two, one."

Together, in an odd dance, they inched their way across the ledge. Josephine slid her fingers through the ivy, never letting go for more than a second. Ansgar counted down before every step, urging her gently to remain calm, to breathe, and to let him guide her. He still smelled of smoke even after changing into the monk's robe, but somehow the scent now reminded her of childhood bonfires, when she and the children from neighboring farms had visited to roast apples on long sticks and subsequently burned their mouths on the charred peels and tangy-sweet juice.

"Almost there," Ansgar said. "Are you all right?"

She inhaled deeply. His body was as warm and comforting as a quilt—in spite of the man's thin frame. Since they'd met, she'd perceived him as cold and grim. Perhaps her first impressions had been incorrect. A truly cold man would have left her on the cliff and rushed off to claim the wish he wanted. Instead, Ansgar had chosen to shepherd her, step by step, to safety—risking his own life.

"One more step," he said.

And then they reached a large, flat rock topped with a single fir tree and a few sprigs of sharp-looking grass. Ansgar released her from his arms and sank to the ground. Relief and embarrassment coursed through her as she tried to catch her breath. Ansgar sat next to her, making her feel even more awkward. The wind gusted, and she missed his warmth—for purely practical reasons, of course.

"I must apologize. I don't know what came over me," she said. She found a fir cone beside her and picked at its crisp brown scales, for she could not bring herself to look him in the eye. "I have never been afraid of high places before."

Ansgar started to reply, but a plaintive yowl echoed over the landscape. She grabbed his arm. "It's him. Thierry."

"Or an injured rabbit. Or some faerie creature attempting to lure the unwary to their doom."

She stood. "I'm certain it's Thierry. That way." She pointed to the east.

"That's the direction we were taking, so let us continue. I suppose I should be thankful that you're feeling motivated by that horrid noise. If we are abducted by trolls, at least you will go smiling."

Earlier in their acquaintance, his sarcasm would have bothered her. Now, she almost liked it when he sneered. If Ansgar Steuben was wrinkling his nose and saying something haughty, he was being authentic. And was that such a terrible thing in a world full of pretenders and tricksters, where someone could look sweet and good while concealing dreadful moral failings—like thievery, for example.

Like stealing a treasured recipe from the very person who had risked his life to save her and Thierry.

She set off at a brisk pace to keep from confessing everything to Ansgar. As she charged ahead of him and followed a path trodden into short grass, she made a plan: she'd copy the recipe and return the original to his bag while he was sleeping. Everything would be fine. Borrowing was not a crime.

When she won the wish, she would have almost no reason to feel guilty.

Seventeen

nsgar sensed a different kind of magic in the air. Even without a map, he knew they would soon reach the Seven Ovens.

The ground rose steeply before him. How weary he was of climbing. How he hated rocks and spindly spruce trees and roots that tripped him. He hated brightly colored mushrooms and silly, fluffy little ferns. He despised pine cones and chattering squirrels. Gods above, he hated squirrels. He kept his eyes trained on Josephine's shoulders and the dark hair spilling over them like coiled ink. Which might have been part of the reason he kept stumbling.

His chest hurt from panting for breath, but if she could keep walking, so could he.

Her footsteps slowed. "Perhaps that was not Thierry I heard, and only a fox or a strange bird. He would not have given up yowling for help so quickly. He's a determined...man."

The temptation to mock Josephine's belief that the cat was her husband lasted but a brief moment, and brought Ansgar not a jot of pleasure. He chose to say nothing.

"It's getting dark," she said as she clambered over a boulder.

"We should find a place to camp. If it was Thierry I heard before, he's probably safely arrived at the Seven Ovens by now, anyway."

"Agreed."

Josephine stopped. She held onto the silver trunk of a sapling as she surveyed the area. After a few minutes, she pointed. "I think there's a flat space beyond those trees. Do you see it?"

He nodded and set out to investigate. He would not waste his breath on discussion because whether the space was flat or as lumpy as a newly planted potato field, it would be their home for the night. They could not continue on this terrain with candles in their hands.

Twigs snapped behind Ansgar as he walked. He knew the pattern of Josephine's footfalls well after all the miles they'd traveled. It was imprinted in his mind, as was the shape of her eyes and the curve of her jawline. Somehow, the shapes that comprised Josephine's form had replaced his memories of Truda's appearance. He could barely recall Truda's face, and he hated himself for that. If only he could have easily reached the shard of Truda's looking glass he'd put into his pack, he would have rubbed it between his fingers. He wanted to believe that in touching the glass he could renew his connection with his lost wife, while at the same time he knew both Truda and their bond had been expunged from the world. Erased like a singular pattern of frost from a sun-warmed windowpane.

And Josephine was that sun.

His lip curled in a sneer. It was Old Ansgar mocking whatever Ansgar he had become on this godforsaken quest. He dropped his bag on a patch of moss and tried to run a hand through his hair, but his fingers tangled in the sticky, filthy mess of it.

"That moss will make a good mattress," Josephine said as she came alongside him.

He yanked his hand free of his hair and wiped it on his robe. "Indeed. It looks positively luxurious," he grumbled. A hint of smoke tickled his nose, and he remembered how close they were to the Seven Ovens and the contest. He sat beside his pack and smiled up at her sheepishly. "Forgive my ill humor. I'm sure you are every bit as tired and hungry as I am, and yet you remain ever cheerful. Are you quite certain you have no magic of your own?"

She grinned as she lowered herself to the ground. She petted the moss as if it were a dog. "I am quite magic-less, I assure you. But I am weary, and I could eat the bark right off a tree if I had the teeth for such a feat."

Ansgar's smile became genuine. "Food is a disagreeable topic to broach when one is starving, but I fear that I must broach it. We are close to the Seven Ovens. I think the time has come for the baking lesson. We may not get another opportunity."

"But we have no ingredients here, and no oven." She hugged her knees and rested her chin atop them as if she were ten years old.

Ansgar looked away from the too-charming vignette and examined his dirt-stained fingernails. "We do have a few ingredients that Jacques left behind. Nothing I would dare to eat, given what happened before when we sampled his food, but we could go through the motions, as it were. We can imagine we have all we need, and you can teach me the necessary principles."

"I would rather not touch any of that food. We should have thrown it away long ago. If we are going to imagine baking, we might as well imagine it fully. Sit beside me here and close your eyes, *monsieur*."

He obeyed, all too aware of her body's proximity. He breathed deeply and willed his heart to beat in an ordinary rhythm. Her scent made his chest ache. It should have been repulsive, the mixture of smoke and sweat and whatever herbs she'd last rinsed her hair with, but it made him yearn desperately to pull her closer.

"Now, you have a recipe, correct? First, imagine gathering your ingredients and placing them on the table. Flour, honey, eggs, salt, spices. Whatever is listed on the recipe. Next, you'll measure carefully, adding to the bowl only what is stated. One teaspoon means one, not two. Sloppy measurements can cause your cake or biscuits to be hard as rocks or ruin their flavor. Now, when you mix, be sure that all the ingredients mix evenly, without dry patches. Are you listening?"

"Yes." He was trying his best.

She continued to speak in her cheerful way. In his mind, he pictured her measuring and mixing, with a smear of flour on her nose and her cheeks pink from the heat of a nearby oven. He imagined approaching her from behind and setting his hands on her waist, making her laugh and receiving a swat from her floury hand.

"Have you fallen asleep, Ansgar?"

"No!" he protested rather too loudly. He opened his eyes and met her gaze. In the twilight, her eyes looked dark as onyx. "Well, perhaps I did briefly lose track of your words. It has been a long day."

"A very long day. Perhaps when we arrive at the Seven Ovens, the saint will let us practice together before the contest."

"I fear I'm doomed to lose no matter the number of lessons I receive." Honesty made his cheeks burn. She held his gaze as she never had before, and time stood still. He felt fifteen years old again, confused by emotions too big to wrestle to the ground, feelings too beautiful in their agony to banish easily. How could he love this woman? How could he compete against her when he wanted to give her everything?

"You could win," she said. "In fact, I think you will."

He lifted a hand to cradle her cheek. The coolness of her skin surprised him. The air had taken on a chill since the sun had set, but he felt as though he contained glowing embers. "Is that what you want, Josephine?"

She covered his hand with hers but made no effort to remove it. "Don't," she whispered.

"Don't what? I will tell you what I do not want to do. I do not want to ignore what is between us anymore. I see in your eyes that you understand me. Perhaps that you feel the same."

Her cheek heated under his palm. She lowered her gaze. "You

insult me, Monsieur Steuben. I am a married woman on a quest to save my husband, and you said you'd come on this pilgrimage to save your wife. What has this all been for, this journey, the trials, the risks, if not to recover our loved ones? And as I have borne Thierry over the miles, as I carry him in my heart now, you still carry your wife. I have listened to you speak of her. I have seen the look in your eyes as you remember her."

"I grieve for Truda as one grieves the dead. That I do not deny. But the difference between you and me is that while I grieve and carry her memory, I have come to accept that she is dead. She will not return from beyond the grave, and neither will your husband. He is not in that cat, Josephine. I would wager my very soul on it." Something shifted inside him as he confessed his belief that Truda was gone. He had not accepted it fully before, and now that he had, the guilt he'd felt for wanting Josephine fell away from him like shed reptilian skin. He felt reborn.

If only she could experience the same newness. He gazed at her with hope.

She pried his hand away from her face. "Thierry is neither dead nor gone," she said coldly. "And it is none of your concern either way. Please do not speak of it again."

It was like being slapped without physical contact. But it left a mark. Perhaps he should have put his hope to bed then, or dug a deep grave for it, but he chose not to. He simply tucked it into a corner of his heart and bade it to live and thrive until a later time.

He would not give up on her.

She moved a few feet away from him and lay down on the moss. "We should sleep. Good night," she said dismissively.

Using his lumpy bag as a pillow, Ansgar stretched out under the canopy of branches. The wind had ceased, and a single cricket chirped in the brush. If he had sensed magic earlier, he felt it all the more now, surrounding him, overarching him in the stars that peeked between the boughs, and within his breast. This magic was like nothing he'd known in his life as a wizard. It was simple goodness, yet complex in its depths. It was light and wholeness, strength made of gentleness.

Perhaps it was love, and he'd never loved before.

He folded his hands over his pounding heart and listened to Josephine's breaths slow as she surrendered to sleep.

Josephine awoke with a start. Her skin was damp with sweat, the result of her flight from the dark beast of her nightmare. Shivering, she sat up and reached for her bag to get the blanket she should have covered herself with before falling asleep. When they'd stopped for the night, exhaustion had so overwhelmed her that she'd put off looking for the necklace Jacques might have stolen. No wonder the predator in her nightmare had resembled her brother-in-law.

Hazy moonbeams slipped through the trees. The sun would soon rise and wake Ansgar. Another opportunity to secretly copy and return his recipe might not come. Her nerves, still agitated by her nightmare, caused her already accelerated heartbeat to race. Once again, checking her pack for the pendant slipped lower on her list of priorities.

Ansgar looked peaceful slumbering with his arm tucked under his cheek. His bag sat behind his head, as if he'd rolled off it during the night—luckily for her. Sleep erased decades from his face and added softness to his features. She wanted to despise him for suggesting she had romantic feelings for him, but it was hard to hate someone who'd saved her life. It was also hard to hate someone whose silly looking calves and bony knees stuck out from under their bunched-up religious robe. Men's legs were funny things; hardly more attractive than those of a farmyard turkey. Perhaps that is why women in novels fell in love with owlish professors and dowdy poets—dazzled by their minds far more than any physical attribute. Not that Ansgar Steuben's face held no appeal. He had a strong jaw line, a straight nose, and deep-set eyes of a stunning blue found only in the summer sky. When it wasn't all creased by a scowl, his brow might be described as noble.

Ansgar mumbled and rolled over, putting a few more inches of space between his head and his bag. What was she doing standing there staring? If he awoke and caught her...

Josephine hurried to pull her pencil and notebook out of her bag. When she'd first stolen the recipe, she'd tucked the yellowed paper inside her shirt. Soon after, when Ansgar had been fetching water, she'd folded the recipe and stuffed it into her pocket for safekeeping. Its faint crinkle had been a bit of an annoyance—and she'd been afraid Ansgar would hear it and make inquiries. To be rid of it would be a relief.

Tiptoeing, she left the camp. She wandered a little to the west, until she found an ancient pine to rest her back against. Pinkish gold light filtered down onto the page. Time had all but erased some of the words, but she did her best to copy the recipe accurately. She didn't know much German, and the old style of lettering sometimes baffled her. Reducing the recipe to a reasonable size from enough to build a wall challenged her mathematical skills. She could only pray she wasn't making errors that would cost her the prize.

Birds twittered above her and flitted from branch to branch as dawn took over the sky. The second she copied the final word, she stood and stuffed her notebook and pencil into her trousers pocket. A squirrel scampered ahead of her as she made her way back to the camp. The sound of Ansgar's gentle snoring was lovelier than the birdsong, for it offered reassurance that she still had time to secretly return the recipe.

She crouched close to Ansgar's head and opened his bag. She found his little journal near the top, quickly inserted the borrowed page, and replaced the journal. He continued to snore as she crept back to the place where she'd slept. As she covered herself with her blanket, she reveled in how much lighter she felt. The stolen recipe's presence had weighed more heavily on her conscience than she'd realized. She could endure the splinter of guilt it left behind, knowing she'd done what had to be done for Thierry's sake.

Where was her husband now? Where was the cat? Were they truly one and the same, or was Ansgar right when he said Thierry's soul had departed the world? The wizard did have experience with the supernatural. All she had was a feeling. A bit of faith as flimsy as the paper the magical recipe had been written on.

She could be wrong. She shuddered and pulled the blanket closer. She wasn't ready to be a widow. Or to remarry for security. Her hand felt for the necklace at her throat, to touch it for comfort and the memory it stirred of her strong *grand-mère*. But the necklace was not there.

The days had run together, and her memory was cloudy from tiredness. When had she last seen the necklace? Before Jacques had rummaged through their belongings in the cottage? Her stomach sank. She yanked the top of her bag open to dig for the cloth-wrapped pendant.

"Good morning, Josephine," said Ansgar in a drowsy voice. "Have you been awake long? You should have woken me."

"I have not been awake long," she replied, her hand still deep inside the bag, touching, seeking.

"It is hardly conceivable," Ansgar said as he stood and stretched. "Today we finally will meet Sainte Yvette of the Seven Ovens."

Her fingers found a piece of cloth wrapped around something the right size. *Thank heaven.* Now she could breathe again. She released the object and pulled her hand out of the bag. "I only hope we find Thierry first," she said.

"It is possible that he is already at the Seven Ovens. I would not be surprised if Jacques has taken him there. Does that man know about your theory connecting Thierry and the cat? Perhaps he has designs to wish Thierry out of cat form as well. For the sake of brotherly love and loyalty."

Josephine eyed Ansgar with astonishment. There had been no teasing in his voice at all. He just stood in front of her, in his unflattering robe with his bag hung over his shoulder, his mouth neither smiling nor sneering. Was this because of the feelings he'd confessed last night, or was he playing some new game? She could not think of what to say, so she nodded like a dumb marionette.

"Ready to proceed?" Ansgar asked.

"Yes." She grabbed her bag and followed Ansgar. He had been treating her with greater kindness lately, but had he truly changed? In this magic-tainted landscape, how could she know if anything was real or trustworthy?

Well, she'd soon part from Ansgar for good. She tried to imagine walking home with a restored Thierry, but it was difficult to picture anyone but the irascible German at her side.

She and her traveling companion had been together too long, too familiarly. They had forged a strange bond through surviving shared dangers. But it had to end. She was a simple, home-loving, married woman, and he was a complicated, magically trained, somewhat arrogant man of the world.

He offered his hand to help her up a steep slope of jagged, red-brown rock. She accepted his aid because in doing so, she could climb faster and reach the Seven Ovens sooner. Because his grip was always sure and reliable, and not because she remembered that same hand tenderly cradling her cheek. Would she miss him after they parted? She shivered at the thought. Or perhaps she shivered because of the little breeze that teased her hair and rattled the leaves.

"What is that sound?" Ansgar asked, cupping a hand to his ear.

With all her heart, she hoped to hear Thierry's plaintive meow, but instead she heard the rumble of rushing water.

Eighteen

A plateau stretched before them, carpeted with short grasses and orange flowers. Ordinary flowers with petals instead of flames, Ansgar noted with gratitude. Unfortunately, the pleasant land came to an abrupt end where it met a swath of churning, rushing water.

Just when Ansgar had thought the remainder of the journey might be easy, a river blocked the path to the Seven Ovens. The dark water ran fiercely, as if fueled by a mountain's worth of thawed snow, throwing off cold spray and drenching his skin and clothes as he stood on its bank. He glanced at Josephine, who'd been disturbingly silent all morning. She stared at the water as if it had offended her more deeply than he ever had—an accomplishment, to be sure.

"You don't suppose there's a bridge somewhere nearby?" she said.

"The poem we copied mentioned that a bridge would appear, but not when or where. It also mentioned 'a pinch of sand from river drawn.'"

The look she gave him was one of wide-eyed disbelief mixed with stubborn denial.

He considered suggesting screaming a few curse words, as foul language brought him comfort on occasions such as this, but he held his tongue. He'd heard her curse on two or three occasions during the journey, and he would not have been surprised to learn that he'd already been a bad influence in that regard. The metaphorical dog she'd lain down beside, only to end up infested with fleas. In truth, he had no desire to see her become more like him in any regard. The world needed Josephine as herself, in her most unsullied, honest form.

"What is that, carved into that tree trunk?" Josephine asked, pointing to a huge pine tree not far from the water.

Ansgar drew close enough to read the words someone had hacked into the bark. Josephine joined him there as he read, "Every pilgrim, by his own hand, must reap three grains of river sand. To the bed you must now dive, and pray the shore to reach alive."

Josephine shivered. He could relate to her dread. He hated swimming. It brought back horrid memories—and without insulating feathers to shield his body, he'd not feel warm again for days.

"I have a confession," Josephine said, touching his sleeve. Her damp hair was frizzing up, expanding like a thunder cloud with plans to obscure the sky.

"I thought we already knew all of one another's secrets," Ansgar said wryly.

Unsmiling and pallid, she stared into the rushing water. "I cannot swim."

"What? But the pond, when the bees chased us—"

She shook her head. "It was not deep, and splashing sufficed until we could stand."

"If you're going to bake for the wish, you must learn quickly, Josephine. The poem said that grains of river sand must be mixed into each contestant's dough."

"I know, I know. But..."

"You're trembling." How he wanted to hold her close and

soothe her—but she would probably stomp on his foot or slap him if he tried.

"I cannot help it. This is the end of my journey. If I go into the river, I'll drown. I may as well turn back. Thierry will remain a cat, wherever he is, and I will learn to live as a widow."

"Josephine." His hands gently clutched her shoulders and he turned her to face him. "There is one secret I do not think I revealed to you when we ate the mushrooms, although I could have forgotten telling it. You see, for a very long while, a number of years, I was a duck."

"Ha." Her reaction contained no mirth. "I'm afraid that no amount of humor will make me feel better, but thank you for trying."

"I am as serious as cholera. I was bewitched, as punishment. I wore white feathers and spoke only in quacks. I ate grubs and fish and thought only duckish thoughts. Suffice it to say I am an expert swimmer."

"Congratulations. I expect you'll succeed in the task with little effort." She tried to step backward, out of his grasp, but he did not release her.

"Wait, you ridiculous woman. What I am saying is that I would help you, if only you'd allow me to. Will you allow it, or will you remain mired in stubbornness?"

Tears welled in her eyes. "I don't know. That water looks deadly. I don't want to die, Ansgar."

"I swear by every deity above and below that I will keep you safe in the water."

"Wait. Why should I believe this duck story? Why should I believe anything you say?"

He didn't want to lie to her again, but he had to convince her to trust him—which seemed altogether ironic. An appeal to her romantic side ought to win her over quickly. He thrust a hand into his bag and pulled out the wrapped shard of mirror. Carefully, he unfolded the cloth to reveal the silvered glass. "This is why. My wife, Truda, was once trapped inside this glass, as I was once trapped inside a duck's body, and as you believe Thierry is trapped within the body of a cat. I know your anguish. I have lived through your pain and his, having earned that pain. I have made mistakes, Josephine. Now, as your friend, I advise you, I implore you, not to make a choice you will regret for the rest of your days. If you turn back now, you will lose more than a wish. You will make yourself a dwelling within a shard of bitter remorse. A trap you might never escape."

She glanced at him, then stared at her feet as if they could offer her wisdom. Her hand strayed to her throat, probably seeking the absent pendant. After a minute of silence, she took a deep breath and released it as a sigh. "All right," she said.

"You still sound doubtful."

She shrugged. "Of course I'm doubtful. If I'm carried off by the current, you have one less competitor to be concerned about. Better odds of winning the wish."

His brow furrowed and he let go of her. "That stings. I thought we had an understanding, after all we've endured together. An unspoken agreement to see each other through until the saint makes her choice."

"I am simple in many ways, but I understand that we are rivals. You have said so several times along the way."

"You are not simple in *any* way. Time and time again, you have shown yourself to be resourceful and clever. Brave and determined. And things have changed between us. I have changed. Look at me, Josephine."

As if she hadn't heard him, she bowed her head and messed with her hair, making some attempt to gather it into a knot again. Wet curls stuck out from her head like little springs, defying her. She said crossly, "Let's go in if we're going in."

"No. Not until you look me in the eye." He released her shoulders and put the piece of mirror back into his bag, willing his hands not to tremble with fear, for she was correct that the river looked deadly. He needed her faith to bolster his courage.

As a duck, he'd never navigated such a turbulent body of water. This churning river made the lakes and streams of the Igel-wald look as dangerous as mud puddles. Dread tied his guts into knots, but he would not reveal his trepidation to Josephine.

"Fine." She met his gaze for two seconds before looking away.

"Will you trust me?"

"I will try."

After dropping his bag, he kicked off his damaged boots easily. He watched Josephine crouch to untie and remove her boots—which were also badly damaged from their hiking and scrambling. She yanked her dirt-stained stockings off and dropped them onto the pile of boots.

"Take my hand and do not let go," Ansgar said as they approached the river's edge. "When I say so, take a deep breath, as deep as you can, and hold it. I will swim to the bottom as fast as I'm able, towing you behind me. You must not panic, Josephine, or you could doom us both. Understand?"

She grabbed onto his hand. Clung to it. "Take in that breath now," he instructed. He filled his lungs as full as he could, and then he pulled them both into the rushing water.

Under the water, the current felt slower. The water was cool, but not as frigid as he'd expected. He opened his eyes to a cloudy, blue-gray tinted scene: bits of weeds and little fish floating past as he towed Josephine down, down.

The dark river bed came into view. Ansgar swam to a pillar of rock and dove toward its base. Frightened fish darted away from them as they each reached to claim a handful of sand. Ansgar gave Josephine a puffed-cheeked smile before pushing off from the pillar with his feet and launching them back toward the surface.

Josephine's hand gripped his harder. Her arm flailed but he did not let go. Ansgar cast a glance back at her. Her eyes were wide with panic. He knew she'd breathed in water. She thrashed and kicked. Screamed without making a sound.

Quickly, he maneuvered his body to wrap an arm around her chest. He swam hard, swiftly, driven by the greatest terror he'd ever known. He could not lose Josephine. Not now. Not ever.

He breached the surface and lifted her head above the water as he fought to swim the last few yards to shore. When he hauled her onto dry ground, she'd ceased struggling. Her skin was blue-gray and her eyes were shut. She neither coughed nor breathed.

With both hands, he shook her as he cried, "Josephine! Come back to me, my love."

Carefully, he rolled her onto her stomach. He pushed on her back, trying to force the water out of her. He prayed as he rolled her onto her back. He covered her mouth with his and tried to blow air into her lungs. But she remained limp as a rag doll.

The world seemed to tilt sideways. This could not be happening. Time stood still yet raced and unspooled and spun out of control. He needed to think of a solution, but all he could do was feel: love and loss, regret and fear. To live on without her when he'd never had a chance to truly share a life with her seemed unbearably tragic.

Truda's voice spoke within his mind, reminding him of one of the first lessons she'd taught him about how to survive in an emergency or battle situation. *Use whatever is at hand.*

The only resource he had at hand was magic—and not much of it. Would it be enough to drive the water from her lungs? And if he did purge the river from her, could she still be revived or had death already claimed her soul?

He rolled her onto her back. He cradled her face with his hands and closed his eyes. With every ounce of his will, he commanded his magic to awaken and do his bidding.

The cold kiss of raindrops on her cheek woke Josephine. Or was it the coughing fit that shook her? Either way, the first thing she saw upon opening her eyes was the tearstained face of Ansgar Steuben. He looked as if he'd just stumbled home from a war, ashen, undernourished, and bedraggled. Stranger still, he was kneeling with her in his arms and muttering what sounded like a German prayer of thanks.

What could have happened to cause the surly man to weep and pray? And why did her chest tingle as if she'd inhaled starlight?

"Take deep breaths," he said, easing her onto the ground. "That's right. You're going to be fine."

She stared at him as she sat up. River water streamed down her forehead and dripped onto her sodden clothes. Her memory returned in a rush. "I drowned," she said.

"Indeed you did."

"You saved me. How did you...?" She winced as the answer came to her. "You used your magic, didn't you? That is why you look ill, and why I feel reborn." She reached to lay a hand on his arm, too overwhelmed with gratitude to speak for a moment. She didn't know much about magic, but the effort had clearly cost him health and strength. He looked older and frailer. Perhaps even humbled. Tears filled her eyes as she said, "Ansgar, I can never repay such a debt."

"How many times have you saved my life this week? No, there is no debt between us." He stood, paling more as he tugged his robe straight. "We must go. The Seven Ovens await."

She shook her head. "Forgive me, but I refuse to enter that river again. I would only drown again, and as worn out as you must be, you would die if you tried to save me."

"Look there. Downstream." With a pointing finger, he directed her gaze to a place almost shrouded by shadows. A bridge stood in the distance, a graceful arch of white wood crowning the fitful waterway.

"Has that been there all along? How did we miss it?"

"It appeared only after we dove for the sand."

"'A passage bought with fervent tears,'" Josephine quoted. Her excitement about the bridge faded fast. "I lost my handful of sand. I cannot bake for the saint without it."

"Worry not. You need only a few grains. I'd wager you have enough lodged under your fingernails to suffice."

Now that he'd mentioned it, she could feel the irritation of the grains beneath her nails.

Ansgar got to his feet and fetched a small envelope from his bag, one that held the only spice he'd managed to carry since the journey's beginning, due to the fact that the envelope's pointed corner had caught in the inner stitches of the bag when Jacques had upended it. "Here," he said. "Empty out the cardamom seeds and use this to hold the sand."

"Thank you." She dumped out the small, black seeds and handed them to Ansgar before using her thumbnail to force the grains of sand out from under her fingernails. After she closed the envelope, she allowed her companion to help her to her feet.

"And now we go," Ansgar announced rather grandly.

"Now we go," she echoed.

Side by side, they walked toward the shining bridge.

It was difficult for her to look at Ansgar without being overcome by guilt. Using his magic had cost him greatly. His skin was ashen and purple half-moons hung under his eyes. His movements were stiff, as if his joints pained him with every step. Yet in her eyes, he looked more heroic than ever.

Thierry would have let her die. He would have left her alone on the riverbank to continue his pursuit of the wish without a backward glance. This thought—this truth—sent an unpleasant shiver through her.

"Are you cold? You could wear your blanket as a cape, and if it is not sufficient to warm you, I'll give you my blanket to add."

Who was this man? Certainly not the arrogant, self-centered aristocrat she'd met at the old church days ago. Ansgar had said they'd changed, and he was right. So much had happened to them both. Things too big to be forgotten.

"I will be fine once we've been moving for a while," she said. "My clothes will drip themselves dry, I imagine."

"As you wish," he replied.

They neared the bridge. Up close, it shimmered as if painted with pearl dust. As they crossed, the roar of the river seemed less like the voice of a monster now that she knew she would not have to submerge herself in it. Still, she'd be happy to put the place behind her.

On the other side of the bridge, the land was carpeted with bright green blades of grass interspersed with tiny red and yellow flowers. A path wound gently up the hillside. She felt strong, thanks to Ansgar's magic, and could have climbed a mountain without tiring, but she doubted the German could have ascended three flights of stairs without resting.

She glanced sidelong at him. He looked no worse, thank heaven. Still, his appearance alarmed her. He could have been a specter sent to wander the wilderness, something made mostly of shadow.

They crested the hill. In the distance, beyond one last knoll, seven plumes of dove-colored smoke meandered heavenward. "I had almost come to believe the Seven Ovens were nothing but a myth, and that I was stuck in some never-ending nightmare," Josephine said.

"As had I," Ansgar replied. "But here is the evidence, finally, before our eyes."

The path angled downward, speeding their progress. "Are you nervous about baking for the saint?" Josephine asked. "Do you wish me to review the basics with you again as we walk? I would be happy to do so."

"I have not forgotten a single word of your previous instruction. Nor will I ever, Josephine."

"Do you need to stop to rest? You sound unlike yourself.

Come, there is a nice patch of dry ground by that tree."

"No, we must not," he said emphatically, in a commanding tone much more in keeping with her experience of him. It was oddly comforting. "If we are late to the contest, the saint might not allow us to bake."

"Neither will you be able to bake if you die before you get there. You look as if that could happen at any moment. You're scaring me. Please let us stop and rest, if only for a few minutes."

"Do you care for me, then?"

"Of course I do."

"As a friend," he said. "Or as a brother in arms, perhaps?"

Her face heated as she realized the meaning of his inquiry. She changed the subject. "Do you think the saint will provide us with anything at all? I know we were supposed to bring our own spoons and spices and such, but surely many of the other pilgrims lost supplies along the way. We cannot be the only ones for whom the journey proved perilous. And what do you think the others will bake? There are endless varieties of spiced cakes. Do you think the gingerbread from different countries varies in both texture and flavor?"

She continued to blather, making certain to avoid meeting his eye. The ground leveled, becoming a meadow of waist-high, amber grasses. It was a relief to tread on flat land, and a greater relief that Ansgar made no attempt to interrupt her ongoing chatter.

"I wonder if the saint provides rooms for the pilgrims, or if we'll spend the night on the ground. It would be lovely to sleep in a bed..." She kept talking all the way across the meadow and up the next hill, hardly pausing for breath. She refused to allow Ansgar a moment to speak. She didn't want to hear a confession of love from him. Not now, not ever.

Her heart beat much faster than warranted by the amount of physical exertion, as if the thing knew it was in grave danger. For if the German spoke tenderly to her, her heart might shatter. Or, more likely, melt into a useless puddle of sorrow.

How silly she was to think of her heart in such a way. Life was not a romantic tale, and her heart was just a lump of unemotional flesh. If her husband never praised or coddled her, that was her lot in life. At least Thierry had provided a nice home for her. The home she hoped to return to with him.

Where was Thierry? All she could do was hope the wish would reach him wherever he had gone—and that when she finally returned home, he'd be there, back in man-form, waiting for her. Probably looking cross because she'd taken so long.

She heard herself rambling on to Ansgar about clean dresses and comfortable shoes. A few more steps and she expected to be able to view the Seven Ovens of Sainte Yvette. Beside her, Ansgar panted, which was worrisome. He needed a warm bed, a hot meal, and someone to nurse him back to health. Perhaps the saint would have an infirmary where he could recuperate, or a prayer to restore his vigor.

At the top of the hill, they stopped in unison. Words failed Josephine as she surveyed the scene in the little valley. A half-circle of quaint, simple stone houses faced a circular herb garden. Beyond the garden stood a crescent of hive-shaped clay ovens: seven of them, with coils of smoke puffing out of their chimneys. Near each oven was a sturdy work table. On the far side of the village, at the very edge of a pine forest, she spied a little church with a bell inside its spire.

Oddly, not a soul could be seen. Perhaps the pilgrims and saint were worshiping inside the church.

"We're here," Josephine said, devoid of the joy she'd expected to feel upon reaching their destination.

"Indeed we are," Ansgar replied, sounding just as numb. He began to stride down the slope which led to the settlement.

She took a deep breath as if she were about to dive again into dangerous water, and then she followed him.

Nineteen

A nsgar let gravity pull him downhill, surrendering none of his meager energy to the act of walking. If he'd had any magic left to spare, he would have conjured a good warm wind. He felt chilled to the marrow of his bones, and besides, Josephine wore wet clothes that needed drying lest she fall ill.

If he was honest with himself, she was the primary reason he'd drum up a tropical breeze. She was the primary reason he kept breathing, in fact. Every inch of his body hurt. His soul felt thread-bare, if such a thing was possible, and every fiber that remained of it pined for Josephine.

He would die for her. Literally. What a fool he'd become.

The closer he came to the herb garden, the more scents he could identify in the midst of the ovens' wood smoke: sage and thyme, chives and basil—and even nolgresse and havage, two rare plants with magical properties that Truda had always grown. If he could make a tea from havage leaves and jasper mint root, it might boost his energy and restore a shred of his magic.

Josephine was unusually quiet as they stepped into the village. He gave her the briefest of glances. She wore a funny little scowl, as if equally angry and puzzled. She was probably thinking about the blasted missing cat, or worrying Jacques would leap out from behind one of the cottages.

Gods, he'd murder the fellow before he allowed him to harm a hair on Josephine's head. That was the truth, not an exaggeration. He should have done so before.

They halted at the edge of the garden. The faint sound of religious chanting mingled with the bright songs of the birds hopping among the plants and perching in nearby trees.

"I believe they're inside the church," Ansgar said. "We should use this time to acquaint ourselves with this place. Perhaps we might find something to eat or drink. A stream or spring to wash our faces in."

"I see lettuces in that corner." Josephine pointed to a section of plants. "And some radishes, I think."

"I have always detested radishes," Ansgar said. "But I'd eat a bushel of them presently. Dirt and all."

She smiled. "I would not recommend that. We cannot risk offending the saint by ravaging her entire crop."

"A wise thought."

As Ansgar trailed behind Josephine, fine gravel crunched beneath the worn, scorched soles of his formerly beautiful boots. She stopped, knelt, and plucked a few leaves of lettuce. How lovely she looked, encompassed by greenery, with her hair tumbling halfway down her back. Her profile, freckled and sharpened by hunger, held his attention captive. She lifted a fistful of lettuce to him.

"Thank you," he said before stuffing the crisp leaves into his mouth. It was, without a doubt, the best lettuce in the world.

Josephine sat back on her heels and nibbled a leaf. She moaned in pleasure, as if she'd just eaten something prepared by the best of chefs. He imagined spoiling her at his table, feeding her the sweetest grapes, the flakiest pastries, the best cheeses...

"Radish?" She popped up from the ground and startled him out of his reverie.

He ate the radish under her gaze. It tasted peppery and earthy, and better than he'd expected.

"Not so bad?" she asked.

"Not bad at all. One more?"

A mischievous smile appeared on Josephine's dirt-smeared face. If ever he had the chance to commission a portrait of her, that smile would be the one he'd ask the artist to fix on canvas.

"I suppose one more each would likely go unnoticed," she said. "There are dozens, after all." She crouched, plucked two more radishes from the ground, and then shook the soil off them. She offered the larger one to him. He took it, loath to refuse her generosity. Loath to be the one to dispel the cloud of perfect happiness that hung about them in the saint's garden.

All too soon, the pilgrims, their guide, and the saint would spill out of the church. Once that happened, he and Josephine might never again share a private moment. In the company of others, the rigid rules of polite society would fall into place once more, shutting doors and erecting walls. There was also a chance they'd be tossed out of the settlement, unchosen as they were.

He swallowed the radish as something brushed along his lower leg.

"Thierry!" Josephine cried out. She scooped the orange cat into her arms and kissed its head again and again. "You naughty thing. I thought you were gone forever."

Ansgar turned his back on the scene. With crossed arms, he watched a crow perch on the steeple of the church and let bitter jealousy stew within him. But fate cut his inner tantrum short.

The church door swung open wide and one by one, the four remaining pilgrims stepped out onto the grass. They practically glowed with cleanliness, and had donned clothes made from plain linen in tan and light blue. Martel, Jacques, and a simply veiled young woman followed. They waited in silence until another figure exited the church, a tall, willowy woman clad in a flowing white veil and robes of pale gray silk.

Saint Yvette of the Seven Ovens. Magic emanated from her like mist hovering above dewy grass.

Ansgar fell to his knees.

Josephine heard the huff of Ansgar's breath as he sank to the ground beside her. Was he preparing to pray? That was not something she'd thought she'd ever witnessed. "What are you doing?" she asked. "Are you ill?"

Thierry wriggled in her arms but she refused to release him. As she squeezed and scolded him, motion caught her eye. Martel, four pilgrims, and Jacques followed a statuesque woman dressed in pearly-gray: the saint, no doubt. At her heels scurried another, smaller woman dressed in a simpler veil and vestments. A few other pairs of veiled women trailed after the group. The procession was silent and solemn as they filed toward the cluster of little houses, but when the saint spied Josephine and Ansgar, she turned to lead her followers toward the newcomers.

Josephine could not look away from Yvette. Now her knees gave way so that she, too, knelt on the pebbled path. She blamed magic. Thierry took her moment of physical weakness as an opportunity. He sprang from her arms and fled.

The saint stopped a few feet from where Josephine and Ansgar knelt. "I am Yvette of the Seven Ovens," she said in an airy yet authoritative voice. "With the arrival of Jacques Monfort, I had five bakers. And you are the final two sent by divine grace to make the seven complete. Welcome. You may rise."

Yvette's ready acceptance surprised and relieved Josephine. She'd expected to have to state her case and to beg for a place among the bakers, since Martel had not chosen her. Her heart beat fast with awe and fear. This was the saint who could change her life by delivering Thierry from feline form. She could not afford to offend Yvette in word or deed. She had to obey and stand, but her legs felt fashioned from custard. After half a minute of struggle and concentration, she managed to stand.

Out of the corner of her eye, she saw Ansgar fighting to rise. He groaned as he got to his feet and straightened his back. Again she wished that she could restore the health he'd spent on her.

The saint presented them with the sparest version of a smile. "It is your good fortune to have arrived in time for the second and final practice session before the contest. In one hour, all pilgrims shall be permitted to begin baking. At the setting of the sun, baking must cease. Do you understand?"

Ansgar bowed and said, "Begging your pardon, my lady, but most of our supplies were ruined as we traveled. We have almost nothing with which to bake."

"The packing list you received as pilgrims was a test of obedience, and the bearing of the supplies across the miles was a test of dedication. Because you have tried to be faithful in these things, you may help yourselves now to anything in the storehouse. Sister Genevieve will show you the way. Certain ingredients will not be found there, however, as they were items you were required to gather for yourselves along the way. If you did not bring these things, you must fall upon the mercy of your neighbors." The saint waved her hand to summon Genevieve from her shadow. "Take them to the storehouse, Sister Genevieve."

When Genevieve stepped into the sunlight, she looked even younger than she had when trailing the saint. Josephine, who was of average height, felt tall in the girl's presence. She had a face as round as the moon, and her sallow complexion bespoke a life spent indoors. A bit of wheat-brown hair peeked out from under her veil. None of her features stood out as beautiful, yet together they gave the impression of sweet loveliness. If Yvette were a warrior saint who led men into battle, Genevieve would have been the quiet servant of heaven who tended broken birds or lost children.

The other pilgrims, including Jacques, followed Yvette into one of the cottages—which must have been bigger on the inside than it appeared from the outside. Jacques gave Josephine a haughty look as he passed close to her. She wanted to kick him, but held her foot still so as not to offend the holy women.

Like a traitor, Thierry slunk alongside his reprobate brother. Was Jacques here simply to get the necklace, or had he decided to compete for the wish? Would the saint permit someone who'd not been summoned to win?

Genevieve led them toward the storehouse behind the crescent of houses. As if he'd read her thoughts, Ansgar whispered to Josephine, "How is that man counted among the pilgrims? Jacques came here only to threaten and bedevil you. He should be tossed into the nearest deep hole."

She leaned close to reply, "I do not disagree, but I believe that the saint requires seven contestants. If Jacques does not participate, she might call off the competition until next year. Are you willing to wait another year to have the wish?"

He grunted in answer to her question.

With a large iron key, Genevieve unlocked the arched wooden door of the storehouse. She took two baskets from a pile just inside the door and handed them to Josephine and Ansgar. Enough light streamed through clear glass windows set high in the walls to make candles unnecessary. The bright, whitewashed walls were free of cobwebs, and the slate floor had been swept to a shine. Row after row of well-stocked shelves and oak barrels filled the space. The scent of spices, apples, and pears hung in the air.

In a meek, barely audible voice, Genevieve said, "Take what you require for tonight's practice and no more. It is a sin to waste what heaven has given to sustain and strengthen us. If you are hungry, I will procure a meal for you from the abbey's kitchen."

"That would be most appreciated," Josephine said. Her stomach growled loudly to affirm the sentiment. "Pardon me. We have not eaten much since starting our journey."

"No need to apologize," Genevieve said sweetly. "I will fetch your meal while you collect your ingredients. And help yourselves to the clothes in the cupboards in the back of the room. Our holy saint demands that her seven bakers be dressed cleanly and modestly. When you are ready, meet me by the Seven Ovens—but make haste so you do not miss a minute of practice time. Be sure to lock the door as you leave." Smiling beatifically, Genevieve glided out the door. Her footsteps made no sound.

"Is she real?" Josephine turned to ask Ansgar after the girl had left. "She almost glows with goodness."

"She is as human as you are," Ansgar said. He made his way toward a stack of small wooden casks labeled *wheat flour*. "Have you a list?"

"I know what I need," Josephine said. Shame heated her face as she remembered stealing Ansgar's recipe. Thankfully, he was too busy filling his basket with bottles of spices to notice her appearance.

In silence, they moved among the shelves and gathered their ingredients. Now and then, one of them would hold up a jar or tin of something the other might need, and the offering would be accepted with a nod. Once, Ansgar uncorked a small jar and waved it close to her nose. The fragrance of cinnamon made her nostrils tingle. Never had she smelled such a strong, pure version of the spice. She sneezed, then smiled, and he grinned in return.

As Ansgar sorted through a basket of tiny vials, Josephine paused on the other side of a shelf. She took a moment to examine his face. New creases fanned out from his blue eyes, and hunger had honed the edges of his cheekbones. He had a proud brow line and a straight, regal nose that would have looked at home on a statue of some Greek god. As if he'd sensed her staring, he looked up from his task. She'd always thought of him as cool in demeanor, but the gaze he set upon her now was anything but cool. It warmed her to her toes.

"The cinnamon," she said inanely, because she had to say something. "Did you know it comes from the bark of a tree? A tree that grows in some faraway land we shall never see." She looked away and focused on a jug of oil, but she knew his gaze had not strayed from her face.

"Why should we not see this faraway land?" he answered. He had not moved an inch closer, nor did he reach out to touch her, but his words felt as intimate as any caress. "Why should we not travel together by ship, upon the backs of elephants, astride donkeys, or barefoot to see every wonder of the world?"

"My days of adventure will end with the contest," she replied sensibly. Factually. Ignoring his improper invitation and the thrill it sent through her. To ride elephants and watch the sun set over a turquoise sea, to wander meadows of unfamiliar flowers, to... She cleared her throat and tried to clear her thoughts. "Of course you may travel where you please. You are a free man, and no one will stop you."

He moved around the shelf. Her body tensed as he approached her. She wasn't afraid of him exactly, but her pulse raced like she was about to be consumed by a bear.

"You could stop me," he said when he stood one step apart from her. "With one word, you could command me, Josephine. And I would never regret it if I could never move from this square of tile as long as you remained this near to me. Although to be nearer would be a dream made real."

Her eyes drifted to his mouth. How easily she could kiss him. All she had to do was to lean forward a little and stand on tiptoe. She wanted to, very much, although she knew it would be wrong. But who would know?

"Josephine," he said softly. His voice was dark honey, and she was on the brink of starvation. Gripping the handle of her basket with all her might, she leaned toward him, inch by inch.

In the back of her mind, something stirred. An idea. A suspicion. A warning that something was not right.

She took a step back, and then another. Her elbow knocked a box off a shelf, and it hit the floor with a clatter. Her blood chilled as she pieced together his scheme. He was trying to seduce her so that she'd lose the contest. If he distracted her with a forbidden love affair and the guilt of her own transgressions, he could beat her more easily. This was doubly offensive, since he'd claimed to want the wish to help his cursed wife. Did the wife even exist, or had he made her up?

She asked before she could change her mind. "Were you lying when you said you wanted the wish to break a curse on your wife?"

"I did say that once, but later I told you I told you plainly she was dead. Truda is dead. That is the truth."

Now that he mentioned it, Josephine did remember the conversation. She'd been trying to teach Ansgar to bake, and he'd flustered her by flirting, and then insulted her by insisting Thierry was not inside the cat. At the time, she'd thought he'd been speaking metaphorically about his wife's passing. "So you're confessing that you lied about your wife's curse."

"Josephine, I'm sorry. That was before we were friends, and before I lost my heart to you. I've changed." He rubbed the back of his neck and groaned with frustration.

This time when she met his gaze, she hoped he could see how much she despised him.

"Stop pretending to be in love with me," she said. "I am simple, but not as simple as you hoped. All along, you've been manipulating me. You acted cruel, then kind. You let me save you, and then you saved Thierry and me so I would feel bonded to you by gratitude. It was all a game. And for your grand finale, you meant to win my heart so you could steal my chance to win the wish."

He had the audacity—and the thespian skills—to look hurt by her words. His hand pressed his chest as if to staunch a wound she'd inflicted. "You cannot believe that, Josephine."

"You see? Even now you try to tell me what I believe. Get out of my way. I need to get clothes and find Genevieve. I might have needed you to get here, but I do not need you to win—or to keep me from winning." She brushed past him and marched to the cupboards at the back of the building.

Her hands shook with anger as she sorted through a pile of plain blue linen dresses to find one her size. No longer was she hungry. All she could think of was that she'd been the world's biggest fool. Ansgar had played a tantalizing tune and she'd danced to it—almost into the fire of her own destruction. She could only imagine what he really wanted to wish for. Something utterly selfish, no doubt.

Thierry had not been an ideal husband, but at least he'd never pretended to be something he was not. Other than a cat, of course, and that seemed a minor offense compared to Ansgar's sins.

She draped the dress over her shoulder, grabbed her basket, and fled the storehouse with her eyes dimmed by tears.

Twenty

Ansgar stared toward the open door after Josephine disappeared from view. His gut ached as if he'd been kicked by a large horse. Finally, he convinced himself to exchange the monk's robe for a plain white shirt and simple tan linen trousers. Clean clothes usually made him feel like a new man, but not this time. The loss of Josephine had made him feel older than the rocks of the mountain they'd climbed. He picked up his traveling bag and his basket of supplies and headed outside.

Dazzling daylight assaulted his eyes. He winced. The world had no business being so bright when such a black cloud of misery and confusion crowded his mind. In spite of the uncommon length of his life, he had only truly regretted one thing until now: betraying Truda. He had learned to live with that regret. If he were to lose Josephine, he would never stop regretting it.

If he lost Josephine, he would have little use for the long life for which he'd planned to wish. Without hope of winning her affection, he might as well not try to win the contest at all.

He replayed their last moments together. For a moment, he'd thought Josephine intended to kiss him. His heart had blazed with hope that her feelings might mirror his. What had he said or done to inspire her turn against him? They'd finally become real friends, he'd thought, after their encounter with Jacques at the cottage. With a shared enemy, they'd formed a bond. Or had they?

The blame was his to bear. He could not deny it. She was right when she'd said he'd lied and schemed to take the wish she wanted —although he'd failed to follow through with those plans. Would he ever be able to convince her that he repented of these things? Never in his life had he yearned so deeply to be forgiven.

Slowly, sadly, he walked across the cushiony grass. Behind his breastbone, a tiny frisson stirred: the smallest bit of magic regenerating. For this, he was thankful. He had wondered if saving Josephine had consumed his magic so completely that nothing of it remained. The magic's faint but familiar thrum was a comfort, even if it wasn't enough to charm a housefly to sleep.

Voices drew him toward the half-circle of ovens. There, the other pilgrims chatted quietly as they unpacked baskets of ingredients on the wooden tables. Of course his eye was immediately drawn to Josephine. In the ankle-length, cornflower blue dress, with her face scrubbed clean and her hair pulled back into one tight plait, she looked more like a saint to him than the actual saint. He wanted to fall at her feet in supplication. His once treasured self respect meant nothing to him now. The only thing that kept him from casting himself down before her was the steady, judgmental gaze of Sainte Yvette. From a throne carved from dark wood, she was watching everyone at once.

Ansgar turned his attention to the tables, searching for his own. Of course the only free table and oven were at the very end of the row, next to the station Josephine had chosen. Carefully, as if approaching an easily spooked pony, Ansgar moved into the space. He didn't dare to look directly at her. He couldn't bear it.

What could he say to her? To attempt to explain his actions here in front of the others would be a mistake, of this he was certain. If he stole her focus from the important task at hand, she would detest him more than she already did.

Finally, he settled on asking, "Have you need of anything, Josephine?"

"I do not," she said without emotion. He watched her sprinkle a spoonful of a dark brown spice into a large bowl. She kept her eyes directed on the task. "Mind your own work or you'll never finish before sundown. And do not speak to me again unless it is a matter of life and death."

Her words stung like the punishing slap of a birch switch, but she was correct. He needed to focus on baking. Tonight, after the practice session, he'd decide whether he'd make every effort to win the contest or merely go through the motions. It was a decision he'd reason his way through, carefully, with the goal of figuring out what would most help Josephine in the end—because he no longer cared about anything but her happiness.

Reclining under Josephine's table, the blasted cat purred as it licked its paw. Ansgar gave the thing a hate-filled scowl and wished he had ample magic to turn the cat to stone. The animal obviously had no sense of loyalty or gratitude, the way it wandered from Josephine to Jacques and then back again.

"Only a few hours until nightfall," Genevieve announced from somewhere behind Ansgar.

He set his traveling bag on the ground and unpacked his basket, arranging the ingredients in tidy rows. Someone had placed a crate of tools under the table: bowls of several sizes, spoons, a cup with which to measure, a towel, a rolling pin, a knife, and a baking tray made of red clay. With a prayer to whatever deity might be listening, he opened the journal and prepared to follow the recipe hidden therein.

Cinnamon, ground cloves, ginger, a dash of white pepper.

In her head, Josephine repeated the names of the spices as if they were a prayer. Anything to keep her mind from wandering to the blond man mixing dough and mumbling profanities at the table to her right.

Had she judged Ansgar too harshly? What if she was wrong about his scheming to win, and she'd cast aside her only ally based on a fiction she'd created while famished and exhausted? *Grand-mère* had always advised against spewing mouthfuls of words from an empty stomach.

No, no. He was definitely a scoundrel. His arrogant demeanor, snooty attitude, and foul tongue testified to that. And he had not only confessed to being the partner of a cruel witch, but had practically bragged about it.

"Something to keep you until supper." Genevieve startled her by appearing at her elbow with a plate of bread, grapes, and cheese. Before she could thank the little woman, Genevieve had moved on to deliver a plate to Ansgar.

Josephine eyed the plate of food as she kneaded fragrant thick brown dough in the bowl with both hands. Too bad she had lost her appetite. If practice baking caused her such anxiety, how would she ever succeed on the morrow? She glanced at the pilgrim on her left, considering striking up a mood-lightening conversation about...well, anything, but the mustachioed bald man wore an expression of grim concentration that discouraged her from speaking to him. When she cast a glance around the green, she noted that all of the pilgrims appeared to be quietly, joylessly, focused on their work.

"I suppose it is just you and me, Thierry," she said to the cat that slumbered in the grass near her feet. "And a lot of help you will be, I'm sure."

The pilgrim to her left shushed her like a short-tempered schoolmaster and her face heated. If that was how he was going to behave, she would not feel sorry for him when he lost. When she beat him and took the prize.

"Did you say something?" Ansgar asked from her right. In reply, she shook her head—although she found herself wanting to ask him how he was faring. He'd been so unsure about baking. It had been endearing, that vulnerability he'd shown. *If* it were real and not an act put on to evoke her sympathy.

She strewed flour over the tabletop, dusting it lightly, and then dumped the lump of dough out of her bowl onto it. With aggressive swipes of the wooden rolling pin, she flattened the dough into a rectangle.

"Blast it all," exclaimed Ansgar. She glanced over to see him shaking his dough-covered hands over a sticky mass of dough. "I followed the recipe. Why in blazes is it like this?"

She couldn't stop herself from saying. "Add flour. A little at a time."

As if she had just granted him the prize, his face lit with a smile. Was he inebriated? For goodness sake, she had only offered him a few words of simple advice. But his smile was so bright and boyish, she couldn't help smiling in response.

"Thank you, Josephine," he said in a voice heavy with emotion.

Lowering her gaze to the dough before her, she used a knife to cut out the shape of a heart. Carefully, she transferred the heart to the clay baking tray, and then repeated the steps twice more. Dealing with her flesh-and-blood heart was so much more difficult than making heart-shaped cakes. Her actual heart missed the horrid German who stood almost in arm's reach. It yearned to hear his apologies and forgive him. It wanted his friendship.

Thierry had always said she was too soft and gullible. The cat rolled onto his back and bumped into her boot. When he was a man again, Thierry would not entertain her friendship with another man, so she could squash that notion now. The memory of Thierry's endless list of stifling rules chilled her although the oven behind her was roaring. He might be changed after being basically reborn, she reminded herself. Where there was strictness before, there might be grace.

Tomorrow she would know—if she won. To win, she had to focus. She had to banish both Thierry and Ansgar from her mind.

Once more, she consulted the stolen recipe. She'd used all the proper ingredients in the correct proportions. All she had yet to do was repeat the spell-like poem at the bottom of the page. Bowing over the tray and whispering, she said the words—and hoped Ansgar would not recognize them. Not that she should give a fig what he thought, or care if he discovered she'd borrowed his special recipe.

If there was magic in the words, she neither saw nor felt its effects. The cakes looked exactly the same as before. They looked utterly ordinary, and ordinary would not win the saint's favor. Perhaps when she'd reduced the recipe, she'd miscalculated the measurements. But the sun was inching down the sky and she had no time to make another batch of dough. This was only practice, she tried to reassure herself. Tomorrow, she would use the special honey she'd harvested according to the riddle, and whisper her sweetest memory over the bowl. Perhaps those two additions would make a difference.

Doubt crept up her spine like a many-legged insect as she turned to push the tray into the hive-shaped oven with a long paddle. Using the stolen recipe might be the gravest error of any she'd made in her lifetime. One of the gravest, since she should not have stolen the recipe in the first place.

Why had she thought that heaven would let her get away with it?

Twenty-One

Inside a one-story meeting hall behind the church, the seven bakers and Martel chose seats at a long table. Ansgar sat across from Josephine, who looked weary and worried. She stared at her plate while surprisingly jovial conversation flowed between those who had traveled together. Jacques joined in with enthusiasm, laughing more loudly than anyone with manners would dare to while dining. As dishes of plainly prepared vegetables and fish were passed, Ansgar eyed the other pilgrims in turn.

A sapling-thin man of perhaps fifty years, with short gray curls, very long arms, and a heavy Greek accent, who wore a dark blue scarf knotted at his throat.

A brawny French woman with a wide face, chapped cheeks, and chestnut brown hair artlessly bound in a tight bun, somewhere between twenty and thirty. A farmer by trade, he heard her mention to Genevieve, her neighbor at the table.

A diminutive Frenchman with a curled mustache and very little hair atop his shiny head, aged forty or so. Ansgar recognized his accent as Parisian, and if made to guess, would have pegged the man as a shopkeeper of some kind—a seller of books or table linens.

A plump, fair-haired young man, no older than twenty, who always looked on the verge of weeping. He'd come from a seaside town in the south of France, Ansgar heard him explain to Josephine, and needed the wish to heal his mother of some crippling malady that kept her bedridden and in constant despair.

Jacques did not belong among them any more than a rabid wolf would have. Ansgar watched him joke with the Greek fellow as he swirled the wine in his goblet. How had the swine convinced the saint to add him to the company of bakers? Or had she not required convincing, since he'd found the hidden Seven Ovens on the right day, when there were not yet enough contestants present?

When Jacques met his gaze coldly, Ansgar blinked with pure disdain. He looked away to focus on an earthenware vase stuffed with orange flowers. He was not intimidated by Josephine's slimy brother-in-law. He'd eaten frogs of better character back when he was a duck. Clearly Jacques had come to the Seven Ovens to harass Josephine until she handed over the necklace. Wait until he found out Josephine had "lost" it.

Ansgar patted the pocket of his new trousers, the current hiding place for Josephine's necklace. He'd return it to her, but only after Jacques was gone. Pity he'd never been able to figure out what magic the pendant held. He'd tried on a few occasions, when he'd had moments alone, to unlock its power with his own, but whoever had placed the spell on it had done a fine job of securing its secrets.

One of the silent sisters of the convent refilled his glass goblet with cool red wine. He sipped it slowly, enjoying its slight bitterness. Across the table, Josephine lifted her fork to her mouth without enthusiasm, like a child faced with a dreaded plate of overcooked vegetables rather than a half-starved woman given her first decent meal in ages. He was nervous too, he wanted to tell her. Try to eat. You need your strength, my dear.

How she would frown if he called her "my dear."

She set her cutlery on the table. The look of misery and exhaustion she wore broke him as much as her earlier rejection had. To see her without the usual spark of hope in her eyes tore a hole in his heart.

In legends, weighty vows were sworn in grand settings: on windswept mountaintops, inside ancient cathedrals, at the feet of fearsome kings. But Ansgar made his vow at a dinner table peopled by wish-desperate wanderers dressed in dull-toned, borrowed clothes, over a plate littered with fish bones. He took his vow in silence, and swore it to himself alone, by whatever magic still lived within his frame.

I will see Josephine happy and safe if it costs me everything I have and all that I am, he vowed. *If it costs me my life, so be it.*

Josephine's bed was too soft, her nightdress was too clean, and her stomach was too full. Her freshly washed hair and skin smelled too much like lavender, and the bedchamber felt too safe from dangers. A hazy moonbeam drifted through the window to bathe the room in silver light, but it did nothing to soothe her restlessness.

A thief did not deserve such luxuries.

In contrast to her unease, Thierry slept on the bed alongside her ankles, vibrating with gentle purrs. Someone, probably Genevieve, had brushed him until his fur shone and tied a pretty white bow around his neck. His fluffy tail twitched as he dreamed.

To be lost in dreams would be grand, as long as they were good dreams. But Josephine had known before getting into bed that she'd not fall asleep easily. Worries about the contest swirled through her mind. And guilt. Guilt so wide and deep one would need a boat to cross it in a day.

A few hours ago, her practice gingerbread had come out of the oven as she'd expected: ordinary in every way. Neither crisp nor over-inflated, dull brown, and barely spiced. Nothing to bring tears of joy to anyone's eyes, least of all the eyes of a saint used to tasting exceptional delights. In her heart of hearts, Josephine knew that no matter how many spices she added, the cakes she made from the stolen recipe could never be exceptional. Ansgar's magical recipe would not work for her, a woman without a single spark of magic who had no right to meddle with it.

A chill ran down her spine. What if the original author had imbedded some kind of curse amongst the words of the recipe so that no one could succeed in baking something delicious or even edible when using a copy? What if she would come to harm for trying? She had to relinquish it to Ansgar. Immediately. To attempt to destroy it seemed risky, given that the paper she'd copied it onto might now carry a curse. Her knowledge of magic was so limited. She needed to make a confession and place the evidence in the wizard's experienced hands, or she'd be dogged by fear throughout the contest, and perhaps ever after.

She slipped out of bed without disturbing the cat. Quietly, she pulled the pale blue linen dress over her head and jammed her feet into her well-worn boots. She took the copied recipe out of her travel bag and slid it into her pocket. Her heart pounded so hard she thought it might bruise her ribs as she opened the front door.

By moonlight, Josephine took the short path to the cottage next door, knowing that within its thick stone walls, Ansgar Steuben slept.

Twenty-Two

Ansgar dreamed of tribal drums. His eyelids fluttered as the beat grew louder, nearer. No, it was not drums, but someone pounding on the door.

"One minute," Ansgar shouted. He rubbed his eyes, and the cozy, moonlit interior of the one-room cottage came into focus.

The intensity of the knocking implied that the visitor had dire news to share. Perhaps the settlement was ablaze, or a flock of angry dragons circled overhead. Maybe the saint had decided to move the contest time to five minutes from now.

He grabbed his trousers from the bedpost where he'd hung them. He pulled them to his waist, glad he'd elected to sleep in the nightshirt he'd found on the bed. Impossibly, the knocking grew louder.

"Patience," he grumbled as he strode across the room. He yanked the door open, swearing when it collided with his big toe. And then he gasped.

The last person he'd expected to find on the doorstep was Josephine.

The moonlight was kind to her and cruel to him. The way its light caught the silver strands among her loose, wild curls, how it made her skin look the blue-white of night-fallen snow—these sights caused him the worst kind of agony. That he could not touch her was nothing short of torture, but her posture and expression warned him to keep his hands well to himself.

"What do you want?" he said gruffly. "You should not be here. If you're seen, we'll both be disqualified for immoral behavior. The saint's rules—"

"Be quiet." She shoved him hard enough to make him stumble backward, and then she stepped inside and closed the door. Blushing, she said. "That was unkind, and I apologize, but I must speak to you alone."

"It could not wait until morning?" Not that he would be able to sleep now. Every nerve in his body was wide awake and buzzing like he'd been struck by lightning. Was he dreaming? Had she actually just shoved him and addressed him rudely?

"It most definitely could not wait." She reached into her dress pocket. "I have something to confess, and something to give you."

She was trembling, and he was almost too astounded to stand, so he gestured to the two chairs by the low-burning fire. "I have something to give you, as well," he said. "Shall we sit?"

"Yes, please. I think that would be best."

Ansgar had hardly settled into his chair when she thrust a piece of paper toward him. "Take it," she insisted. "I beg you."

He glanced at the handwritten page. "A recipe? I do not understand. Are you unwell, Josephine? Your eyes have a most feverish glint."

"I am a thief. That recipe is stolen. I copied it from the page in your journal."

"You did what?" He felt his eyes widen to their full capacity. The shock lasted less than a second, after which he was tempted to bellow with laughter. Sweet Josephine, a thief! He bit his lip and tried to look offended.

In truth, her announcement delighted him. He loved that she never stopped surprising him, and that the more he knew her, the more he wanted to know. He loved her, and he would forgive her anything, but he'd let her wriggle a bit before offering words of pardon.

"Ansgar, must you pretend to be so thickheaded? I am confessing that I stole your recipe to use in the contest. I repent of it. I do not want the thing or any magic attached to it." She stood and clenched her hands into fists at her sides. "Tell me you forgive me so I can leave before someone discovers us alone together."

He leaned forward and casually took up the iron poker to stir the embers in the hearth. "However did you manage such a feat of thievery?"

"Does it matter?"

"Of course it matters," he said. "I prefer to know my weaknesses, so I can address them."

"You showed me the journal after we ate the mushroom soup, and then you fell asleep. I took the recipe page out then. Eventually I copied it and returned it to your bag."

"That blasted mushroom soup. But well played, my dear. Are you a wolf in sheep's clothing, or just an unusually clever sheep willing to do whatever it takes to win that wish?"

"You should be furious, not amused." She frowned as if she'd sniffed something rancid. "If you're going to laugh at me instead of forgiving me, I will just leave. I need to sleep before the contest."

"Sleep you have just denied me? Your game continues, yes? I'm guessing the recipe was unsuccessful, so you're now seeking to hobble the leg of this proverbial race horse by ensuring that I come to the contest drowsy and dim-witted."

Her mouth gaped open. His mouth curled into a smile that lasted until she huffed and started to march toward the door. He leapt from his chair to chase her. With one hand, he caught hold of her wrist. "Josephine, wait. I should not have teased you. I—"

"Unhand me. I'm not wasting another minute on you. I should have burned the recipe and kept my secret. I knew you were a snake from the beginning, the kind that looks pretty until it bites you and sucks out your soul."

He released her arm but darted to block the door. At his back, the wood felt cool through the linen of his shirt. "That is not how venom works. It is an injection of poison."

"Then you're a special kind of snake. Now let me go or I'll scream and wake the entire settlement."

"I will let you go for a price."

"In ten seconds, I will scream. And when the others come, I will tell them you tried to seduce me, and they will believe me. Ten. Nine..."

"Wait," he pleaded. "The price is that you hear this: I love you, Josephine. If every word that ever fell from my lips before now was a lie, if there is no other shred of goodness within me, that much is true. I would rush into a hundred fires to save you. I would give every drop of magic that could be wrung from my bones to buy your happiness. I love you, and that is all. That is everything." He opened the door and stepped out of her way.

"One," she said, ending the countdown. "You don't give up, do you? Nice try, but I'm immune to your venom or poison or whatever you prefer to call it." She kicked him hard in the shin and rushed into the night.

Her necklace. It was still in his pocket. He'd meant to return it, but things had escalated so quickly. Perhaps tomorrow. She might want to wear it for luck.

Ansgar stepped out onto the doorstep and watched Josephine run with her hair streaming behind her. What had he expected her to do when he confessed his love? Kiss him? That would have been wondrous—but a miracle. Even if she hadn't hated him, she still believed she was married to the wretched cat. Faithful Josephine.

Tomorrow, if she won the wish, she'd finally learn the truth about the spoiled orange feline.

For a moment, Ansgar thought it was raining, but the droplets that dampened his feet had not fallen from the star-speckled sky.

He had not wept since leaving the Igelwald, but he wept now. With his eyes, his heart, his soul.

When he ran out of tears, he felt hollowed out, like one of the vegetable lanterns he'd carved alongside the other village children long ago. They'd set candles inside the shells. Who would be the light inside him if not Josephine?

Her light. When first they'd met, he'd found it glaring and abrasive. He now realized that was because he'd never been in the presence of such brightness. Truda had been shadows and shade. He'd been a young, naïve boy when she'd rescued him from loneliness and obscurity and shaped him into her likeness. He'd never questioned her ways. The love they'd shared had probably not contained a trace of real love, but he'd never stopped to consider it before. Cruelty was not the same as love, was it?

Yet it hurt like a wound. A mortal blow, the slice of a dull blade sweeping from his chest to his gut.

Blast Josephine for changing him this late in his life. This transformation pained him more than the bone-shifting shift from duck to man, and had made him more human than ever before. And as a wretched, emotion-filled human, he would not die happy without her. He would just...die. Unloved, unmourned.

Trembling from the cold mountain air, he left the doorway. The place where Josephine had kicked him throbbed as he lifted his bag from a small table and dug out the piece of Truda's mirror. He held it up to catch the moonlight. A dark splotch of dried blood stuck to one of its edges, a reminder of one of the many times the glass had injured his fingers when he'd tried to caress it for comfort.

It would have been sensible to sleep, but he wandered out the door in his bare feet. He followed the sound of the river. Moonlight bathed the spruces, and owls swooped from branch to branch, hooting somberly. Leaves and needles clung to his toes. His lungs drew in deep draughts of forest-scented air.

The shore of the river welcomed him with soft soil. He stared at the burbling water and clutched the tiny bit of glass between his fingers. This was right, what he had chosen to do. He kissed the unnaturally cool shard and remembered his long-gone wife. He remembered who he'd been with her. That man was as gone as she.

"Goodbye, Truda. Rest in peace, or be blissful in turmoil, as it pleases you," he said as he flung the glass into the river. It disappeared with barely a splash. Not the fanfare one might expect at the end of one era and the beginning of another—and yet he knew that he'd never be the same again.

On his way back to his cottage, he stopped at Josephine's door. The windows were dark. She had probably gone to bed, but he had no intention of intruding. He would not steal her sleep on the eve of baking day. An owl hooted, and a moth flitted past his head as he withdrew the cloth-wrapped pendant from his pocket. He kissed it as one might kiss a holy relic, as he yearned to kiss her face, with reverence and devotion. Whatever mysterious magic the necklace held was hers and hers alone.

With the moon as witness, he set the little parcel on the doorstep. He started to walk away, but turned back. To ensure that the package would be picked up by Josephine and not a passerby or by the vile Jacques, he knocked hard enough on the door to summon her from the deepest sleep. And then he ran.

Soon after dawn's glow spilled over the windowsill, wide-awake Josephine plodded across the floor to answer a soft knock on her cottage door. As she lifted the latch, she prayed the caller was not Ansgar. She could not deal with the man and his yearning eyes and romantic blather now. In two hours, she'd be baking to save her husband, and she'd hardly slept. She felt too weak and dazed to tie her own boots, let alone bake. She had not an ounce of energy to waste on deceitful wizards.

But no one at all stood on her doorstep.

The visitor had left a wicker basket covered with a woolen shawl. Under the shawl, Josephine found a warm pot of tea, two boiled eggs, two soft buns dusted with flour, and a note.

Good morning,

At the sounding of the bells, please report to your work table, bringing everything you need for the contest. You will have until mid-afternoon to prepare a heart-shaped, spiced, small cake to present to the saint. Pilgrims may consult quietly with one another during the competition, but quarreling and physical altercations will result in immediate expulsion from the grounds.

Blessed Sainte Yvette will taste all offerings and then withdraw to the chapel to prayerfully determine the winner of the wish. The winner's name will be announced thereafter, to all assembled.

Yours most humbly,

Sister Genevieve of the Sacred Order of Sainte Yvette of the Seven Ovens

Josephine draped the shawl over her shoulders and carried the basket to the table under the window. She sank into the straight-backed wooden chair and nibbled a bun to keep up her strength, not because she had any appetite. Quite the opposite. Her stomach threatened to heave up every bite.

Outside the window, the branches of a birch sapling bounced as a robin landed near the top of the tree. The sky was gray-blue tinted with pink: gentle, soothing colors that failed to hint that the day to come would be one full of nervousness and striving.

If Ansgar had received the same breakfast, he'd probably already wolfed it down in its entirety. He was what *Grand-mère* would have called "a man of appetites," one who indulged himself in every possible way, with food, drink, games, and women.

Drat. She wanted to smack herself for thinking of the

scoundrel. They'd grown too familiar during their journey. Time and distance would surely erase him from her mind. Soon, heaven willing, she'd have the man version of Thierry back to occupy her days and thoughts. She glanced at the cat that had not yet left the bed. As if he sensed her gaze, he put on a show of stretching and yawning, displaying all of his tiny sharp teeth. That was one thing the human Thierry had in common with cat Thierry: impressive teeth. White and almost frighteningly perfect. Jacques's teeth were the same.

It was strange that Jacques had not tried to meet with her since she'd arrived. The man had always been tenacious. Giving up on obtaining the necklace was unlike him. So what was he plotting?

Josephine brushed crumbs off her chest. The saint valued neatness, which also meant she'd have to tame her hair. She used water from the pitcher to dampen her curls, and then knotted them firmly at the nape of her neck. Without hairpins, this was the best she could do.

From her bag, she took the honey she'd saved after Ansgar had almost died from the bees' stings. Half of it was rightfully his, and she would give it to him peaceably—if he dared to ask for it. Knowing him, he probably would dare.

Ansgar was daring. Heroic, even. He'd rushed through flames to save Thierry. He'd saved her from drowning by draining himself of magic so thoroughly that he'd become ill. Had he truly performed those deeds as part of a grand scheme to win her trust for his own diabolical purposes? *Yes*, she told herself firmly. He had used her in every way he could get away with. One could be both daring and wicked.

Ansgar Steuben was a detestable scoundrel.

And she missed him.

The bell pealed again and again to summon the pilgrims to the competition. It sounded like salvation. For the next few hours, she'd concentrate fully on baking and winning, and have not a thought to spare for Ansgar Steuben. If nothing else, at the day's end, she'd leave him behind. That in itself would be a victory, would it not?

She gathered her things and headed toward the door. But she'd forgotten something. Her necklace. She'd been carrying it inside her bag for so long she'd almost stopped reaching to touch the pendant for comfort. Today, of all days, she wanted the memento of her grandmother with her.

As the echo of the bells faded, she emptied her traveling bag onto the table. She grabbed the cloth-wrapped bundle and opened it. Inside she found a gold wedding band with a chain looped through its center. She'd found it along the roadside when the coach had stopped to water the horses between home and Anneçon, the town closest to the Church of the Three Sorrows. She'd forgotten stashing it among her belongings.

She stared at the scattered items as the truth became clear. Her pendant was gone.

Suddenly it made sense that Jacques had stopped demanding her necklace. He'd already taken it, back when he'd drugged her and Ansgar with food at the cottage. So why had Jacques continued all the way to the Seven Ovens? What other vile plan did the man have in mind? Did it have something to do with Thierry, perhaps?

Disgusted and angry, she shoved everything back into her bag except the chain and ring. She'd have to deal with Jacques later. Now she had to bake.

Now she had to win the wish.

She slid the chain over her head and let the ring fall under the collar of her dress. Its weight mimicked that of her beloved necklace. With heartening memories of *Grand-mère,* she once again took up her basket of ingredients and left the cottage.

Surely the world was on fire.

A bell rang out repeatedly, urgently. The scent of smoke filled his nostrils.

Ansgar sat up in bed and remembered where he was. The smoke was from ovens already lit by the convent's sisters. The day of the baking contest had dawned, and he'd slept past sunrise—something he never did unless ill. He threw back the covers and dressed quickly. He felt almost too well. His heart thudded not with dread but hope. Today held a thousand possibilities. If there was any justice in the universe, Josephine would have her heart's desire before the sun set—whatever that might be. Great gods, he hoped it would make her happy.

He still held little hope for his own success, magical recipe notwithstanding. He would participate in order to make the number of bakers complete, but he was not foolish enough to believe he'd be victorious—nor did he truly want to win. If he could have meddled with the others' efforts to ensure their failure, he would have. Unfortunately, the saint was too shrewd. He'd never get away with it. He'd have to keep his magic to himself and trust fate.

How he detested being forced to trust fate.

The events of the previous night replayed in his mind as he washed his face over a tepid basin of water: Josephine's midnight visit, her confession, his confession. The aching bruise on his shin testified that these things were not a dream. The woman had a strong foot. The pain was no laughing matter, yet he smiled.

The bell continued to clang. He grabbed his still-packed traveling bag, his basket of supplies, and the recipe Josephine had given him. Out the door he flew, almost tripping on a basket someone had left on the doorstep. He picked it up in case it contained things he'd need for the contest, and then took off running. Barefoot, unhindered by his ruined boots, which made him feel younger than he had in decades.

Without the shard of Truda's looking glass, his footsteps seemed to bounce more lightly off the earth.

The crescent of tables came into view. The ovens crackled with already-burning fires, sending tendrils of smoke toward the sharp blue sky. Josephine stood with her hands pressed flat against the tabletop and her eyes focused on the trees in the distance. Was she afraid or just anxious to begin? Her face was white as fresh snow.

Ansgar opened his mouth to say something to reassure her, but as the big bell's echo faded, the chime of a small bell replaced it. Everyone turned to face the saint and Genevieve. The saint's white silk cassock reflected the sunlight like water, whereas Genevieve's robe was plain linen the color of weak tea. Ansgar might have mistaken them for painted statues had their eyes not blinked.

"Good morning," Genevieve said in her high, childlike voice. "The contest will begin when our blessed saint gives the command. But first, I shall read you the list of rules she has scribed upon this scroll."

"Read," commanded Sainte Yvette.

Genevieve unrolled the parchment between her hands. "On this day, hear the words I, Yvette of the Seven Ovens, record here for good and for glory. One: you shall now swear a solemn oath never to speak or write of this place or these proceedings, upon pain of death and eternal suffering. If you do so swear, say 'aye.'"

All together, the pilgrims agreed.

The saint nodded, and Genevieve continued to read. The rules were as one would expect—no stealing others' ingredients, no loud speaking or singing, no presenting previously prepared baked goods, no leaving the area except during specific break times. Ansgar tapped his toes against the dewy grass, impatient to begin creating although he had no faith in his skills.

"The final rule is this," Genevieve said. "You must incorporate the ingredients specified by the poem you encountered along your journey here. No allowances will be made for misinterpretation or failure to procure the needed items."

Gasps came from a few of the pilgrims. "Great," Jacques mumbled.

Ansgar glanced at Josephine, and she returned his gaze long enough to nod knowingly. They'd solved all of the poem's riddles together. The jar of honey sat on her table, they'd brought sand from the river, and they knew to speak their fondest, happiest memory over the dough before baking. They'd been a good team.

"Hear now, before you bake, the tale of Sainte Yvette," Genevieve said. "When our blessed saint was but four years old, an angel appeared before her in her mother's garden. 'Dear child,' said he, 'I charge you to be a good and obedient daughter. When you are grown, your task will be to find the recipe for the best spiced cakes in all the world. With this recipe, you will calm the temper of a king and end a war, thus saving thousands of men and steering the course of history. Each year until the perfect recipe is found, you shall send a message to those fated to compete. Seven will be chosen, and seven must bake. These seven shall present an offering of their best gingerbread. I give you one wish a year to offer as a prize. Once the proper and best recipe is in your hands, great bells shall ring of their own accord as a sign unto you that your search has come to an end.'"

"Sainte Yvette has lived a good and pious life. Honor her and heaven with the work of your hands this day, and perhaps play a part in saving many lives."

The saint pronounced a flowery benediction and then proclaimed, "You may begin!"

The pilgrims fumbled with bowls and spoons, jars and bottles. Ansgar took a deep breath, gathered his courage, and walked toward Josephine's table with the copied recipe in hand.

Twenty-Three

J osephine whacked an egg against the edge of a small dish and tipped the white and yolk out. She never cracked an egg without remembering her grandmother. *Grand-mère* had taught her many things as she showed her how to bake. Little lessons about life. She'd even offered wise-sounding advice when breaking eggs. "Look for the treasure in the brokenness, child. The beautiful consequence. The unexpected cure." It didn't matter that half of *Grand-mère*'s proverbs made no sense. Every time Josephine remembered one, it was like being folded into one of the old woman's lavender-scented hugs, and that was a priceless gift.

Thierry's growl alerted Josephine of Ansgar's approach. She agreed with the cat's sentiment. If only she could have hid under the table with the animal. But she had too much work to do to spend time cowering from scoundrels.

"Take your portion of the honey and go," Josephine said when he arrived at her side. She would not allow the man to distract or sabotage her. She waved a wooden spoon. "It's there. Did you bring a jar? Never mind. Dump half in that blue dish and take the rest."

"Thank you, but that is not the primary reason for my visit."

He slid the recipe toward her. "I want you to have this. Use it to bake and to win the wish."

"No. It is a cursed thing. Take it back." She shoved it toward him with the spoon. "I'm using my own recipe. If I win, I win fairly."

"If I give it to you and you use it, you will win fairly. There is no sin in using a gift, Josephine."

Genevieve approached them. "I remind you that you must speak quietly and amicably. There will be no second warning, only expulsion."

"My apologies," Ansgar said with a small bow. He turned away and hurried back to his own station, leaving the copied recipe on her table.

Genevieve leaned close to whisper, "Is there a problem? Has this man acted in a way you believe warrants his disqualification? I will fetch our blessed saint to hear your grievance if you wish."

"There is not a problem," Josephine said. "He meant well, I think." She measured flour and dumped it into a large, yellow-glazed bowl, recalling her *grand-mère*'s recipe. Since the age of ten, she had known it by heart. Everyone had loved *Grand-mère*'s highly-spiced little cakes. She hoped the saint would love them as well. She'd add the special honey, the grains of river sand, and the sweet happy memory of baking with her beloved grandmother, and trust heaven for the rest.

As soon as Genevieve wandered away, Josephine picked up the copied recipe between her finger and thumb as if it were something putrid. She turned to her oven, opened its door with the hook provided, and flung the paper into the flames. It exploded, sending a shower of sparks out of the oven's front and chimney. Josephine shrieked. She leapt backward to avoid being singed, but several embers seared her cheeks and throat.

Her earlier theory that the copied version could be dangerous had been correct. How stupid she'd been to impulsively throw it into the oven!

"Are you hurt?" Genevieve clutched Josephine's arm. Shock had rendered her motionless, dazed, and chilled. At her other side, Ansgar stood, although she had not seen him arrive there.

She blinked hard in an attempt to clear her vision. "I'm fine. Please don't expel me from the contest. I didn't know that would happen. I only meant to burn an unwanted scrap of paper…"

"It was my fault, and my recipe," Ansgar said to the saint's assistant. "Had I known that it had the potential to explode, I would have warned her. Please believe that I'd sooner cast myself into the oven than see Josephine come to the least bit of harm. I deserve the blame and the penalty."

"My heart tells me you both have spoken truly. Neither one of you will be punished for this unfortunate accident. Ansgar, return to your station. Everyone else, continue to work. All is well." Genevieve patted Josephine's back. "I will acquire some salve for your burns, and brew a calming tea for your nerves. You will continue to compete, won't you? Our blessed saint would be disappointed were you to quit."

Josephine nodded. She pulled out a short, three-legged stool from beneath her work table and sat upon it. She would allow herself a few minutes to catch her breath. Thierry jumped onto her lap and purred soothingly.

The gazes of the other contestants kept wandering her way, but she did her best to ignore them. Better to face humiliation now rather than later. Perhaps the incident would even work in her favor— if the saint added points for perseverance.

"Are you certain you're unharmed?" Ansgar asked from his station in a voice too soft to draw a rebuke from Genevieve. "I will help you in any way I can, if you will allow me to."

The man also deserved points for perseverance, but she'd award him with nothing. For all she knew, the exploding recipe had been yet another part of his many-layered plan to defeat her, and the smooth declaration he'd loosed before Genevieve had been another verse in his endless litany of lies.

Josephine pasted on a smile but didn't look toward Ansgar. "I am perfectly well," she said cheerily. "And you have helped me already in too many ways, Monsieur Steuben." She set Thierry on the grass and rose from her seat.

As she brushed a bit of soot off her dress, she tried to ignore the slight dizziness and headache brought on by the explosion. In light of all her recent challenges, these small discomforts were nothing. Less bothersome than a moth flitting past.

She took up her spoon and resumed mixing.

By noon, Ansgar dripped with sweat. The saint's settlement sat high in the mountains, but the sun blazed down as if they were in a desert, while the heat from the ovens made the atmosphere almost as stifling as the hellish landscape from which he'd rescued Josephine's cat. Never had he expected to be that hot again, but here he was.

With the tip of his knife, he etched a swirling design into the unbaked, heart-shaped cakes on the tray. He'd impressed himself. The dough had come together nicely, and if scent gave a true indication of flavor, these hand-sized confections would be delectable. His triumph. In truth, any success he achieved in baking could be attributed to the old, magical recipe he'd stolen. That recipe, which he'd taken from Gretel's husband, Lukas Beckmann, had been used by Lukas's grandfather to build Truda's gingerbread house in the Igelwald. It had resisted him a little, but in the end, and thanks to Truda's training and Joesphine's baking lesson, he'd been able to coax the recipe to do as he willed.

As the poem had instructed, Ansgar had added the special honey he'd almost died for, the grains of sand from the river bottom, and a whisper of his favorite memory. Before placing the tray in the oven, he'd sprinkle a dash of his personal magic over the cakes.

Choosing the strongest of his fond memories had been a challenge. Of course Josephine featured in all of them. Every memory he had of Truda was tainted in some way by spite or selfishness—most often hers, but sometimes his. Those recollections were dark-edged things, like forged love notes singed around the edges by the fires of profanity. His best memories of Josephine shone like a handful of gems, each one pretty and without blemish.

Her face as she accepted the cat from his arms after he'd saved the beast from burning.

Their joyful meal of pilfered vegetables in the saint's garden.

The moment she came back from the dead, revived by his magic.

In the end, he'd settled on the picnic of radishes. Only she could have convinced him to eat such a vile vegetable. He'd enjoyed it, too, in all its sharpness. But not as much as he'd enjoyed Josephine's teasing smile and bright laughter, and the way she'd looked at him without malice or suspicion for that brief and beautiful half-hour. That one curl that kept poking her in the eye, the speck of something shiny on her cheekbone, that maddening dimple in her chin, how she'd shaken the dirt off the radishes so expertly, the slant of the light, the sweet, earthy scent of the garden...

Josephine was scowling at her dough as she rolled it out. The dark brown lump flattened in submission, forming a neat rectangle. His rolled-out dough had been the shape of some undiscovered continent, complete with bays and peninsulas. She paid him no mind as he stared.

What memory had she sunk into her bowl of ingredients? Something sweet from her childhood on the farm, like feeding lambs or riding a pony through a wildflower meadow? Gods help him, he could not bear the thought that she might have chosen her wedding day. But surely not...

"Are you going to put those in the oven or do you expect the sun to bake them?" Genevieve asked, startling him out of his reverie.

"The oven," he said. He rarely blushed, but he might have if his face had not already been flushed from the heat.

Genevieve leaned over the table to whisper to him. "You love her, do you not?"

Ansgar lifted the tray of cakes and turned away from her. Josephine, not his personal emotional state, was all that mattered. "That is of no consequence."

"Love, of no consequence?" Genevieve's already high voice rose an octave. "There is nothing of greater consequence. Love holds the stars in place and calls the seedlings forth from the soil. Love fuels the beating of the heart and the rush of the wind over the sea. Love blesses and begets. In truth, without love there would be nothing. All would cease to exist."

"Very poetic," Ansgar said, too tired to say more, and disinclined to share his secrets with the sister. He gathered some of his magic and whispered it over the tray. There, as long as he didn't burn the cakes, he'd done his best by them.

When he opened the door of the hive-shaped oven, a blast of hot air almost blinded him. He used a wooden paddle to place the baking tray in the center of the oven, and then shoved the door shut.

He turned, expecting to see Genevieve, but she'd already moved on to another pilgrim's table. He lifted the pitcher of water and drank it dry, but his thirst remained. The temptation to make it rain nagged him, but he was loath to waste what little remained of his magic on manipulating the weather. Circumstances could arise that would require his remaining magic, circumstances related to the woman at the neighboring table—who was currently cutting out neat hearts from dough.

Who, with no magic at all, had resurrected *his* heart from its shriveled, dead state.

From the center of the crescent of tables, someone shouted,

"Water! Bring water!" A few of the other bakers rushed to aid the mustached Parisian, dousing his flaming shirtsleeve with the contents of their pitchers. After the fire went out, he wept loudly as Genevieve led him into one of the cottages.

Seconds later, the oven at the opposite end of the crescent exploded with a bang. The baker, the stout farm woman, dove under her table as the oven door flew toward the gardens. Black smoke poured out of the oven.

"I'm fine," the farm woman insisted as Jacques pulled her to her feet. "No need to fuss."

"Too much magic," the Greek pilgrim at the next table said, shaking his head. "We talk of this on the way here. I tell her not to use that kind of magic, that it not end good if she do. These ovens too old, you know? The gentle magic is the thing. Gentle and sweet, like the cakes, no? Better to use no magic at all. Add sheep fat instead."

"Of course," Ansgar said.

The saint emerged from the church, where he presumed she'd been praying, and strode toward the work stations. "If no one has perished, keep baking," she called out to the pilgrims. "Where in the world is Sister Genevieve? That woman and her wandering off..."

"Why does Genevieve seem more saintly than that woman?" Ansgar asked Josephine, not expecting an answer.

"I think your cakes are done," she said. "They smell done."

Ansgar swore. He'd let distractions get the better of him. He tore open the oven and removed the tray with the paddle, full of dread that his hearts would be black as pitch and half as edible.

On the tray sat three perfect gingerbread hearts imprinted with curlicues and whorls. The scent of cinnamon, cloves, and honey rose from them, strong and pure.

For the first time, he believed he might stand a real chance at winning. Had he made the worst mistake of his life? If he gained the wish and a hundred more years but never Josephine's heart, what purpose would those years serve? But would it not be worse if another one of the competitors won?

He sank onto his stool to weigh his options, all the while watching Josephine scurry about to finish her work. The charming wrinkle of worry that creased her forehead did not help his concentration.

<h1 style="text-align:center">Twenty-Four</h1>

Breath held with apprehension, Josephine wielded the long wooden paddle. She withdrew her baking tray from the oven and tipped the paddle to slide it onto the tabletop.

She exhaled with relief. The three heart-shaped cakes were pretty enough. Their edges had not spread, they'd risen evenly, and they had a rich brown color. All that remained to do was to decorate them as *Grand-mère* had, with white frosting vines and yellow frosting flowers. In her mind, she heard her grandmother's voice: *Take your time*, ma chérie. *Let them cool completely before you begin.*

Out of the corner of her eye, she saw Ansgar arranging his offering on a dark blue plate. He had left his cakes plain, but he'd garnished the edges of the dish with freshly picked dandelions to add brightness. Would this please the saint? Josephine had no way of knowing whether the holy woman preferred a simple presentation or elaborate embellishment. From the uncomplicated dishes they'd been served at meals, Josephine could not imagine the saint favored excess.

The clouds overhead thickened, hiding the sun and providing a little relief from the unseasonable heat. Thank heaven, for the frosting would surely melt into ugly puddles if the sun continued its cruel assault. The heat from the ovens was brutal enough. She wiped her damp brow with her sleeve and set to mixing the frosting.

"Pilgrims, you have less than one hour to complete your offerings," Genevieve warned from near the center table.

Josephine's stomach churned. As she stirred together egg whites and sugar, her hands trembled. She glared at her hands and willed them to stop shaking. With anything less than a steady grip and utter confidence, she'd never be able to craft the intricate leaves and flowers that would make her cakes a delight to the eye and not just the palate.

"May I offer any assistance?" Ansgar asked from his table. "It seems I have a bit of spare time."

"No, thank you," Josephine said firmly. The last thing she needed was his meddling. What did he mean to do to help, "accidentally" knock her offering onto the grass? Bespell the cakes with bitterness by breathing on them?

Thierry rubbed against her ankles. The familiar caress of his soft fur comforted her. With a quiet purr, he reminded her why she had taken on this challenge. She'd trekked all this way for Thierry. To save her husband from life as a cat, and thereby save herself from life as a penniless widow.

"Thank you," she whispered to the cat. "Just think. If all goes well, you will soon be a man again. I will bake your favorite apple tart as soon as we are home. You can eat at the table again. Unless you've grown fond of lapping from dishes on the floor." She giggled, picturing her staunch husband with his face in a bowl of soup, something as likely to happen as the moon raining down bits of brie.

Hopeful, happy thoughts of home inspired her as she carefully applied frosting to each cake. She modeled the flowers after those she'd seen growing in the saint's garden, taking her time to accurately shape the petals and leaves.

Finished, Josephine stepped back to assess her work. Every vine and blossom, every flourish was perfect. *Grand-mère* would be proud. She had done her best. Whatever happened next was up to fate and the saint.

As she closed her eyes to pray, the church bells pealed to command the pilgrims to set down their tools.

Ansgar tapped his toes on the patch of bare dirt under his table, where his back-and-forth movements had worn away the grass. The bells had tolled and the offerings had been delivered to the table near the church, but the saint had not yet appeared. What was keeping the woman? He was tempted to go find her, but restrained himself. There was something about Yvette that inspired fear. If she hid the ability to toss lightning bolts like javelins, he did not want to inadvertently volunteer to be a target.

As instructed by Genevieve, each pilgrim waited at his or her work table. Ansgar scanned the half-moon of tables and the other four remaining contestants. The Parisian whose sleeve had caught fire and the stout farmwoman had never returned from their trips to the infirmary.

Of all the competitors, the tall, curly-haired Greek fellow looked the most confident. He stood with his hands on his slim hips, grinning like he'd already conquered them all. If there had been a cliff nearby, Ansgar might have shoved him over it.

The plump, blond young man shed silent tears, as he always seemed to be doing.

Jacques leaned against his table, arms crossed over his chest, looking bored.

Josephine. Ah, Josephine. Weariness subdued her usually sunny features like a shadowy veil. She was still lovely, yes, but lovely like a misty valley just before daybreak, somewhere hidden and secret that needed no magic to be extraordinary. She looked less nervous now, and somberly resigned to her fate.

By the gods, he hoped she'd win.

A breeze ruffled the beige linen cloth of the offering table. Genevieve rang a small silver bell, and a moment later, Sainte Yvette emerged from the church. Her robe matched the sky, and a starched white wimple covered her head. She strode slowly across the grass, as if reluctant to crush a single blade. As if she was unbothered by the fact that five people had worked all day in the blazing sun to bake for her pleasure.

Without a word, the saint walked along the edge of the table and examined the plates of heart-shaped cakes. She turned on her heel and walked past them again, this time stopping to poke a few of the cakes with her fingertip, and to bend over to sniff the others. Her face remained utterly expressionless.

Genevieve moved to the end of the judging table. "Thank you for your entries," she said. "Our blessed saint will now taste the cakes. Before she does so, if any one of you has something to confess which would affect your qualifications to compete for the prize, speak now, that you might be forgiven or cast aside, according to Sainte Yvette's divinely inspired will."

No one said a word. Indeed, all stood still as graveyard statues. A cool draft passed through Ansgar's body. With his sensitive eyes, he perceived it as it moved along. A long swath of magic glimmered as it circled the pilgrims one after another. He'd read about this type of magic in books but had never seen it employed. It was used to root out false friends or to reveal someone hiding behind a glamour, if he remembered rightly. One thing was certain: he didn't like the way it prodded him with its icy tendrils.

The magic gathered into a swarm of shimmering purple sparks, reformed into the shape of a person, and leaned to whisper into the ear of Sainte Yvette.

"Did you feel that?" The Greek pilgrim rubbed his arms as if to warm himself. "Like someone just walk over my grave."

"Quiet," demanded the saint. "I will now taste these offerings. Let all living flesh keep silent. Let time itself hold still."

Josephine's cat yowled and darted toward the forest. The Greek slumped to the ground in a faint, and Genevieve signaled for a sister to come care for him.

Ansgar shivered with foreboding. The simple baking contest had become something dark and dangerous. He glanced at Josephine, who'd gone pale as milk. She met his gaze with terror-filled eyes.

The earth trembled faintly under their feet as the saint took her first bite.

Twenty-Five

Josephine knew they weren't supposed to move, but fear drove her to Ansgar's side. She grabbed his hand and held on as if it could keep her from passing out like poor Dimitrios had, or from falling into whatever hole might open up to swallow them. Anything could happen, and she did not want to die alone.

Thierry, in usual Thierry fashion, had abandoned her to take care of himself.

A gust of wind rattled the tree branches as it roared over the mountaintop.

"Forgive me, and I will forgive you," she said, disobeying the saint's demand for silence. "If I have wronged you or misjudged you...I do not want to die as enemies, Ansgar. Even if we are still enemies, or—"

"I hold nothing against you," Ansgar said. He squeezed her hand. "Let us face this bravely, as friends."

"Yes," Josephine said. She inched closer to him so that her arm pressed against his. Her entire body shook, but he stood as firm as the rock faces they'd scaled together.

The saint set down the cake she'd nibbled and picked up another. This one was Jacques's, Josephine thought. When the saint gagged and spat out the bite, Genevieve rushed to offer her a cup of water.

"At least we know he won't win," Ansgar whispered mischievously.

Josephine bit her lower lip to quell a nervous giggle. She closed her eyes. If she kept watching, she would throw up.

Thunder rumbled. She gripped Ansgar's hand harder. He pulled her closer, so that her side nestled against his. "I'm here with you," he said. "It will be over soon. Breathe, Josephine."

"Soon," she repeated, leaning against him. The world, though shaking with thunder, felt safer with him near. She didn't care if he'd been plotting against her, or if his current efforts to comfort her were part of an ongoing wicked plan. Right now, she needed him.

The wind ceased, and the thunder's rumblings faded away.

"The tasting is done," Genevieve declared. "You may follow Monsieur Martel to the Garden of Wishes, where Sainte Yvette shall render judgment in due time."

"That sounded rather ominous," Josephine said as she loosed Ansgar's hand. It would not do for the saint to see her holding hands with someone to whom she was not married. But what if Sainte Yvette had already seen? Would the saint believe her if Josephine claimed she and Ansgar were only friends? That she had sought nothing but momentary comfort from her fellow pilgrim?

Ansgar frowned. "I must say, I expected the awarding of the wish to be a more joyful occasion. Those holy women look as if they bit into the same bad lemon."

"The very worst of lemons. Come, we should catch up to the others."

Led by Martel, the small parade meandered around the side of the church, treading a path worn into the short, rough grass. The tall building cast a long shadow there, and the coolness of the air felt like a blessing to Josephine. She watched for Thierry among the gravestones and evergreens, but saw no sign of the cat.

Everyone but Ansgar passed her by. He matched her stride at the rear of the somber procession.

"Who do you think will win?" Josephine asked him—although the thought of not winning made her sick to her stomach. "I stopped watching the tasting after the saint spat out that burnt offering."

Ansgar snorted a laugh. "Not Jacques. Definitely not Jacques."

"At least I can rest in the knowledge that he won't be using the wish against me. He already has everything Thierry owned, and my necklace."

"He has the necklace?" Ansgar sounded genuinely surprised.

"I noticed it was missing last night. Did you know he proposed marriage the week after Thierry died? I think he was willing to do anything to get his hands on that necklace."

"That scoundrel did not propose!"

"Three times, actually. The first time, he brought me a bucket of live snails to cook for him and a green hair ribbon, as if that might sway my decision. But tell me how you proposed marriage to your wife. Did you pick her twenty bouquets of bluebells and kneel before her? Did you recite poetry you'd written about the rare color of her eyes?" She was babbling again, too anxious to stop herself.

"Truda hated bluebells and my attempts at poetry. I brought her the gift of an amber ring wrought by faerie artisans on the darkest night of the year. I asked her plainly and she answered plainly, and we wed the next day under the oldest oak tree in the Igelwald. But to this day, I am unsure if I came by the thought of proposing marriage on my own or if she planted it in my mind with an enchantment."

"You sound as though you don't care if she tricked you into asking for her hand."

"It mattered not. I wanted nothing in the world but her, and I knew she adored me wildly. I was young, so young, and she was the queen of my heart as surely as she was the queen of the forest. But she is gone from this earth now, Josephine. This is a different world, and I am a changed man."

Josephine felt the meaning of his words as much as she heard it. His yearning woke butterflies in her belly. But as much as she wanted to be loved, she could not simply cast aside her marriage vows. She shushed the butterflies and tried to picture a happy reunion with her un-felined husband. Would the wish transform him in an instant? Would he fall into her arms murmuring his thanks, kissing her again and again? No. He might give her a word of thanks, but Thierry would not be Thierry if he showered her with gratitude or affection.

She stumbled, this time over a rock. Ansgar caught her by the arm. "Are you all right?" he asked.

Josephine pulled her arm out of his grasp. "I'm fine. Just ungraceful."

Thierry would have let her fall on her face. He would have laughed and called her a clumsy cow, and invited others to mock her. That was the old Thierry, of course, the one not chastened by life as a cat. If Ansgar had changed, Thierry could.

"Josephine?" Ansgar said quietly, tentatively. "Would you slow down for a moment? I know we have already forgiven each other for past misdoings, but I must be forthright about something. Your necklace."

Her already taut nerves tightened further, like a snagged row of knitting. She slowed her pace to match his. "My necklace?"

"You see, I found it on the ground after Jacques ransacked our belongings. I kept it with me, hoping to discover its secret when given the time. I intended to return it to you when you came to me with the recipe last night, but you departed before I had a chance. And so I visited your cottage sometime after midnight and left it on your doorstep, wrapped in cloth. I knocked loudly enough to wake the dead, to draw you out to find it."

Josephine had known him long enough that his misdeed did not surprise her. Perhaps she should have been angry, but what good would that do? It would be better to hold to their pact of mutual forgiveness, especially with the saint's judgment looming, to be as pure in heart as possible for the awarding of the wish. Mostly, she felt sad not to have the heirloom with her. She touched the ring-on-a-chain she wore in place of the pendant and said, "I heard nothing. I must have slept hard in the brief time I was asleep. There was a basket on my doorstep this morning and nothing more."

"Perhaps you overlooked it. I'll run to the cottage and check, if you wish."

"No. Stay with me," she said, sounding more desperate than she liked. "We can look after the ceremony."

"Very well. And again, I'm sorry," he said with boyish earnestness. If she had not wholly believed his recent claim that he'd changed, she did now.

"Forgiven," she said, meeting his gaze long enough to catch sight of his small smile of relief. "We should catch up with the others."

They hurried to round the corner of the church. The Garden of Wishes appeared before them. Josephine tripped over her own feet, but recovered her balance without assistance. This garden was not at all what she'd envisioned.

Tall, emerald green hedges full of sharp silver thorns formed the garden walls. Anyone who attempted to climb over them would be torn to shreds. Within the walls, white gravel paths ran alongside square patches of fragrant herbs and bright flowers. Bees and butterflies sipped lazily from the blossoms or fluttered above them as they walked. After a few minutes, they stepped onto a half-acre of trimmed lawn. There, two curved stone benches faced a raised platform, and on the platform sat a throne flanked by ivy-covered columns.

It was the throne that most shocked Josephine. Its gleaming, gilded back reached heavenward like a spire carved with whorls and grimacing faces. Red velvet cushions lined a seat wide enough for two, and the arms of the chair boasted carvings of open-mouthed dragons' heads, complete with vicious teeth and serpents' tongues. This was not the seat of a humble saint, but a monumental chair fit for a bloodthirsty queen. To make matters more frightening, a long sword stood in a rack to the left of the throne.

"Not a very saintly piece of furniture," Ansgar whispered, giving voice to her musings. "Will Yvette behead the losers, do you think? You know, I strongly suspect that she is not a saint at all. At least not in the conventional sense."

Josephine shuddered. Every minute held unknown possibilities, both bad and good. The pilgrimage had taught her as much.

As if to reinforce that sentiment, a young woman stepped out from behind an enormous rose bush alongside the stage. Dressed and veiled in the same beige linen as Genevieve, the woman sang softly, hauntingly, while Martel and the pilgrims took their places on the benches.

Ansgar sat next to the Greek, Dimitrios, who trembled like a dog left outdoors too long in winter. Josephine sank onto the cool bench beside Ansgar, but everything within her wanted to pace or flee. Or to awaken from this strange dream and find herself at home under her favorite quilt. But then she spotted Thierry padding along the edge of a patch of lavender. She would be brave for him. He was counting on her, whether he knew it or not.

But her eyes kept wandering to the sword, and consequently, her knees shook under her skirt. Her hands went cold. Drat Ansgar for suggesting the saint might behead the losers.

As the song ended, Genevieve walked to stand beside the singer. She proclaimed, "All rise for the procession of the blessed Saint Yvette of the Seven Ovens."

The pilgrims and their guide stood and turned toward the entrance of the garden. As the singer began a new song, five more young women stepped onto the lawn. Dressed in light gray robes and veils, they carried bejeweled plates topped with the baked offerings. They moved so smoothly that Josephine wondered if they were floating above the ground.

The scent of cinnamon and honey drifted through the garden. The women formed a line on the opposite side of the platform from Genevieve and the singer, plates held steadily at waist level. *How serene they look*, Josephine thought. *Surely their faces would be grim if murder was imminent.*

The singer fell silent, as did the birds. Sainte Yvette approached slowly, as if she had all of eternity to reach the golden throne. The gravel crunched under her calfskin slippers. Her expression was both calm and proud. She passed the pilgrims and ascended the steps to the throne, and then she spun to face them. With a queenly smile, she lowered herself onto the cushions.

"Be seated," Genevieve said to the pilgrims.

"The hour has come," said Sainte Yvette. "My judgment shall be final and unquestioned." She glanced at the sword long enough to make evident the price of dissent. "Come, daughters of the Seven Ovens. Bring the offerings unto me."

The women scaled the steps. Three stood to the saint's right, and two to her left.

"You were all given the opportunity to confess any reason you might be unfit to win the sacred prize, and yet not one of you spoke. I now call Jacques Monfort to stand."

A few of the pilgrims gasped. Jacques stood.

"Speak plainly and truthfully, for I do not suffer liars," the saint said. "How did you come to seek the wish when you were never called to do so?"

Jacques shifted his weight from one foot to the other. "The truth. The truth...the truth is that I overheard my brother's widow speaking of it, a wish that could change her life. Why would I not desire the same? Why would anyone ignore such an opportunity? Luck has never been on my side, my lady, so I followed her on the pilgrimage. I thought...I wanted... And my brother. I brought him here because I think he's stuck in a cat. If I won, I could wish for him to be free—"

"Stop!" Sainte Yvette commanded. "Cease your lying! Be grateful for my heart of mercy, Jacques Monfort, for the sword of justice calls out to smite you."

Jacques fell to his knees. "All right. The truth. Until a few weeks ago, all I wanted was a certain pendant of Josephine's—until I overheard her speaking of the wish. Since then, I have wanted both, because I believed one could help me unlock the other's secrets.

"It's been spoken of in my family for ages, the pendant, although no one could say from whence it came. The story was the pendant's magic could turn anything into gold—if only the holder knew the words to unlock its power. It was the women of my family who kept it close, generation after generation, always trying to figure out how to get the magic to work. But times grew hard. My great-great-grandmother gave it to Josephine's family in exchange for food when her children were starving. The next summer, when she tried to buy it back, Josephine's ancestor refused to sell it. With the pendant in their possession, the family moved away, and although we Monforts searched for decades, we couldn't find them. Until my brother, Thierry, heard a rumor when passing through Valerienne. The pendant belonged to a spinster there, the daughter of a poor cabbage farmer. Thierry married Josephine within the week. Under the law, what was hers belonged to him.

"Thierry tried to unlock the pendant's power, but he was a quitter and a coward. I could succeed. I know I could, if I could have what rightly is mine. Forgive me for speaking falsely before, Sainte Yvette, I beg you. And for whatever else I have done—"

The ground rumbled underfoot as the saint's face darkened. "Whatever else you have done? You dare to speak as if you do not know your sins! You came not as a true pilgrim, but with a plan to threaten and rob the called. You have lied, stolen, and plotted treachery. You would use my wish to take advantage of a newly widowed woman, one of your family, no less. Get from my sight and never return, or I will spill every drop of your ignoble blood."

Red-faced, Jacques rose and stumbled toward the gate. Josephine gawked at him, confused and dismayed by his speech.

"Good riddance," Ansgar mumbled. He crossed his arms and smiled smugly.

The saint stood and placed her hand on the pommel of the sword. "Wait, Jacques Monfort. You carry something that does not belong to you. Return it now, or meet the blade of justice."

Josephine looked over her shoulder to see Jacques halt. Before him, blocking his escape, stood two tall sisters with swords drawn.

Jacques turned to face the saint as he reached inside his shirt to grab something. "Take it. I have wasted enough of my life chasing it. I'm sure it's nothing but a useless object of superstition anyway." The silver chain caught the light as he cast the necklace onto the ground, and Josephine recognized it as her necklace. He ground it into the dirt with his heel and then brushed past the guards.

"Bring the pendant to Josephine," Sainte Yvette said to one of her guards.

As the sister set the pendant in her palm, Josephine barely contained a sob of relief and sorrow. Jacques's rough treatment of the pendant had caused a spiderweb-shaped fissure in the stone that could never be repaired. She was happy to have it back, but sad that Thierry's brother had damaged the heirloom she'd treasured.

"Wonders never cease," Ansgar muttered.

The saint sat again. "Judgment will continue," she said.

Josephine clutched the pendant. Her stomach sank. If Jacques could be expelled for thievery and deception, so could she. She deserved the wish no more than he had. It broke her heart that Thierry would remain confined in a cat's body forever because of her mistakes.

She rose from the bench before she could change her mind.

Her heart beat fast as a frightened bird's. Behind her, Ansgar cried, "No, Josephine."

"Blessed Sainte Yvette," she said. "I have something to confess."

The revelation that Jacques had stolen Josephine's pendant from the cottage doorstep in the night had stunned Ansgar, but the horror he now felt eclipsed all other emotions.

Ansgar had known little deaths before. When he'd changed from a man to a duck, and from a duck to a man. When he'd seen Truda fade from the looking glass the day Gretel had taken the throne of the Igelwald. But this was worse, this feeling of perishing. To lose Josephine now would be the worst version of death he could imagine.

He shot to his feet and reached for her arm. "Please," he begged her. "Not now."

Josephine took a step forward. "On the journey here, I stole a recipe from this man, Ansgar Steuben. I intended to use it to win."

"But she repented," Ansgar interjected. "She returned it. I forgave her. The recipe she used in the contest was her own. Is not a forgiven sin erased from existence?"

Sainte Yvette nodded. "It is as you say, sir. Otherwise, Josephine would have already been banished. Now sit, both of you."

Ansgar looped his arm through Josephine's and tugged her back onto the bench.

"You should not have defended me," she whispered, and was immediately shushed by a scowling Genevieve.

"Bring me the winning gingerbread," Sainte Yvette said.

One of the women brought her a plate, and after a low curtsey, placed it into her hands. Ansgar strained to see which offerings lay on the plate, but the jeweled trim blocked his view.

"The one I have chosen tastes of childhood afternoons. Of a *grand-mère's* soft embrace, and love not tainted by the evils of the larger world. There is no other magic baked into this heart, and none is needed." The saint stood and held high half of a cake decorated with flowering vines. "Who has offered this to me?"

Josephine's sob came before she slowly lifted her hand. "I have, Sainte Yvette." She fell sideways as she wept, colliding with Ansgar's body.

Tears slid down his face as he embraced her shaking shoulders. Had he ever cried for joy before? It was a glorious thing indeed to be so overcome with pure happiness, like swallowing a sunrise whole. He had loved the darkness for so long, never imagining how it would feel to be filled with this kind of light.

"Josephine Monfort, you are the winner. Write your recipe on the scroll Sister Francis provides, and you shall receive the wish of your heart."

As the pilgrims applauded politely, a young woman brought a tray containing parchment, ink, and a quill pen. Josephine's trembling fingers could hardly grasp the quill to write her *grand-mère's* recipe. She hoped the saint would be able to read the scribbles she jotted.

Bells rang out from the steeple of the chapel in loud and joyful peals, just as the story had said they would. A cheer rose from the sisters and the pilgrims.

"Come to the throne, Josephine, and receive your prize," Genevieve said as Francis bore the scroll away.

Josephine sniffed and wiped her eyes on her sleeve. "May I have one minute to compose myself?"

"Of course," Genevieve said. "Consider well what you will wish for, and approach the throne when you are ready."

Dimitrios passed a handkerchief into Ansgar's hand and gestured to Josephine. "Give to our winner, please, with the congratulations from my heart."

Ansgar nodded his thanks and pressed the handkerchief into

Josephine's hand. She blew her nose loudly, and he almost laughed. If he could adore her completely in such an uncouth moment, what a delightful life they might have shared—were it not for the cat.

Thierry rubbed against his ankles and purred loudly.

As much as he wanted to hate the cat, he found he was too full of love for Josephine to summon one bit of vitriol.

"Josephine?" he said quietly as she dabbed at her eyes. "Congratulations. I hope your wish brings you every joy."

She bumped her shoulder against him. "Have you been bespelled? That is not something surly Ansgar Steuben would say."

"Perhaps."

She stood. He peered up at her pink cheeks, the freckles under her eyes, and the untamed curls that framed her face. He memorized the nervous twitch of her mouth. "Come with me?" she said. "I'm a little afraid of that woman and her big sword."

"Yes," he said simply. He would go with her as long and as far as she needed him to, until age hobbled him or the ground became his everlasting coverlet.

She took his hand and they approached the throne with the cat following at their heels.

Twenty-Six

Josephine walked slowly to avoid tripping in front of the saint and the other pilgrims. Besides, the occasion felt too sacred for rushing. And she needed time to think.

She needed time to decide what to wish for.

Certainly she wanted Thierry to not be a cat, but was such an existence so bad? She would keep him warm and fed for the rest of his days, and he could nap and carouse as much as he cared to.

Ansgar's fate weighed on her far more heavily than Thierry's. Since the start of their journey, he'd aged visibly. His blond hair had gained more streaks of white, and the lines in his face had deepened. When he'd used magic to save her after she'd drowned, he'd paid dearly—with years of his life as the currency.

When she thought of him dying, her heart sank like a sack of stones thrown into a lake.

One more stair step stood between her and the saint. She paused to glance over her shoulder at Ansgar, and sorrow welled up inside her chest. At no point in her marriage vows had she sworn not to love anyone else as a friend. She could allow herself that.

And what was love without action? Empty words. As worthless as seeds not planted.

"Kneel," said the saint when Josephine reached the top step of the dais.

She obeyed. Her rushing blood turned to fire, then ice. This was what she'd waited for and journeyed for and almost drowned for. Held in the saint's curled fingers was a glass vial that flashed purple. The wish.

Thierry sat on the step beside her, tail undulating. Nothing about his presence comforted her. In fact, the orange cat looked dangerous, as if about to leap onto helpless prey and tear out its throat. The knowledge that Ansgar stood behind her was far more encouraging, no matter that he'd been her enemy as often as he'd been her friend.

Sainte Yvette extended her hand, palm up and open. The vial gleamed as she said, "Josephine Monfort, because your offering of gingerbread has well pleased me, I grant you this one wish. Use it to secure the desire of your heart."

The cat sprang forward and snatched the vial with its teeth. Quick as a striking snake, the saint grabbed the sword and brought the flat side of the blade down on the cat's body, pinning the animal to the floor.

"Thierry!" Josephine shrieked.

The cat hissed. The vial rolled out of its mouth and spun on the dais floor.

"Shall I finish it?" Sainte Yvette asked. "This foul creature has plagued you from before your journey began, has it not?"

"No!" Josephine leapt to the cat's side. "Please! Let him go!"

Sainte Yvette lifted the sword. Thierry jumped up and fled.

Ansgar retrieved the fallen vial and held it out to Josephine. This time, when she looked into his blue eyes, she saw calm resignation. He smiled and said, "Take it. You've earned it."

Josephine did not reach for the vial. She said quietly, "You have changed."

"Of course he has, my dear, for that is the purpose of the pilgrimage," Yvette said. "Those who arrive here no better than when they left home have no chance of winning the wish. The magic of the Seven Ovens makes certain of it."

"I should not have won, then," Josephine said. "I was a better person at home, an obedient, respectful wife of good character. On the way here, I schemed, stole, and worse." She pushed Ansgar's outstretched hand away. "You must take the wish, Ansgar. I don't deserve it."

"No." With his empty hand, Ansgar gripped her upper arm gently and turned her body toward his. "Look at me, Josephine. The prize is yours. You out-baked us all. You are a woman of strength, virtue, and surpassing loyalty. And you have journeyed too far on behalf of that cat to not find out if it's your husband."

She shrugged out of his grip and exclaimed, "I don't want the cat to be my husband, you ridiculous German."

His mouth gaped in surprise. Josephine flushed from head to toe. She wanted to melt into a puddle, slip through the cracks in the platform, and seep into the ground. Instead, she stood unable to move under the intense gaze of a saint, her servants, and the exasperating man who'd made her question everything.

Ansgar's heart skipped a beat, and then launched into an erratic rhythm. The odd tapping in his breast would have alarmed him had he not known to attribute it to Josephine's declaration. *I don't want the cat to be my husband, you ridiculous German.* The sentence echoed in his head like a stanza of song.

Could she mean that she wanted him instead? He gave her a questioning look, but she'd closed her eyes. He could no more decipher her expression than he could read a wall of hieroglyphics. The skin of her cheeks bloomed red, then pink, then white, as if she were an enchanted rose.

"I am a seer of such mystical attachments," said the saint. "That cat is bound to you by neither promise nor enchantment."

Ansgar dragged his attention from Josephine to the saint. He'd been right all along then.

Sainte Yvette added, "I will keep and care for the animal if you would like to be free of it, for mice are wont to nibble the grain in our storehouse."

"But what of Thierry, my husband?" Josephine's voice swelled with grief. What a testament to her goodness, Ansgar thought, that she would mourn the man who treated her so abysmally year after year.

"He is deceased, my child," the saint said gently. "He awaits the resurrection of the dead like all mortal men who rest beneath soil and stone."

"You are certain? But the cat. He was so like Thierry, and came to me just after Thierry died. I do not understand."

"The cat is nothing more than a cat. Wily and shrewd, to be sure, and possessing of a measure of faerie blood. Neither truly good nor wholly evil, but self-absorbed and fond of comfort. Perhaps heaven sent the animal to comfort you as you mourned, or perhaps the creature found you by chance. Some things cannot be known."

"Just a cat," Josephine said disbelievingly. Trembling, she sank onto the platform. Ansgar sat next to her. "May I put my arm around you?" he asked.

She nodded. Tears streamed down her cheeks as she wept or laughed, or wept *and* laughed. He did not need to name her emotion, only to support her through it.

His arm settled around her. His insides warmed, like he'd drunk a kettle of perfectly brewed tea. "Would you permit me to tell you a story?"

"You may," she answered with a sniffle.

"Once upon a time and long, long ago, there was a boy who

lived on the outskirts of a village at the edge of a huge, dark forest. He was the tenth and final son of a farmer, a puny and frail thing. As soon as he could walk, he was taught to tend his family's flocks of ducks. They were a mean breed, apt to snap and peck and befoul his small feet with excrement. The other children mocked him for always being filthy and ragged.

"As the years passed and the boy grew, he dreamed of a different life: one in which he'd be respected and powerful. And then, in his sixteenth year, he met a young woman in the market square. She smiled at him as if he were beautiful and desirable. As if feathers did not stick to his breeches and she didn't notice the patches on his shirt or the shabby shoes he'd bought used from a peddler. The boy smiled back.

"'Come with me,' she said. 'It's a fine day to sit by the river.' Enchanted by her lilting voice, he followed her like a pup at its mistress's heels. In truth, he would have followed her to the very ends of the earth.

"Beside the water, she took his hand and stared into his palm. 'There is magic in you,' she said. 'I felt it the instant I saw you. It sleeps in your bones, the gift of a grandmother long dead.'

"The young man thought she was making sport of him, but he didn't mind. All afternoon, they lazed on the riverbank. At twilight, she kissed him, slowly and beguilingly, and the magic in his bones sparked to life. The sparks became embers that promised to kindle into flames. Into power. How hungry he was for power, and for her. But she broke their kiss and stood.

"'I will return for you in a year and a day,' she pledged. 'Be ready.'

"When she returned, he was ready. They'd exchanged passionate letters by way of her pet crow, and he'd fallen deeply in love. Or deeply and willingly under her spell. He abandoned his flocks and his family. She led him deep into the Igelwald, where she lived in a simple wooden house among the woodland animals and faeries. She was their queen, as she was his. That she was neither kind nor gentle bothered him not. He adored her fierceness and free spirit.

"Her name was Truda, and she taught him the ways of magic; how to use the power that lived and grew in his marrow—but not to spend it all lest he kill it and himself. She crafted cloth on an enchanted loom and dressed him in finery. He brought her bouquets of herbs for potions: meadows-eye and deerwort, golden thornbramble and prickled sage. They fought and frolicked, and he drank in her lessons like a thirsty leaf sucking in rainwater.

"She changed the sad, scorned little boy into an arrogant, confident wizard. Once they wed, he commanded the forest as her prince. They reigned over the Igelwald, feared and honored by every creature that dwelled there. Surrounded by the magic of the forest and imbibing potions made from rare elnissa berries, they remained young for decade after decade. Each year, they grew closer to one another and gained power.

"He thought it was true love, but there is neither pain nor darkness in true love. If it was love at all, it was only a shriveled shadow of it.

"This he should have learned when he sinned against her and was brutally punished. With full knowledge of his hatred of water-fowl, Truda cursed him to become a duck and bound him to wander the Igelwald until he satisfied the conditions of a compli-cated curse.

"That very summer, while the duck swam and preened, blight destroyed every last elnissa bush. Without the means to maintain her youthful appearance, the witch's face wrinkled and sagged. Her body ached and shriveled. The only other remedy she knew against aging was one brewed from the flesh and bones of children. She was evil enough to use it, and to have a cottage constructed from gingerbread to lure tender little ones to her door.

"She did not account for the cleverness of a girl called Gretel. I will spare you the entirety of the tale, but know that Gretel conquered Truda and eventually took her place as queen—vowing to rule kindly and justly. In that winter, the duck turned back to a man, stole the gingerbread recipe, and set out to make a new life for himself beyond the Igelwald.

"With gems he'd carried off from the witch's hoard, he planned to live a life of wealth and indulgence, to leave broken hearts in his wake but never gain a scratch on his own heart. But it wasn't enough, in the end. His youth started to fade as his wife's had, and he soon would perish—unless he won the favor of a saint who had a fondness for gingerbread.

"On the way to the pilgrimage to meet the saint, he met a woman. She was neither young nor old, but crossing that narrow ledge of time that bridges youth and experience. She talked too much, had hair as wild as the wind, and carried more hope in her heart than any mortal he'd ever encountered. She was brave with bees, skilled in soup making and riddle-solving, and utterly unable to swim. And she broke the wicked wizard into a thousand fragments, so that he had to puzzle how to fit himself back together again. She stole his recipe and his heart, and returned one but not the other—as was well and good.

"The wizard was happy in the end. Reborn. She'd taught him to see the wonder in the world again, and that kindness is not weakness. He would love her until the day he died, with a true love that eternity could not erase."

Josephine stared at him as if he'd turned back into a duck before her eyes. She didn't blink or move. A minute passed, perhaps two. Had his revelation transformed her to stone? When she awoke from her trance, would she pummel him with angry fists and banish him from her sight?

He sensed the time had come for him to leave, as he'd known when to leave the Igelwald behind. This time, though, his heart was full of peace. He lifted her limp hand to his lips and kissed her cool knuckles. "Thank you for everything," he said. "Good bye, Josephine."

Ansgar descended from the dais with aching knees, a sore back, and waning magic. He reckoned he couldn't move a nervous frog off a lily pad with it. He was as dirty and poor as he had been as a duck-harried child, and he had never felt more achingly human.

Twenty-Seven

Josephine could not move. All she could do was to stare after Ansgar.

Nothing she'd believed was true—or at least most of the things she'd believed.

Thierry was dead and gone. She was no one's property, and owed no one a wife's fidelity.

She knew now she could survive almost anything. She would be fine—if not great—on her own. If Ansgar could be reborn, so could she.

Ansgar.

Facing her, he'd looked concerned, but also compassionate. Less harried. More human. His hair was a mess, like a haystack blown apart by a storm. Flour besmirched his shirt collar. And he had, in no uncertain terms, confessed his love for her a moment ago.

Josephine loved romantic novels. Her favorite, dog-eared passages contained heroes declaring their everlasting devotion. None of those pages had stolen her breath like Ansgar's speech had. She was without air, without words, stunned.

The slim vial she clutched only deepened her bewilderment. In her palm, she held a million possibilities, the chance to, in an instant, acquire fortune, fame, power, or possessions, and she didn't want any of it. All she wanted was...

All she wanted had said good bye and was walking away.

She sprang to her feet.

Ladies do not run, Thierry would have said as she leapt from the platform and plunged headlong after Ansgar, past the still-seated, remaining pilgrims. *Ladies do not shout*, he would have scolded when she cried out, "Wait! Stop!"

Thierry had no hold on her anymore.

Ansgar stopped. He turned to face her. Gasping for breath and dizzy, she grabbed his arm to steady herself. "Wait," she repeated foolishly, for he stood motionless. "Don't go."

"I'm here."

"I need to...I want to say..." She opened her palm and showed him the vial. "I don't want it."

"Josephine, we discussed this. You won the prize."

"It is not the prize I want. You are. You are all I want."

Before he could reply, she pulled him close, stood on tiptoe, and kissed him. At first, he laughed against her mouth, but then he quieted as she kept on kissing him. He embraced her and kissed her back fervently, weakening her knees so she had to cling to him to stay upright. She had never been kissed like this in her life. Perhaps she'd never been alive at all. Heaven knew her heart had never pounded so intensely.

Ansgar's hands cradled her face. He gazed at her with adoration. "Josephine. Always surprising me."

She smiled, feeling it all the way to her toes. "I meant what I said. I want only you. I love you."

"And I love you." Ansgar took a single step back. His eyes sparkled as he extended his hand toward Josephine, palm open. "I have changed my mind. I want the wish."

⚜

Dusk threatened to settle over the mountains, adding an otherworldly radiance to everything it touched. Ansgar had always loved this time of day, when the sun kissed the landscape goodnight and the landscape blushed golden in response.

But the glow of twilight did not compare to the rosy glow of Josephine as he requested the wish.

She tilted her head and said, "And you call me surprising? But you may have the wish. One of us should use it after all we endured to get it." Josephine placed the vial in his outstretched hand. It was as cool as spring water and quivered faintly, as if alive.

Together, they walked back to Sainte Yvette. She sat on her throne sipping from a goblet in a queenly manner. Genevieve stood beside her, smiling serenely.

"I knew you would return," Genevieve said when Ansgar and Josephine stopped at the bottom of the steps to face the throne. "I'm so pleased."

In contrast, Sainte Yvette addressed them sternly. "The wish will lose its potency when the sun sinks behind the mountains. You must wish soon, or not at all."

"I give the wish freely to Ansgar," Josephine said. "If that is permissible?"

"It is yours to keep or to give," the saint replied. "I see he holds the vial. You were not coerced to give it away? It is a priceless, once-in-a-lifetime thing, this wish."

"As I said, I give it freely," Josephine replied.

"Let it be done," the saint said. But then she lost her grip on her goblet. It fell to the floor, spilling red wine across the platform. Yvette's eyes rolled back. A low, humming sound came from her open lips.

The audience of pilgrims and holy sisters gasped.

Genevieve fell to her knees. "A vision! Everyone must kneel, quickly. The saint receives a message from above."

Ansgar knelt beside Josephine, his fingers tightly clenching the vial. He knew Yvette was not merely putting on a performance, for he could feel the presence of something otherworldly and powerful.

The saint gripped the arms of her throne and declared, "Lies have been spoken. Untruths which must be unveiled. Ansgar of the Igelwald, once a wizard, once a duck, across many miles and years have you borne a falsehood and a curse."

His blood became a rushing stream of ice. He had no idea what she meant, but there was anger in her voice. Would he die under her wrath before he could use the wish?

The saint continued. "The former witch-queen of the Igelwald, Truda of Lunneburg, ruled cruelly, serving her own pleasures before those of her subjects of leaf and flesh. The eldest oak tree of the forest, her wisest councilor, once offended her by calling her wicked and suggesting reform. She cursed him with a blight, from which he would perish within hours, but before he did, he cursed her in return: no longer would any berry or herb of the forest keep her body from aging. He meant to punish her vanity, and to teach her the humility she needed to rule rightly.

"Instead, she found a way around the curse. She supped on children and stole the essence of their youth to smooth her wrinkles and harden her bones."

Ansgar remembered the wise old oak and its sudden death during his time as a duck. All of the animals had mourned the passing of the tree they'd loved as a grandfather and friend.

"When the day came that Truda realized her efforts could no longer outpace her body's decay, not long before she lured future queen Gretel to her cottage, she also realized that the husband she'd turned into a duck would not remain a duck forever. When he became a man again, he would be the same as he'd been when she'd cursed him: still handsome, still full of vigor. What would prevent him from leaving her?

"And so Truda set another curse upon Ansgar. Drawing on ancient magic and much of her own power, she brewed a potion which she then sprinkled over the duck as he slept. It would do him no real harm if he remained a faithful spouse and never strayed from the Igelwald. He would age as any man inside the forest, day by day, year after year. But if he chose to leave her and the protection of the Igelwald, Ansgar would be cursed to age much faster than an ordinary man. Every day would be as a week or a month. A month could be as a year. Truda enjoyed leaving some things up to the whim of the magic.

"The curse bonded to the man within the duck. If ever he left their forest home, Ansgar would pay the price. And so he has, since the day he set foot outside the Igelwald's borders. This is the truth. The truth has been spoken."

Sainte Yvette shook fitfully and then fainted. Genevieve rushed to the throne, as did the sisters who'd been holding plates. They fanned her with their hands and the ends of their veils. One pressed a cup of water to her lips. The sisters murmured prayers and wept softly.

Ansgar stared at the throne as he tried to comprehend the message.

Truda had cursed him twice and never spoken of the second curse. Of course they had not spent much time conversing after he'd escaped duck form and discovered her spirit trapped inside a mirror, but if she had truly cared for him, she would have at least warned him not to leave the Igelwald. If she'd loved him at all, she would have told him how to break the terrible curse before she slipped out of the mirror forever.

Truda had never loved him. That truth felt like an anvil dropped onto his chest. Still kneeling, he gasped for air.

"Ansgar?" Josephine's hand squeezed his arm. "What's wrong?"

He dropped the vial. Panic seized him. His heart beat too fast, too hard. Truda was about to win the game she'd been playing with him since the day they'd met. Nothing had ever mattered to her but her happiness, her power. If she could not have him, then neither could the world.

His hands grabbed for Josephine. He stared into her beautiful, fear-filled eyes. Something to remember for eternity, wherever he'd spend it.

"What can I do?" she asked desperately, and then she shouted, "Someone help him! Please!"

Twenty-Eight

Josephine cried, "No!" But it did not stop Ansgar from slumping to the floor, unconscious. She fell on her knees beside him. His chest rose and fell sharply as he continued to fight for breath. He was alive, but for how long? She took both his hands in hers as she wept.

Broken. Truda had broken him, that witch. Cruelly, purposefully, like Jacques had broken her necklace.

Everything gets broken, her grandmother's voice said in her head. *The breaking lets the goodness that's inside come out. The egg for the recipe, the bird for the sky, the love that's too strong to die. Look for the treasure in the brokenness, child. The beautiful consequence. The unexpected cure.*

She reached into her pocket to touch the broken pendant. Her fingernail caught in the crack of the stone. In trying to pull her nail free, she felt the stone fall into pieces. Carefully, she scooped up the fragments and brought them out to examine them. In the middle of the bits of black rock, a crystal shaped like a tiny star sat. When she poked it with her fingertip, tingles ran up her arm.

"What you hold there, little one, is more powerful than the wish you won today," said Sainte Yvette. Thanks to the assistance of two of the sisters, the woman sat straight and proud in her throne again, pale but otherwise unchanged by her vision. "It is far better than the ability to change things to gold. Since history began, few have been blessed to own the cure for any curse."

"What did you say?" Josephine stared at the saint.

Genevieve clapped with joy, like a child given a new toy. "Do you not see, Josephine? You can cure him."

"You can banish the curse and reverse its effects, yes," Yvette agreed. "But if he dies before the cure takes hold, the magic will have been wasted."

"What do I do? How do I use it?"

"Place the token on his heart and declare him cured," Yvette said, as if Josephine's ignorance of magic was absurd.

Quickly, she pressed the little star onto Ansgar's heaving chest, holding it in place. "By this gift, you are cured. Please, Ansgar. Be cured. Be well." Under her hand, she felt sparks of power, warm and sharp and sinking into his body.

His breathing calmed and slowed. He opened his eyes and smiled at her.

"What miracle have you wrought?" he said. "I have not seen so clearly in ages. My eyes can hardly stand the sight of you."

She laughed and helped him sit up. "I will choose to take that as a compliment."

"You have taken away the curse? But how?" His smile, although younger now by years, still caused creases around his blue eyes. Good. She'd grown quite fond of those little lines. She would have hated to see them all erased. He still looked like himself, a man of experience—but not a man with one foot in the grave.

The bells rang out the hour.

Sainte Yvette stood. "Explanations must wait. The sun is setting. Wish now or forfeit the wish."

Ansgar reached for the vial he'd dropped, and then got to his feet. He offered Josephine his hand, tugging her to stand close beside him.

"Ansgar Steuben, the wish is yours," said the saint.

He looked into Josephine's eyes. "Are you still sure? Now that I'm well—"

She nodded. "I trust you to wish for both of us."

The saint said, "First, you must open the vial."

He pulled the cork. White vapor swirled out like smoke from a chimney. It filled the air with the scent of a spring rainstorm.

"Now speak your wish," the saint said.

Ansgar fell to his knees before Josephine. He peered up at her tearstained cheeks, the endearing smudge of dough on her chin, and the faint lines etched into her forehead by time, and he loved her more than he'd ever loved anyone.

"This is my wish," he said. "But only if it is also yours, Josephine: that we could spend the rest of our earthly days together. That you would allow me the honor of breaking bread with you every morning, noon, and evening; that your kiss would be my last memory every night before sleep comes to claim me, that your sorrows will be our sorrows, your joys our joys. That if you fall, I bear the bruise. That you will believe me when I tell you that you are the most wondrous, most vexing creature I have ever known—and that I desire nothing in the world but you."

"You may wish for only one thing," the saint said.

Josephine sank to her knees, facing him. "None of those things are things to waste a wish on, Ansgar Steuben."

His heart sank—but then she smiled.

"If you are asking for my heart, it is already yours. If you are asking for my hand in marriage, that will have to wait. I have been a daughter and a wife, and an unwilling widow, but I have never had a day to be just myself. And as mean as Thierry was, he was my husband. I must mourn him, if only for a season. Do you understand?"

He reached for her hands and took half a second to marvel at how perfectly they fit in his. "Then let this be my wish," he said. "I wish that when we wake tomorrow, we find ourselves in a comfortable cottage overlooking the sea, a place where we can dwell whenever we grow tired of .adventuring. A house with two sides and two doors. You will have space to grieve, to rest, and to dream. And when you are ready, we will knock down walls together as husband and wife, and make it one home."

"It is a perfect wish," Josephine agreed.

"So be it," said the saint.

The air shimmered for a moment, then stilled as the last of the wish vial's vapor drifted skyward. The magic in Ansgar's bones warmed, testifying that the wish's magic had done its work.

"I ask your pardon if what I'm going to do is against the rules here," Josephine said to the saint. "But I'm going to kiss this man."

Yvette smiled more broadly than Ansgar thought a dour saint could. "Do as you will," she said.

Josephine placed her hands on his cheeks, leaned toward him, and pressed her mouth to his. An hour ago, he'd felt a hundred years old but now as he kissed her back, he felt fifteen again. Full of butterflies and starshine. He felt foolish and ridiculous, and so in love that he no longer cared if he was foolish and ridiculous.

The pilgrims cheered and the sisters applauded.

The kiss lasted so long that when Ansgar lifted his head to catch his breath and gaze adoringly at Josephine, everyone else had gone, and moonbeams played upon the empty throne.

Twenty-Nine

I t was Josephine's idea to visit the storehouse. After the wish-granting ceremony, she'd been ravenous. She could have devoured a table full of anything—except gingerbread. Should she have been grateful to that spiced cake? Probably. But the memory of the stressful baking competition was not one she cared to entertain at the moment.

She and Ansgar sat on the floor and shared a picnic of cheese, dried fruit, and a bottle of some sort of mead. He teased her for suggesting the unsanctioned purloining of food, but she called it their betrothal supper and insisted that had they asked for it, Genevieve would have brought them the food on a platter. Several platters. They ate a lot of food.

Insects trilled in the trees and bushes as they closed the door and left the storehouse behind. Without discussion, they wandered through the gardens and toward the main gate. The night was fair and still, perfect for strolling.

The moonlight made Ansgar's hair look like fine filaments of silver. Josephine was tempted to touch it, to test whether it felt unnatural. Since they'd met, and until only hours ago, she'd tried to ignore the hint of magic that emanated from him at all times, invisible to the eye yet somehow as present as a swarm of tiny gnats. Now she accepted and loved it, for it was part of her beloved.

After everything she'd endured when wed to Thierry, how mad it was to be risking her heart again. But she had faith that this relationship would be different. With Ansgar, she'd share adventures, mischief, and a lifetime of kisses. She blushed as she remembered their first ardent (and public) embrace, but she did not regret it in the least.

Ansgar held open the ornate iron gate that separated the Seven Ovens from the outside world. They'd spent only two days in the saint's little community, but Josephine counted them as two of the longest days of her life. And two of the most meaningful.

By pale-blue moon-and-star light, they followed the path. "I don't remember these tall ferns," Josephine said. "Is this the way we came?"

"There was only one path that led to the gate, but given the ever-shifting route we took as pilgrims, this might not be *exactly* the way we came. Do you want to turn back?"

"No, not yet. This night is too lovely to miss." Yellow light flickered to her left, and Josephine stopped. "Over there. Do you see that?"

They exchanged a look, then waded through the waist-high ferns, hand in hand. The light grew brighter, revealing an arched doorway flanked by tin lanterns. Beyond it lay a shadowy churchyard.

"Fascinating," Ansgar said. "I do believe the saint has granted us a shortcut back to the place the pilgrimage began. A portal, if you will. I rather thought Yvette enjoyed letting people suffer their way through long and arduous journeys."

"Perhaps she has decided we've suffered enough traveling. Unless...it could be a faerie trick. Do you think we should trust it?"

He closed his eyes for a moment and drew a deep breath. When his gaze met hers again, he said, "Its magic feels benign to me. I say we use it, unless you object?"

"I have no objection, but I do confess I'm tired."

"We will rest soon, *liebling*." He squeezed her hand. "Shall we go through together?"

"It's too narrow. You go first."

"Nonsense." He scooped her into his arms, and she laughed. As she rested her head against his shoulder, he carried her under the iron arch.

Josephine had expected the magic portal to do something as they passed through, to buzz or hum, or to send a jolt of coldness through their bodies, but nothing of the sort happened. The lack of drama almost disappointed her. What a change for the woman who had hated leaving the safety of her cozy parlor. She would crave another adventure with Ansgar soon, she reckoned. After a good rest, of course. One that included vats of tea and platters of crispy potatoes. Chocolate cake. A hot, deep bath scented with rose petals. Snuggling against Ansgar while reading a fat novel near a crackling hearth.

After leaving the churchyard, Ansgar stopped at a fork in the path. A light breeze shook the boughs of the fir trees surrounding them. He set Josephine on her feet, and then frowned. "We cannot be far from the town, but blast me if I remember which way to go."

"Does it matter? Wherever we lay our heads, the wish will take us to our seaside cottage before we wake. I'm simply looking for a nice patch of moss to bed down on." She yawned and rubbed her sore eyes.

He tugged her along playfully. "A lovely thought, but I am afraid you chose a man who hates sleeping out-of-doors, or on lumpy mattresses in cheap inns. One who absolutely abhors spending a single night in a smelly, straw-strewn barn. I should have warned you, I suppose."

"Oh, I have been well aware of your snobbery since we met. You dressed in that fine suit to climb a mountain, did you not?"

"Snobbery? Just because I like nice things..."

She slipped her arm through his. "Now, now. No need to fuss. I take you as you are. Also, I think you will survive a few hours of sleeping in the forest."

"I have my doubts," he said wryly. "Wait. I remember that strange willow tree over there. I noticed it out the carriage window. If we keep walking, we'll soon come upon a rather grand house with a 'for sale' notice affixed to its door." The devilish look he gave her made heart skip. "I'm quite skilled at lock picking."

"Snobbish and a criminal. I have never been more in love."

"I am beginning to think that your sweetness was nothing but a ruse, madame!"

"And I know for a fact that you are not the cold monster you portrayed. An actual, loving heart beats in your chest."

"It is a new heart, recently acquired. Nevertheless, I would thank you not to have that printed in the newspaper."

"I will accept bribes," she teased.

An instant later, she found herself spun around and held tightly in his arms. "Bribes? I have not a coin to my name at present, but I could pay with a kiss, if you will allow it."

Dizzy, she nodded. "One kiss will suffice."

He kissed her thoroughly, until she had to push him away to catch her breath.

When she could speak, she said, "That is only a down payment, of course."

With his hands tangled in her hair, he whispered, "I look forward to bankruptcy. But let us find sanctuary first. Come along, *liebling*."

Only minutes passed before they stood before a three-story, stone mansion with a "for sale or lease" sign nailed to the door. Quickly, they skirted the house and found the back entrance.

His skill at lock picking should have disturbed her. It felt wrong to offer a prayer of thanks for it, but she did. And when he picked her up to carry her over the threshold, she thanked the heavens even more fervently.

The dark stairs creaked under his feet as he climbed them. His sure grip kept her close to his body. She tried to commit the moment to memory. He smelled of cinnamon and sweat, wood smoke and damp wool, and his eyes were hazy with desire. He was everything she'd never wanted, and she loved him more than she'd believed possible.

With his boot, he shoved open a bedroom door. Slowly, he lowered her feet to the floor. He kissed her forehead. "You're not easy to say good night to, Josephine Monfort," he said in a low voice that made her knees weaken. "I shall be counting the days until we are wed."

"Good night," she said as he closed the door and left her alone in the dark.

She sat on the bare mattress, wide awake, and listened to Ansgar's footsteps in the room next door. There was a crash, and then another.

In the morning, the wish granted by the saint would come true, but in this borrowed house, as her future husband collided with furniture and swore loudly, she could not have been happier or more full of hope.

The sound of gulls woke Ansgar. Stupid, noisy scavengers. He loathed them, as he loathed most birds. He was also keenly aware that the mattress beneath him was lumpy, his pillow was too thin, and the blanket covering his body scratched his skin. But when he glanced down at his chest and saw Josephine nestled there, he forgave the birds, the bed, and every other thing that had aggravated him during this singular moment. This miracle.

After eight months of living as the fondest of neighbors, yesterday they'd married in the sailors' chapel overlooking the waves. He'd spent the night before the ceremony secretly bedecking the chapel with evergreen boughs, ivy, and dozens of white candles—to give Josephine the wedding she'd envisioned as a girl. She'd cried with joy because he'd remembered what she'd said about her dream wedding back in one of the pilgrimage's many sanctuaries. And then she'd kissed him, which made having hands stained with indelible pine sap more than worthwhile.

A sea breeze ruffled the window curtains. He kissed his wife's hair, in which was tangled a crushed crown of bridal flowers, but she did not stir. Well and good. He wanted to linger this way for as long as possible. He wanted to compose sonnets about the way the light streamed through the window and lit her bare toes where they stuck out from under the blanket.

How he would have hated this version of himself once, before the pilgrimage. He hardly recognized this new Ansgar. Strangely, he felt closer to the boy he'd been before meeting Truda. Like everything was possible, and a thrilling life lay just around the bend. Like he could be a good man who did good things.

He held his hand up to admire the simple gold band Josephine had slipped onto his finger during the wedding. If it was a little tight, he didn't care, for he intended to never remove it. He loved the fact that she'd found it along the road to the pilgrimage, a lost thing she'd not been seeking, and then carried it with her from that day forward. He and the ring had much in common.

"Darling?" Josephine shifted to peer sleepily into his face. Her smile was a slice of pure joy. "Isn't this perfect? Did you know that although you did the wishing, every one of my wishes has also come true?"

"If those confounded gulls would cease their yawping, I would not mind staying here forever," Ansgar said peevishly. She kissed his chin and made him regret complaining.

"You're terribly grumpy for someone waking up with a new bride."

He tightened his embrace. "This is me happy. I have never been happier."

"We can move to the city if you wish. Or deep into the countryside, where gulls dare not roam."

"Do you not understand, woman? I need the wretched gulls, and this horrid blanket, and this thin-as-toast pillow, for if I were but a fraction happier, I might die of it. And the last thing I want to do is to leave you. The notion that I might have only thirty or forty more years with you is the worst thought I have entertained in my life. Far worse than memories of bee attacks and walking through fire."

"Think positively, *mon chéri*. Think of the good things ahead. All we will share in this wide world." She sat up and hugged her knees to her chest. "We will grow old together. Very, very old. If I have to seek out another wish to make that happen—"

"No. No more wishes. Magic has defined enough of my life. Let love define what I have left. It will be enough, and more than enough." He pulled her back into his arms and kissed her. He forgot the gulls and death and everything but Josephine.

The bed shook. Josephine screamed and pushed him away. At their feet stood a huge, charcoal-gray cat. Ansgar swore and propelled his body back against the headboard. "Where did that beast come from? The bowels of hell?"

Josephine laughed and shooed the cat onto the floor. "Your new life of love does not include loving cats, then?"

He sneezed. "Dear gods, please tell me you do not want to keep it."

"I have had enough of cat-husbands," Josephine said. She shooed the animal off the bed. "I will find him a new home after breakfast."

Sighing deeply with relief, Ansgar let his head fall into his inadequate pillow. One tiny feather flew into the air and then descended, fluttering slowly. If it was his, he couldn't be bothered to care.

Acknowledgments

Getting a book out into the world is a grand and daunting adventure, and one that is best not undertaken alone. And so I want to thank some of the people who helped me get Ansgar and Josephine's story into your hands.

Thank you to my husband, John, for supporting and believing in me. I love you!

Thank you, Christine, for being the best buffalo in the world. Let's go back to Ireland now.

Thank you, Laura Z, for being my writing partner and helping me get this done. Your support and encouragement are priceless gifts, and I treasure our wacky friendship more than I can say.

To Amber K, the founding member of the Official Ansgar Fan Club, thank you for loving our grumpy wizard-duck-wizard, and for your wonderful suggestions and inspirational pep talks. It's hilarious that we became fast friends because of an evil duck, but I'm so grateful.

To Alaina, Tanya, and everyone at OHB, my deepest gratitude. It's such a pleasure working with you all.

Thank you to my son's cat, Tod, for being the inspiration for the infamous cat-husband of this tale.

To every family member, friend, and reader who has supported me with kind words, bars of chocolate, or by purchasing my books, I could never thank you enough. Keep reading, and share your favorite books with others!

Last, but never least, I thank God for giving me words to write, the life to write them in, and his love that never fails.

The Gingerbread Legacy

The Gingerbread Queen

The Gingerbread Thief

The Springborn

The Mermaid's Sister

The Gold-Son

Gretchen and the Bear

The Peddler's Reward

About the Author

In the wake of her thrilling past as a theater student, restaurant hostess, nurse aide, and newspaper writer, Carrie Anne Noble now crafts enchanting fiction for teens and adults. Her debut novel *The Mermaid's Sister* won the 2014 Amazon Breakthrough Novel Award for Young Adult Fiction and the 2016 Realm Award for Book of the Year. Her other books include YA fantasies entitled *The Gold-Son* and *Gretchen and the Bear*. Carrie lives in the Pennsylvania mountains, where she enjoys taking walks, frolicking with her half-Corgi, and hosting the occasional mad tea party. Connect with Carrie online at www.carrienoble.com.

A small press bound by the belief that every voice matters.

Sign up for our newsletter to learn about new releases and more.
https://oliver-heberbooks.com/subscribe/

Follow us on social media:

facebook.com/oliverheberbooks

instagram.com/oliverheberbooks

amazon.com/oliverheberbooks

youtube.com/@OliverHeberBooksPublisher